Smells Like Treasure

by
Suzanne Selfors

LITTLE, BROWN AND COMPANY
New York   Boston

Also by Suzanne Selfors:

To Catch a Mermaid
Fortune's Magic Farm
Smells Like Dog

Copyright © 2011 by Suzanne Selfors

Little, Brown and Company

Hachette Book Group
237 Park Avenue, New York, NY 10017
Visit our website at www.lb-kids.com

Little, Brown and Company is a division of Hachette Book Group, Inc.
The Little, Brown name and logo are trademarks of Hachette Book Group, Inc.

The publisher is not responsible for websites (or their content) that are not owned by the publisher.

First Paperback Edition: April 2012
Originally published in hardcover in May 2011 by Little, Brown and Company

Library of Congress Cataloging-in-Publication Data
Selfors, Suzanne.
Smells like treasure / by Suzanne Selfors. — 1st ed.
    p. cm.
Summary: Farm boy Homer faces another challenger for his uncle's spot in the Society of Legends, Objects, Secrets, and Treasures, but Dog's hidden ability to smell treasure guides the duo as clues lead them to fantastic mansions and hidden islands.
ISBN 978-0-316-04399-1 (hc) / ISBN 978-0-316-04402-8 (pb)
[1. Adventure and adventurers — Fiction. 2. Dogs — Fiction. 3. Buried treasure — Fiction. 4. Secret societies — Fiction. 5. Mystery and detective stories.] I. Title.
PZ7.S456922Hom 2011
[Fic] — dc22
                        2010041541
    10 9 8 7 6 5 4 3 2 1

RRD-C

Book design by Saho Fujii

Printed in the United States of America

This book is dedicated to
Maxine Rose Nagramada,
my extraordinary
soccer-playing niece, and to
Joe Nagramada,
an extraordinary
sock-eating corgi.

CONTENTS

"Sometimes a map doesn't take you where you want to go."

—Drake Horatio Pudding

Dear Reader,

Once again, let me assure you that this is a happy dog story. At no point in this story will a dog die. I hate stories about dogs that die, and so I will never, ever write that kind of story. That is my solemn promise.

In fact, I believe there should be some sort of punishment for people who write stories about dogs that die. Maybe they should be forced to peel gum off the bottoms of movie-theater seats, or file old people's toenails, or clean the shark tank at the zoo. That's what they deserve after bringing such terrible unhappiness into our lives.

Because who wants to break into tears while reading a book? Not I. The pages get all soggy and people turn and stare and ask, "Why are you reading that book and crying?"

"Because the dog just died," you blubber, wiping snot from your nose. And then you ask, "Why? Why did the dog have to die? Why not the cat? Huh? Why is it always the dog?"

Who wants to go through that?

So find a nice cozy place, get yourself something yummy to snack on (I prefer chocolate-covered pretzels, but popcorn is also good), and don't worry about anything because the dog in this story will be just fine. He might face some dangers and he might run amuck, but he will most assuredly be alive on the very last page.

Happy reading.

PART ONE

MILKYDALE

1

Destiny

There are two types of people in this world—people who sit by their mailboxes and wait for a delivery from the Map of the Month Club and people who don't.

You might be asking yourself, What kind of person would sit by his mailbox and wait for a map? An image might pop into your head of a nerdy sort of person with messy hair and pants that are too short. A soft sort of person who'd rather sit in his room and dream about treasure than climb a tree or ride a bike. A smart sort of person because map reading uses 2.5 million more brain cells than watching television.

Did you know that the person you've just imagined is Homer Winslow Pudding? And that's what he was doing one Saturday morning in June—sitting at the end of his driveway, right next to his mailbox, waiting.

The grass blade he'd been chewing had turned to mush, so he picked another blade and slid it between his teeth. Then he tilted his head, listening for the rumble of the mail truck's engine. To Homer's right, Grinning Goat Road disappeared into a horizon of green, goat-dappled hills. To his left, the road wound past the neighbor's farm and disappeared around a bend as it made its way to the town of Milkydale. Tall birch trees lined the road, the ends of their slender branches swaying in the morning breeze. Except for a pair of chattering blue jays that perched on a nearby fence post and the occasional bleat of the goats, all was quiet. Homer checked his Quality Solar-Powered Subatomic Watch—an extremely rare apparatus. Only two exist in the entire world.

"She's late," Homer said. "The mail lady's late."

"Urrrr." The dog who lay at Homer's feet moaned.

Homer reached out and scratched Dog's belly—a rather round belly for a dog of such short stature. Dog's back leg kicked rhythmically, as if he'd gotten a sudden urge to chase a rabbit. Homer knew the exact spot on Dog's white belly that triggered this little dance. He knew many things about the dog who'd come to live with him three months before. Such as, when Dog stuck his nose into Homer's sleeve, Dog was feeling afraid. When he howled, he was feeling lonely. And when he started sniffing the ground and digging—well, that meant he was about to uncover something amazing.

Dog's leg froze mid-kick. Then he rolled onto his paws as a rumbling sound sent the blue jays flying. Homer narrowed his eyes and focused on the horizon. *Come on, come on,* he thought, imagining the long cardboard tube with its gold Map of the Month Club sticker. *Please be the mail truck.*

Sure enough, the blue mail truck chugged around the bend and stopped at the Puddings' mailbox. "Howdy, Homer," said Twyla, the mail lady.

"Hi," Homer said, pushing his curly bangs from his eyes. Excitement lifted him onto his toes, and he peered through the open window as Twyla rummaged through a box. Then she handed Homer a stack of bills, a farm equipment catalog, and the latest copy of *Goat World*, with its big headline: WHAT TO DO IF YOUR GOAT EATS A SHOE.

"I still can't get over those ears," she said, looking down at Dog. "They're like a pair of wet towels."

Dog's tail *thwapp*ed expectantly against Homer's leg.

"I know what you want," Twyla said. She reached into her coat pocket, then tossed out a bone-shaped dog treat, which Dog practically inhaled. "Are you going to the opening day of the fair?"

"Yep." Every year of his twelve years, Homer had gone to the opening day of the Milkydale County Fair. Aside from his birthday, opening day was his favorite day of the year because it marked the end of school. Good-bye, English composition. Good-bye, Victorian literature. Hello, summer vacation.

"Wish I could go. I've never been on opening day. I'm always working." Twyla strummed her fingers on the steering wheel. "Well, I'd better—"

"Wait," Homer said. "Don't you have my map?"

"Your map?" Twyla frowned.

"It's the first Saturday of the month." How could she have forgotten? She'd been delivering his maps since last Christmas. The Map of the Month Club had been a Christmas present from his late uncle Drake.

"Gosh, Homer, I don't see it."

"Could you look again?" He didn't want to insult her, but Twyla did have a wandering eye, and because of this wandering eye she sometimes delivered the wrong mail to the wrong address. She crashed the mail truck into quite a few trees, too.

She looked again. "I don't see a map. Oh, but lookey here." She held out a small white envelope. "It's for you. Special airmail delivery. I wonder how it got into my truck."

The envelope was addressed to Homer W. Pudding at Pudding Goat Farm, Milkydale. Since there was no return address in the upper left-hand corner, Homer turned the envelope over. A golden glob of wax sealed the flap. Four letters had been pressed into the middle of the glob: *L.O.S.T.*

Homer gasped.

This was way better than a map from the Map of the Month Club. "Thanks," he said, stepping away from the truck.

"Have fun at the fair," Twyla called as the mail truck resumed its swerving course up Grinning Goat Road.

Homer stared at the four letters—*L.O.S.T.* The secret Society of Legends, Objects, Secrets, and Treasures had sent him a letter. It had never before sent him a letter. Until three months ago, he hadn't even known the Society existed. Until three months ago, he hadn't known that Dog existed, either.

Both L.O.S.T. and Dog had been secrets kept by Homer's treasure-hunting uncle, Drake Pudding. Just before his tragic demise, Uncle Drake had decided that one person—his favorite nephew, Homer—would inherit the secrets. And that is why Uncle Drake had hidden a L.O.S.T. membership coin on Dog's collar, and why he had bequeathed Dog to Homer. It was the mysterious coin that had sent Homer on a wild adventure three months ago to discover the meaning of the initials and to learn the truth about Dog. And what, you might ask, was this truth?

That Dog could only smell one thing—treasure!

"Do you think...?" Homer looked down at Dog. "Do you think L.O.S.T. is inviting me to become a member?"

There was only one way to answer that question. Homer tucked the rest of the mail under his arm, then reached into his pocket and grabbed his Swiss army knife. But just as he was about to slide the blade under the wax seal, a red truck chugged around the bend. Homer closed the knife, then stuffed it, along with his letter, into his pocket. L.O.S.T. was a secret, and he intended to keep it that way.

The red truck turned into the Pudding driveway, then stopped. The front window rolled down. "Did the mail come?" Mr. Pudding asked, leaning his thick forearm on the window's ledge.

"Here it is," Homer said loudly over the truck's sputtering. He held out the pile.

Mr. Pudding took the mail and set it on the seat. "I don't see a map tube. Aren't you supposed to get your new map today?" In his younger years, Mr. Pudding had wanted to become a cartographer. Though his goat farming duties had pushed that dream aside, he still enjoyed reading maps and would occasionally sit with Homer and study the latest delivery. But he wasn't keen on treasure-hunting maps. "Give me a good solid map that's real," Mr. Pudding often said. "Not a map that's one-half dreams, one-half bunk."

"Twyla didn't have it," Homer explained. Under normal circumstances, not receiving the Map of the Month Club map would have been a huge disappointment. But something else—maybe something better—had been delivered. He stuck his hand in his pocket. The golden wax seal was cold against his skin. "The map must have gotten lost."

"Twyla sure knows how to lose packages," Mr. Pudding said as he rubbed his chin. "Did you finish your chores?"

"Yes. All of them." He'd fed last night's dinner scraps to the chickens, collected their eggs, put fresh straw in their nesting boxes, filled the goats' trough with water, milked their largest goat, carried the milk to the kitchen, and swept the front porch. *Please don't give me more chores*, he thought, eager to run straight to his room and read the letter.

"What do you think of the dogs?" Mr. Pudding asked.

"The groomer did a right fine job." Max and Lulu, border collies both, hung over the side of the truck bed, their black-and-white coats shiny and tangle free. "I want them to look their best."

On most days, Mr. Pudding didn't care if his farm dogs had mud on their paws or twigs stuck to their tails, but this wasn't most days. That very afternoon Max and Lulu were scheduled to compete in the dog agility trials at the Milkydale County Fair. The border collies were Mr. Pudding's pride and joy—hence the sign that hung next to the mailbox.

PUDDING GOAT FARM
Home of the Champion Pudding Border Collies,
Winners of Four County Fair Blue Ribbons.

Homer reached up and patted Max's silky black head. "They look good."

Gus, the farm's other border collie, barked from the nearby pasture, where he was guarding the goat herd. Too old to compete, Gus had won his share of ribbons in his prime.

Mr. Pudding stuck his head out the window, his gaze dropping to Homer's feet. "What's he eating?" he asked with a scowl.

"Oops." Homer reached down and pulled a stick from

Dog's mouth. One of Homer's main chores was to make sure Dog didn't eat things he wasn't supposed to eat. Since Dog had been born without a sense of smell, anything could be mistaken for food. He'd been known to eat flowers, slugs, cardboard, whitewash, magazines, boots, and toothpaste.

Dog looked up at Mr. Pudding, his red-rimmed eyes sinking into folds of skin, his ears hanging to the ground as if they were filled with sand. "That's one droopy dog," Mr. Pudding said with a shake of his head. "Too bad he can't herd. Too bad he's not like the rest of the dogs." Then he put the truck into gear and drove up the driveway.

Dog wasn't one bit like the rest of the dogs. The Puddings' border collies were specimens of perfect breeding, elegant in form. While they had legs made for running, Dog, a basset hound, had legs made for waddling. While they had coats of shiny hair that rippled in the wind, Dog's short hair didn't do anything but fall out and get stuck in the carpet. While the border collies had noble names, Dog's name was plain old Dog. Compared to the rest of the dogs, Dog stood out like a raisin cookie on a platter of frosted cupcakes.

Homer knelt and patted Dog's head. "Don't you feel bad. You wouldn't like going to the groomer. She cleans *everything*. And those dog agility trials are real boring.

All they do is run around and jump over things. You wouldn't want to do that even if Dad had invited you." Not that Dog could do those sorts of things. It's difficult to jump when you're shaped like an overstuffed sausage.

But if Mr. Pudding knew that Dog could smell treasure, he'd treat him like a king.

"Come on," Homer said, hurrying up the driveway. "Let's go read this letter."

The Pudding driveway was steep and long, and both Homer and Dog were out of breath by the time they reached the top. The driveway ended at a pretty front yard. A little path led to a house built from river rocks. A white picket fence surrounded the vegetable garden, and just beyond were the cherry orchard, the old red barn, and the hills where goats grazed on grass, clover, and wildflowers.

Just inside the kitchen window, Mrs. Pudding stirred something. Homer knew that if he tried to sneak past her to get to his room, she'd probably give him another chore. So, after looking around to make sure the coast was clear, he sat on the corner of the porch. A quick slice with the Swiss army knife and the seal came loose. His hands trembled.

Imagine a secret group of people whose lives were dedicated to the very thing that Homer dreamed about. Imagine the kinds of stories they could tell of the places they'd visited, the wonders they'd seen. His uncle had been a member of L.O.S.T., and Homer had met two other members, Ajitabh and Zelda, friends of his uncle's. They'd told Homer that it was his right to take his uncle's place. It was only a matter of when.

Not only did Homer desire this membership, but he also needed it. He'd promised his late uncle Drake that he'd continue the quest for the most famous pirate treasure of all time—the lost treasure of Rumpold Smeller. But Homer was twelve years old, so he'd need help organizing and funding such a grand quest. That help could come from L.O.S.T.—but only if Homer was granted membership.

"Whatcha looking at?" A little boy popped his head around the corner of the house. The boy was Squeak, Homer's little brother. He clutched the handle of a red wagon. A baby goat lay in the wagon, nestled on Squeak's favorite blanket. Since most farms in Milkydale were goat farms, baby goats had been popping out all month like weeds in a carrot patch.

"It's a letter for me," Homer told him.

"I like letters," Squeak said. "I'm naming this goat Butter, 'cause she looks like butter." He leaned over and rubbed his freckled face against the goat's back. "She smells like butter, too."

"That's nice," Homer said, only half listening as he pulled out a single sheet of plain white paper.

A bolt of excitement darted up his back.

"What's it say?" Squeak asked.

Four words that meant everything to Homer. Four words that would be the beginning of his destiny.

Your time has come.

2
Rumpold Smeller the Boy, Part I

Destinies come in many shapes and sizes. For a boy who lived long before Homer, destiny was a birthright.

Far away from the Pudding Farm lies the country of Estonia—a luscious, forested land covered with lakes and rivers. There, in a white castle with red-roofed towers, lived a boy named Rumpold Smeller. His father was a duke, which is why the family lived in a castle. Now this was very long ago, in the days before fast-food restaurants, or automobiles, or even steam-powered ships. These were the days when peasants worked the land and rich men owned the land. The daughters of these rich men were not allowed to go to school, so they sat around and made needlepoint pillows and tapestries and went crazy from boredom. Most people ate the same food every day because there were no grocery stores, and it was common to identify relatives by the size of their carbuncles—unpleasant, pus-filled pimples. And if your country was at peace, well, it was only a matter of time before someone invaded and set everything on fire.

Rumpold was a well-behaved boy. He listened to his tutor and completed all his assigned studies, such as Latin, geography, and chivalry. He obeyed his parents by not running through the palace like a wild thing and by going to bed when he was supposed to. He was a semiskilled equestrian, which meant that he could ride a horse without falling off. And, like all the sons of dukes, he was trained in the art of fighting with a sword.

Problem was, Rumpold hated fighting. Aggression went against his gentle nature. Instead of working on impaling and thrusting, he used the tip of his sword to draw pictures in the dirt. Instead of knocking out his opponent with the sword's handle, he decorated the handle with paintings of birds and swirls.

The Duke of Estonia worried about his son's lack of

interest in weaponry. He worried, too, about his inclination to spend long hours perched in the uppermost branch of a tree, daydreaming. The faraway look was a permanent fixture on Rumpold's face. The duchess said, "Worry not. He is a boy. All things will change in him when he becomes a man."

One of the benefits of being a duke's son was that Rumpold could have most anything that he desired. If he wanted cake in the middle of the night, then all he had to do was ring a little bell. If he wanted a new kitten, he had to only ask. If he didn't feel like buttering his bread, someone else did it for him. Such a life would turn most children into spoiled brats. But Rumpold remained polite and never said an unkind word about anyone or to anyone.

"He's too polite," the duke fretted. "It's not natural for a boy to be so polite."

"Worry not," the duchess said. "All things will change in him when he becomes a man."

But what the Duchess of Estonia didn't know, as she smiled at her vegetable-eating, homework-doing, authority-minding child, was that all things would change, but not in the way she expected.

For Rumpold Smeller would become known as the most fearsome pirate to sail the seven seas.

3

Secrets Beneath the Bed

Homer bolted up the porch steps.

"Where are you going?" Squeak asked.

"I gotta do something. Come on, Dog." With Dog at his heels, Homer charged through the warm kitchen. The scent of baking cherry pies swirled in the air. "I need to wash up before the fair," he announced, hoping this would keep his mother from assigning more chores.

"Don't run in the house," Mrs. Pudding called as she peered into the oven to check her pies' progress.

If there was anything Dog hated, it was being left behind. If left behind, whether on purpose or by accident, he'd voice his discontent with the loudest howl anyone had ever heard. It was extra likely he'd get left behind if a staircase was involved. It took forever for him to haul his long body up a staircase. And carrying him was a Herculean feat. Homer had learned that if he needed to speed Dog's progress, it was best to push Dog's rump. So up the squeaky farmhouse stairs Homer pushed.

Once they'd stumbled into Homer's bedroom, Homer shut the door. A boy with as many secrets as Homer Pudding should have kept a padlock on his bedroom door. Since that was not allowed in the Pudding household, he slid a chair under the knob, securing the door as best he could.

Maps covered every square inch of the bedroom's walls and ceiling. All those colors and lines might have induced dizziness in someone not skilled in the art of map-reading. But Homer wished he had room for more.

Panting, Dog collapsed onto the carpet, his chin landing on a dirty sock. Homer settled next to him and reopened the letter. The paper was white and plain, with only those four words.

Your time has come.

The letter's author had purposely kept the message vague. No details about where or when, who or how. Homer understood that this was necessary in case someone other than he had opened the letter. He'd have to interpret the message on his own. It could mean only one thing—that he was going to be given the chance to take his uncle's place. And once he became an official member of L.O.S.T., he'd be a *professional* treasure hunter. But when, exactly, would this happen? In a few minutes? Tomorrow? Next week?

"My time has come," he said. He wanted to stick his head out the window and shout those words to everyone. But he especially wanted to tell one person—his uncle Drake. His beloved uncle, with his scruffy mustache and can-do attitude, had understood Homer like no one else ever had.

"Treasure hunting's in your blood," Uncle Drake had often told him. "It's in my blood, too." But now he was gone, eaten by a mutant carnivorous tortoise, and it was Homer's duty and honor to finish what his uncle had started—to find Rumpold Smeller's treasure.

Homer reached under his bed, found the loose floorboard, and pried it off. Then he stuck his hand into the hole and pulled out a book. Dog raised his head and sniffed the air, his tail wagging. Dog had been the one to find the book—he'd been the one to smell the treasure hidden within.

The book, *Rare Reptiles I Caught and Stuffed*, was a rather tedious, scientific account of odd reptilian creatures from all over the world. Very few people would want to read such a book. That's why Uncle Drake had hidden something very important within its pages.

Before his death, Drake Horatio Pudding had found the treasure map of Rumpold Smeller the pirate. He'd cut the map into precise pieces and had pasted those pieces throughout the reptile book. Homer was eager to assemble the pieces. But that would be dangerous because then it wouldn't look like a boring old book, but a true treasure map—the most coveted map in the treasure-hunting community.

So for now, it remained hidden.

"HOMER!" Mr. Pudding hollered from the driveway. "Where are you?"

Homer shot to his knees and pushed open his bedroom window. "I'm right here," he called, dreading what would follow because it would probably contain the word *chore.*

"It's time to go."

Already? Homer glanced at his Quality Solar-Powered Subatomic Watch. Noon in Milkydale. The Milkydale

County Fair officially opened at one o'clock. Corn dogs, raspberry lemonade, and soft-serve ice cream in every imaginable flavor waited inside the fairgrounds fence. But what if, while he was at the fair, someone from L.O.S.T. came looking for him or sent another letter with instructions?

"Um, I think I'll stay home," he said. He'd never said that before. Mr. Pudding's mouth fell open.

"Stay home? Have you lost your mind? No son of mine's gonna miss the dog agility trials."

"But, Dad, I've got some things to figure out."

Mr. Pudding slid his cap onto his head. "You can figure them out later. It's a family tradition to go to the fair."

Homer knew there'd be no arguing with his father. When Mr. Pudding set his mind to something, there was usually no changing it.

Homer closed the reptile book and returned it to its hiding place beneath the bed. He didn't want anyone to see his letter, so he stuck that under the floorboard, too. "Come on, Dog," he called as he slid the chair away from the door.

Downstairs, Mrs. Pudding was putting her cherry pies into boxes. She wiped her hands on her apron and cast Homer a concerned glance. "Is that what you're wearing to the fair?"

Homer shrugged. "I guess so."

"Those jeans are getting too short. We'll have to make a trip to Walker's Department Store." She kissed Homer's forehead. "Now, please go and find your sister. Tell her we're ready to leave."

"Where is she?" he asked.

"In her laboratory."

Homer frowned. As a soon-to-be professional treasure hunter, he knew he'd end up trekking through his fair share of unpleasant places—a cave full of vampire bats, a swamp full of leeches, an underground sewer full of rats. But his sister's laboratory was one place he wished he'd never have to go.

"Do I have to?"

"Yes, you do."

"But it's disgusting out there."

"Homer Winslow Pudding, go get your sister."

4

Gwendolyn's Laboratory

Gwendolyn Maybel Pudding was Homer's fifteen-year-old sister, which made her the eldest Pudding child. While Homer, the middle child, loved to read maps, and Squeak, the youngest child, loved to help around the farm, Gwendolyn was crazy for taxidermy. She'd mastered the art of preserving dead animals when she took a summer correspondence course at age nine. Her dream was to become a Royal Taxidermist for the Museum of Natural History.

Taxidermy is not for the squeamish. After an animal

dies, it begins to deteriorate, which causes a horrid stench. In order to preserve the creature, all its innards must be removed. The inside is cleaned, and the creature is stuffed. Its teeth, tongue, and nails are painted with lacquer. Its eyeballs are replaced with glass eyeballs. It's a wonder anyone wants to do it.

A few years back, after Mr. Pudding opened the door to Gwendolyn's bedroom and stepped in a pile of raccoon guts, he declared that she was forbidden to perform her artistic endeavors in the house. So she moved her tools and chemicals to the old shed and filled the shelves with her work. All of her subjects—field mice, squirrels, foxes, weasels, sparrows, and crows—had been caught by the barn cats or the farm dogs or had died from natural causes. Gwendolyn wasn't a murderer—just a preserver.

GWENDOLYN'S LABORATORY: KEEP OUT OR BE STUFFED! the sign on the door read. Homer knocked and called her name. Maybe he wouldn't have to go in. He knocked again. And again. Then, with a steadying breath, he opened the door.

Gwendolyn stood at her workbench, up to her elbows in some sort of goo. Homer gagged, then plugged his nose. The sickly sweet scent of formaldehyde clotted the air. "Hey," he said.

Dog pushed between Homer's legs and stared up at

Gwendolyn. Homer stared, too, because there was something very different about his sister. Her lips were as red as cherries and her eyelids were smeared with blue sparkles. And, beneath her lab coat, she wore a red paisley dress. "You're not supposed to be in here," she said.

"But—"

"You're interrupting important work." She stirred the goo. "I'm practicing for a real job. Not like you and those stupid holes you dig everywhere."

"Treasure hunting's a real job," he said.

A low growl rose in Dog's throat as his gaze traveled over the shelves. Homer suspected that the stuffed creatures confused Dog. After all, they *looked* alive. But any other dog would have smelled the difference.

"Why are you all dressed up?" Homer asked. "You never dress up for the fair."

"I didn't dress up for the stupid fair. For your information, Homer, I dressed up because I felt like dressing up." After pouring green liquid into a beaker, she dropped in an eyeball. Then she whipped around and glared at Homer. "*Why* are you in my laboratory?"

The eyeball floated in the liquid like a marshmallow in green Jell-O. Homer cringed.

"Hello? Earth to Homer."

"Uh, Mom wanted me to tell you that it's time to go."

"Why didn't you say something?" She plunged her

hands into the sink and scrubbed. "If we're late, I'm gonna be soooo mad." She tossed her lab coat onto a hook. Then, with long, huffy strides, she headed out the door. Homer unplugged his nose and shared a confused look with Dog. Predicting the weather was so much easier than predicting Gwendolyn's moods—no clouds hung over her head to let you know when a storm was about to let loose.

With a final growl at a stuffed raccoon, Dog followed Homer out of the laboratory and into the front yard, where Mr. Pudding stood, his eyes widening as his daughter stomped past. "What did you do to your face?" Mr. Pudding asked.

Gwendolyn groaned and slid into the truck's backseat. Mrs. Pudding set the pie boxes on the floor of the front seat, then turned to her husband. "Don't tease her," she said.

"Tease her? I'm not teasing her." Mr. Pudding rubbed the back of his neck. "I just want to know what she did to her face."

"She has a date," Mrs. Pudding said as she climbed into the front seat.

Mr. Pudding grabbed his chest as if he were having a heart attack. "A date?"

Squeak stood in the truck's bed. "Come on, Max, come on, Lulu," he called. Max and Lulu dashed up the wooden ramp that had been set up for them. They settled in the truck's bed, their tails happily wagging, their freshly shampooed coats shiny and smooth.

"Date," Mr. Pudding mumbled as he grabbed the ramp.

"Hey, Dad, what about Dog?" Homer asked.

Mr. Pudding frowned. "What about him?"

"He needs the ramp, too. I can't lift him."

"You want to take your dog to the fair?" Mr. Pudding asked.

"I can't leave him here alone. He'll howl. And what if he eats something he's not supposed to eat?"

"That's true, dear," Mrs. Pudding called from the front seat. "That dog will make a ruckus if we leave him alone. And he could get into serious trouble by eating something indigestible. Let him come. Homer will look after him."

"Fine." As Mr. Pudding set the plank back in place, he grumbled about Dog not being like the other farm dogs. Homer led Dog to the end of the ramp, then gave his rump a push. While Max and Lulu had mastered the ramp with grace and ease, Dog struggled and wobbled, then slid backward.

"Homer!" Gwendolyn cried, her face pressed against the truck's back window. "Hurry up. We're gonna be late!"

Homer pushed again and again, until finally, Dog stumbled into the truck's bed. Homer joined him. Max sniffed Dog while Lulu licked Dog's long nose. Dog didn't sniff back. Homer wondered if this was considered rude in the canine world, like a person refusing to shake another person's hand. Maybe that was why the farm dogs never hung out with Dog.

Mr. Pudding drove the red truck down the Puddings' driveway. The Pudding farmhouse grew smaller as the truck turned onto Grinning Goat Road. Soon, Homer's bedroom window was just a speck.

Homer ran his hand over one of Dog's long ears. It wasn't easy having to watch Dog all the time. Sometimes it frustrated Homer, no doubt about it. It would be nice to simply open the kitchen door and send Dog out into the yard to do his business. To know that he wouldn't eat anything poisonous and that he wouldn't get lost because he'd wandered off and couldn't track his way back home.

But Dog wasn't *the* most difficult dog in the world. And so what if he wasn't like the farm dogs? So what if his hair wasn't glossy and it didn't ripple when the wind blew through it? So what if he didn't have long athletic legs or the instinct to herd? And so what if he didn't smell like shampoo from the groomer's salon but instead smelled exactly like a basset hound, which was kind of like a rancid corn chip? Dog could do something that no other dog in the world could do. Homer smiled as the secret tickled his insides.

"Homer, what's a date?" Squeak said.

"It's when a boy and girl go somewhere together 'cause they like each other," Homer told his little brother.

"Oh." Squeak buried his face in Max's fur. "That's weird."

"Yeah. Really weird."

Homer reached into his shirt and pulled out a fake Galileo Compass that he wore on a leather cord around his neck. The compass had been a gift from a girl named Lorelei, sent to him just a few weeks ago. She wasn't his girlfriend, not in *that* way. But she was his friend—a fellow adventurer who lived beneath the Museum of Natural History in her own secret lair. He'd met her when he'd traveled to The City three months ago to solve the mystery of the gold L.O.S.T. coin. She'd been nice to him, but then she'd deceived him by kidnapping Dog. In the end they'd saved each other from the evil Madame la Directeur and her mutant carnivorous tortoise and had parted as friends. He'd promised to keep the secret of her lair and she'd promised to keep the secret of his treasure-smelling dog.

Homer imagined her smiling face, her bold pink hair, and the way she clomped around in her sneakers. He wanted to write her a letter, but how do you send a letter to a secret lair?

Someday they'd meet again. He hoped. And when they did meet, he'd be an official member of the secret Society of Legends, Objects, Secrets, and Treasures. A professional treasure hunter.

"We're going to the fair," Squeak said, sticking his face into the wind.

Homer tucked the compass back into his shirt and smiled.

5

Opening Day of the Milkydale County Fair

Mr. Pudding drove into the muddy, pothole-covered parking lot just outside the fairgrounds. Trucks of all sizes and colors filled the lot. Everyone in Milkydale had come for the opening ceremony, as had families from the nearby towns of Plumtree and Turkeyville, and from as far away as the coastal village of Sunny Cove. Some families had arrived in motor homes, while others had set up tents. The fair would run all week, and many families would stay for the duration.

Kids screamed with glee as they ran toward the gates. Even their parents smiled giddily. The fair was usually the most exciting thing to happen in Milkydale. With no shopping mall or bowling alley, with only a single-screen movie theater and a one-room schoolhouse, the village tended to be a quiet, low-key kind of place. Sure, people got worked up when the baby goats were born and when the frogs hatched in Frog Egg Pond, but other than when the library burned to the ground three months ago, most Milkydale days could be described in one word—*ho-hum*.

"I need to deliver my pies to the pie booth," Mrs. Pudding said as the family scrambled out of the truck. She handed Gwendolyn a ten-dollar bill. "I'd like you to take Squeak to the gunnysack slide."

"The gunnysack slide!" Squeak hollered, just about keeling over from anticipation. Last year he hadn't been tall enough to ride the monstrous slide, but the latest pencil line on his growth chart revealed he'd finally passed the three-foot mark.

"Me?" Gwendolyn stomped her foot. "Why can't Homer do it?"

"Gwendolyn Maybel Pudding, don't argue with me. Homer has enough on his hands watching that dog of his. I need you to watch your little brother until the pie contest is over. I'm sure your *friend* won't mind." Mrs.

Pudding checked her reflection in the truck's window. She fluffed her curly hair, then turned back to her daughter. "I'm relying on you, Gwendolyn. I don't want Squeak shooting off the end of the slide and bumping his head."

"The gunnysack slide!" Squeak hollered again, dancing right through a puddle. "I'm finally tall enough," he informed another boy who was hurrying past with his parents. The boys shared an ecstatic giggle.

"Whatever," Gwendolyn said through clenched teeth. "But as soon as the pie contest is over, I'm doing my own thing." She took Squeak's hand and pulled him toward the gates.

Mrs. Pudding handed Homer a ten-dollar bill. "You have some fun before the dog trials begin." She kissed his cheek. Then, boxes in hand, she hurried away, the ruffle on her denim skirt swishing. Homer tucked the bill into his jean pocket, imagining the colossal corn dog he'd buy.

"Good luck," Mr. Pudding called to his wife. Then he opened the truck's tailgate and set the ramp into place. Max and Lulu sniffed the air. The rich scents of popcorn and cotton candy mixed with the pungent scents of horses and cows. The dogs' tails wagged eagerly. "They know why they're here," Mr. Pudding said. "They can't wait for the dog trials."

The farm dogs circled each other, eager smiles on

their faces. While border collies love to work the field, they also love to play. And that's what the dog trials were—a day of fun and games, of jumping through hoops, crawling through tunnels, and racing around obstacles. Those with the best times would compete tomorrow, and then the next day, until the final dogs competed on the last day of the fair.

"I see you've brought the same dogs as last year." The unfriendly voice belonged to Mr. Crescent, the Puddings' neighbor. The sign on his driveway read:

CRESCENT GOAT FARM
Home of the Champion Crescent Border Collies,
Winners of Five County Fair Blue Ribbons.

"I've brought Molly and her pup, Bull," he said as he walked up to the red truck. Two leashed border collies followed. "You remember Molly, I'm sure. Last year's champion." He slid his toothpick to the other corner of his mouth.

Mr. Pudding tucked his thumbs behind his overall straps. "This isn't last year, Crescent, so don't go getting yourself all puffed up. My dogs are good and ready."

"As are mine." Mr. Crescent tucked his thumbs behind his straps. "Good and ready."

As the two men glared at each other, Homer leaned

against the truck. He didn't much like Mr. Crescent, but it had nothing to do with dogs. It had to do with the time Mr. Crescent hollered at him for digging a hole. Homer hadn't realized he'd crossed the property line because he'd been thinking about Angus MacDoodle, a local man who'd found a trove of Celtic coins in his backyard. Homer had gotten so wound up with possibility that he'd forgotten to look around before digging.

As the two men boasted about who would win the blue ribbon, the border collies wagged their tails, greeting one another with licks and sniffs. Dogs don't have much use for blue ribbons, though Homer's dog would probably eat one if given the chance.

"I see you've got that other dog with you." Mr. Crescent pointed to the corner of the truck's bed where Dog lay curled on Homer's coat, fast asleep.

"He's not competing," Mr. Pudding said.

"No kidding?" Mr. Crescent snickered. "I think he should compete. The audience always appreciates a good laugh."

Homer's cheeks burned.

Mr. Crescent tugged on his leashes. "Come on, Bull, come on, Molly. We've got to get you ready. You've got a blue ribbon to win." As they sauntered off toward the dog barn, Mr. Pudding mumbled a few things that needn't be repeated. Then he gathered his own leashes. "You go have some fun, then meet me at the dog barn just before the trials." With a quick whistle, the farm dogs followed him toward the fairgrounds.

Homer looked into the truck bed. No rich scents tickled Dog's nose. No memories of past fairs washed over him. His back leg twitched as he snored. Homer guessed he was chasing something, probably a rabbit. He'd learned from Dr. Huckle, Milkydale's veterinarian, that basset hounds were bred to track prey, like rabbits. But since Dog couldn't pick up scents, rabbits often sneaked right past him. Once, a rabbit hopped right over Dog as he slept in the upper pasture. But in his dreams, Homer suspected that Dog was the king of rabbit-chasing.

The Ferris wheel and the Whirl-a-Tron loomed behind the fairgrounds' gate. The top of the galaxy roller coaster peaked in the distance. The scents of popping corn and cotton candy beckoned. *Next year when I go to the fair, I'll be a member of a secret society*, Homer thought, a grin spreading across his face. He climbed into the truck bed. "Wake up," he said, gently poking Dog's leg. "Let's go get something to eat."

Dog opened one eye, then the other. "Ur."

"Yeah, something to eat."

And that's when Homer noticed it—a little black card,

covered in gold stars, tucked at the edge of the truck's tailgate.

★ ★ ★ **Excelsior the Excellent—★ ★ ★**
Fortune-teller to the Stars.
This card is good for one free fortune told on opening day of the Milkydale County Fair.

6
The Worst Fortune Ever

"Welcome to the one hundred and fifty-seventh Milkydale County Fair," Mayor Sneed called. She stood just inside the gate, waving at people as they entered. Her white blouse was buttoned all the way to her pointy chin, and she wore a big red sash that read: THE HONORABLE MAYOR. Her smile turned sour when she spotted Homer. "Is that the same dog that burned down our library?"

"It was an accident," Homer said, holding tight to Dog's leash. Almost every day, somebody reminded

Homer that he and Dog had been responsible for burning down Milkydale's only library. Homer had given up his real Galileo Compass, which had been sold to fund the new library. Fortunately, the foundation had been poured, and Homer couldn't wait to walk through the doors.

"Well, you make sure he doesn't get into trouble, young man." Mayor Sneed shook a finger in Homer's face. "The first sign of trouble and that dog will have to leave."

"He won't get into trouble," Homer said. As he hurried away, he murmured to Dog, "Please don't get into trouble."

"Hey, Homer." Wilbur, one of the boys from school, knocked into Homer's arm. "Where's your compass? Better get it out or you might get lost." Earl, another boy from school, laughed. Fortunately, teasing Homer wasn't as important as getting to the roller coaster and they dashed past, tickets in hand. Homer rubbed his arm. They wouldn't think he was so funny when he had an entire wing of a museum named after him.

Homer's stomach growled as a succulent scent drifted up his nose. After finding the familiar red-and-white-striped booth, he bought two colossal corn dogs—one for him, one for Dog. Sitting side by side on a bench, they enjoyed their meal. Dog inhaled his in three bites, licking his lips with satisfaction. Homer dipped his in yellow mustard. Then they both washed the corn dogs down with a long drink of lemonade. A brief struggle followed as Dog tried to eat the lemonade cup and Homer had to wrestle it free.

"Come on," Homer said, tossing the mangled cup into the garbage.

They turned onto a side path and walked beneath a banner: ODDITIES AND FABULOSITIES. Stalls lined each side of the path where vendors sold all sorts of stuff—blue fish swimming in bowls, rings that changed color if the wearer told a lie, nets that caught nightmares. Homer was about to try on one of the rings when something sparkly caught his eye. There, at the end of the path, sat a black tent covered in glimmering golden stars. A man in a long black robe stood outside the tent. He smiled at Homer.

"Who's that man?" Homer asked the ring seller.

"He's a fortune-teller," the ring seller said. "But he's a fake. My rings, however, are not fakes. They will always tell you the truth."

Homer reached into his pocket and pulled out the card he'd found. EXCELSIOR THE EXCELLENT—FORTUNE-TELLER TO THE STARS. Homer had never had his fortune read, and he definitely had some questions about his future. He flicked the card between his fingers, thinking.

"Grrrr." Dog stood in the next stall staring at an African tribal mask. Homer had to tug extra hard on the leash to pull him away. "Come on," he said. "Let's go get our fortunes told."

The robed man's smile widened as Homer and Dog approached. "Salutations," he said with outstretched arms.

"Hi," Homer said. "Are you Excelsior?"

"The one and only." He spoke in an odd sort of way, with a voice much higher than one would expect from such a large man. A gentle breeze blew through his long white hair and long white beard. If Homer had to imagine a fortune-teller, say, for a homework assignment, he'd imagine him to look exactly like Excelsior.

Excelsior reached down and patted Dog's head. "And you are?"

"I'm Homer and this is Dog. I've got a ticket for a free fortune told." He held out the ticket and Excelsior took it. Sunlight glinted off a large ruby ring that Excelsior wore on his index finger. On his other index finger, an emerald ring sparkled. He wore both rings over a pair of black gloves.

"This must be your lucky day," he said. "I only printed a few of these tickets." Then he turned, distracted by a scurrying sound.

The sound came from a girl who was walking past the tent. She carried a cage in which sat a brown rabbit. Dog, up until that moment, hadn't noticed the rabbit barn just across the path. But he took notice of the cage as it passed in front of his face, because a pair of red eyes stared warily from between the bars. With a fierce tug, Dog pulled the leash taut, his little legs pumping furiously. "Urrrr."

"No, Dog," Homer said, holding tight to the leash. "Leave the rabbit alone."

The girl glanced nervously at Dog, then carried the cage into the rabbit barn. Dog whined.

"How do you tell someone's fortune?" Homer asked.

Excelsior tucked the card into the pocket of his robe. "Well, there are many methods. The crystal ball is popular but highly unpredictable. Tarot cards often ask more questions than they answer. Tea leaves make a mess, and head bumps can be misleading. I prefer palm reading. A palm never lies." With a sweep of his arm, Excelsior opened the tent's flap and secured it with a cord. Then he raised his eyebrows and waited.

"Okay," Homer said with a shrug. "I'll get my palm read." He tugged on the leash. "Come on, Dog."

Dog whined, then plopped onto his belly, transforming his long body into what approximated a bag of cement—a clever ploy he used when he didn't want to go anywhere. Lying on the ground, he pointed his face at the rabbit barn.

"You can leave him there," Excelsior suggested. "Tie the leash to the tent pole."

"Will you leave the tent flap open so I can see him?" Homer asked. "He hates to be left alone."

"Certainly."

Homer peered into the tent. An oil lamp glowed from atop a little table. Two stools waited. Homer would have a clear view of Dog, and Dog, if he managed to tear his gaze away from the rabbit barn and turn around, would have a clear view of Homer.

After tying the leash to the tent pole, Homer sat on one of the stools. Excelsior sat on the other stool, arranged his robe, then placed a puffy black hat on his head. The lamp's glow spread across Excelsior's face, casting a yellow tint to his beard and mustache. "What is it you would like to know?" Excelsior asked.

Homer glanced over at Dog, who hadn't moved an inch. "My future," Homer said. "I'd like to know my future."

Excelsior fiddled with his ruby ring. "Yes, indeed. But is there something specific about your future? One question that, more than any other question, you would like answered?"

Homer couldn't ask when he'd become a member of L.O.S.T., because a secret society must remain a secret. So he decided to ask about Rumpold Smeller's treasure.

But how could he do that without giving away too much information? If he asked, "Will I find what I'm looking for?" Excelsior would probably ask, "What are you looking for?" So Homer thought about it for a moment, then asked, "Will I be successful on my quest?"

"Ah. A quest." Excelsior's eyes widened. "Is it a noble quest?"

"I think so." He pushed his curly bangs from his eyes. "How do you know if it's noble or not?"

"What is the purpose of the quest?"

"I made a promise to someone and I want to keep that promise."

"Then it is a noble quest. And there is nothing more important in life than a noble quest. I shall help you find the answer to your query." Excelsior reached out and took Homer's left hand, turning the palm faceup. Even through the black gloves, his long fingernails prickled Homer's skin. "It is the left palm that reveals truth, for it is aligned with the heart."

That makes sense, Homer thought, sneaking another glance at Dog, who was still fixated on the rabbit barn. Homer could practically hear Dog's thoughts—*rabbit, rabbit, rabbit, rabbit, rabbit.*

Excelsior held Homer's palm close to the lamp. "Ah," he said. "How interesting. Did you know that you possess a treasure hunter's line?"

Homer nearly fell off the stool. He grabbed the table's edge with his free hand. "I do? Where?"

Excelsior pointed to a line that ran across the base of Homer's thumb. "I have only seen this line one other time. Will you be seeking treasure on this quest of yours?"

Homer hesitated, his mind racing. It couldn't hurt to admit such a thing. Everybody in Milkydale knew that Homer wanted to be a treasure hunter. "Yes," he said. "But I can't tell you what kind of treasure."

"I understand." Excelsior narrowed his eyes. "A noble quest for treasure is a serious quest indeed." Then he ran his gloved fingertip across Homer's palm, stopping in the center. He gasped and leaned closer, the ends of his long white hair brushing the tabletop. He ran his fingertip across Homer's palm again and stopped in the exact same spot. He gasped louder.

"What is it?" Homer asked, leaning so close that he and Excelsior bumped foreheads.

"A fork in the road," Excelsior whispered.

They both sat up. Homer fidgeted at the edge of his stool. "A fork?" he asked, the suspense unbearable. "What does *that* mean?"

Excelsior let go of Homer's palm, then shook his head. "Dear oh dear. This is most unfortunate."

"What?" Homer asked. "What's unfortunate?"

"Is there anything else you could do besides search

for treasure? Is there something that your parents would like you to do? Something that's...*safe*?"

Homer didn't like the direction of this conversation. "My dad wants me to be a goat farmer. That's pretty safe."

"Yes, that sounds like a much better plan."

"But I don't want to be a goat farmer." Homer held out his palm. "I don't understand. What does the fork mean?"

Excelsior tapped a finger on the table. He looked long and hard at Homer. "You will not like the answer. Do you still want me to read your palm?"

A chill crept over Homer. He stared at his left palm. What other secrets hid between the lines? "Maybe we should go ahead and read the bumps on my head." He looked up hopefully, but Excelsior said nothing. Homer swallowed. "Okay, I want to know. What do you see?"

With a sigh, Excelsior pointed to a line that ran diagonally across Homer's palm. "This is your life line. You see how long it is? You see how it reaches all the way across?" Homer nodded. "It's a long life line. But you see here? You see where the life line splits? That is the fork. One route is long, the other is short. Very, very short."

"You mean...?" Sweat broke out on Homer's palm.

"An untimely end awaits you if you take the wrong route."

"An untimely end?" Homer wiped his palm on his

jeans. "But how do I know which route is the wrong route?"

"It's all there on your palm. Your treasure-hunting line feeds into the shorter life line. It's all very clear. A palm never lies."

"But—"

"But nothing. The fact is etched in skin and blood." Excelsior smiled knowingly and then said the most horrid words Homer had ever heard. "It's very simple. Treasure hunting will kill you."

7

The Black
Rabbit of Doom

Treasure hunting is dangerous. Really, really dangerous. Treasure hunters typically have shorter life spans than, say, fortune-tellers or baseball players or even crocodile wranglers. And the causes of death tend to be dramatic—falling off the edge of a volcano, getting crushed by a giant boulder, being eaten by a carnivorous tortoise. Homer knew all this. But still, when someone tells you right to your face that you're going to die if you pursue your dream, it's not such a nice thing to hear.

"How soon will treasure hunting kill me?" Homer asked Excelsior.

"Oh, very soon. Very, very soon."

One half of Homer's brain said, *How can that guy possibly know anything from the lines on my hand?* But the other half of Homer's brain screamed, *Listen to that guy!*

"You must take this seriously," Excelsior said. "I have been telling fortunes for many years now, and I am never wrong."

That's when a crash sounded. Homer whipped around. Dog scrambled to his feet and started barking. As Dog pulled on his leash, the tent pole bent and the tent's ceiling sagged. "Can't you control your dog?" Excelsior asked in an extra-high voice.

Homer hurried outside. A boy had dropped his rabbit cage next to the rabbit barn. The cage door hung open. A black rabbit poked its head out of the cage, wiggled its nose, then hopped onto the ground. Dog pumped his hind legs, straining against his leash. "Dog," Homer said, trying to untie the leash. "Stop pulling." The pole bent further.

"My rabbit!" the boy cried as the rabbit hopped in confused circles.

"Grrrr." With a burst of energy, Dog yanked with all his might. The tent pole snapped and the leash came free. Dog made his escape just as the tent collapsed and covered Homer in a sea of glittering stars. Flailing his arms, Homer struggled to get clear of the heavy fabric. Finally, a patch of sunlight peeked through and he crawled out. "Dog!" he cried, struggling to his feet.

"He's chasing my rabbit," the boy said, pointing into the rabbit barn.

"Sorry about your tent," Homer called as Excelsior stuck his head out of the collapsed tent, his puffy hat tipped over his eyes.

"Remember," Excelsior shouted, "I am never wrong!"

By the time Homer reached the rabbit barn, chaos had hit—overturned cages, escaped rabbits, and dazed, teary-eyed kids lay about. A heat-seeking missile could have caused such destruction but surely not a droopy, overfed basset hound. "Dog!" he called. He bumped into a boy who was trying to catch a pygmy Holland Lop. "Have you seen a basset hound?"

"Yeah, he knocked over my table," the boy said, his lower lip trembling. "My rabbit got out."

"I'm sorry," Homer said, torn between helping the boy and finding Dog before he did more damage. A chorus of barking solved the dilemma. Homer jumped over a gray angora bunny, leaped over a golden hare, then ran out the far end of the barn and turned the corner. His stomach clenched. The barking came from the dog barn. Dog must have chased the black rabbit into the dog barn.

Homer's father was in there, along with the other farmers and their dogs.

"Dog!" Homer called.

The black rabbit appeared, a wild expression in its eyes. It tore out of the dog barn and ran right past Homer. Dog appeared next, bounding after the rabbit, his ears swinging, his stubby legs pumping furiously. Then, like balls from a cannon, border collie after border collie shot out of the barn. Homer pressed against a red wall as they raced past, their sleek black-and-white coats rippling.

"Molly!" "Spot!" "Rover!" the farmers cried, rushing from the barn.

Mr. Pudding cupped his hands around his mouth. "Max! Lulu!"

What followed is best described as a natural disaster. The black rabbit led the dogs on an agility course that had no rules, no borders, no judges or blue ribbons. The dog pack knocked over a lemonade seller, whose cart rolled from his hands and overturned, creating a sticky yellow lake. The dogs knocked over Mayor Sneed, who'd been judging an all-you-can-eat ice cream contest. Her red sash got wrapped around her head and her high heels flew off. The dogs darted beneath a striped tent, where screams erupted as a table of pies flew into the air. Apple, cherry, and peach filling rained down on the unlucky bystanders. Homer stopped long enough to help his mother to her feet. Piecrust clung to her hair. "Sorry about the pies," he said.

The dog pack trampled a balloon seller, charged through a ringtoss game, then darted around the sheep barn. Dog, his leash dragging behind, was no longer the leader, but was doing his best to keep up as the black rabbit headed for the gunnysack slide.

Next to the slide, Gwendolyn and a frizzy-haired boy sat on a bench sharing a tub of popcorn. Homer cringed as the dog pack knocked the bench over. Her legs in the air, popcorn all over her face, Gwendolyn spotted him and screamed, "HOMER!"

"Sorry!"

Momentarily losing track of the rabbit, the dogs skidded to a stop at the base of the gunnysack slide and turned in confused circles. Homer, gasping for breath, caught up with the dogs and looked around. Where was the rabbit?

"Hi, Homer," Squeak called, waving proudly from the very top of the slide. Kids were lined all the way up the stairs waiting for their turns. An exit stairway stood on the other side of the slide for those kids who chickened out and changed their minds once they reached the top. Squeak, unaware of the impending doom, arranged his gunnysack. "I'm gonna go so fast," he said. He waved at

Homer again, then went to sit on his sack but found a black ball of quivering fur sitting on it. "Hey, what are you doing here?" The rabbit, breathing wildly, thumped a warning with its back leg.

Like a black-and-white jet stream, the pack of border collies flew up the exit stairs. The entire slide wobbled. Dog whined, his front paws planted on the first step, waiting for someone to push his rump up the stairs.

"Go away," the gunnysack man hollered, shaking a fist at the oncoming dogs.

Homer froze, watching openmouthed as the slide wobbled to and fro. The wooden beams creaked. "Earthquake!" someone yelled. Parents shouted at their kids to get off. The first border collie reached the top of the stairs and headed toward the rabbit.

"Squeak!" Homer cried. "Hold on!"

But what was there to hold on to? As the rest of the dog pack reached the top, the slide jerked violently. Squeak lost his balance and fell onto his gunnysack, right on top of the rabbit. "Ahhhh!" Squeak cried as, face-first, he started down the slide. The rabbit, its nose aquiver, peeked out from beneath Squeak's chest. The dogs watched from the top as Squeak and the rabbit flew off the end of the slide. Squeak landed at Homer's feet, but the rabbit shot right between Homer's legs. Then it scampered beneath a chain-link fence and disappeared.

Rather than taking the slide, the dogs pushed their way down the other set of stairs, right through the lined-up kids. Parents held out their arms to catch their toppling children. Between all the barking and screaming, Homer could barely hear his own voice. "Are you okay?" he asked his little brother.

"Yeah." Squeak rubbed his backside as a smile burst across his face. "That was a blast!"

The pack of border collies leaped off the stairs, then raced to the chain-link fence. Sticking their noses through the gaps in the links, they barked and barked. But once they realized they couldn't get through, they lost interest, stopped barking, and settled down. Dog, exhausted from the rabbit chase, collapsed next to Squeak.

Parents hugged their frightened children. The farmers began to gather their border collies. People wiped pie filling from their faces, and Gwendolyn and her date picked popcorn out of their hair. Homer sighed with relief. It was over. No one had gotten seriously hurt. For a moment it seemed as if the fair would go on as usual.

But a loud groaning sound made everyone stop, turn, and stare in horror. The gunnysack slide, which had been wobbling back and forth, shuddered, then collapsed in a heap of wood and metal, sending a cloud of gunnysacks into the air.

For a long moment no one said a word. Children and

adults alike stared at the pile of rubble. Squeak's eyes filled with tears. The gunnysack man stared at the wreckage that had once been his livelihood. "My slide," he whimpered.

"What's going on?" Mayor Sneed asked as she pushed her way through the gathered crowd. "Who did this?"

The boy who owned the black rabbit pointed at Dog. "It's his fault. He chased my rabbit."

"That dog?" Mayor Sneed asked. She straightened her sash. "That fat dog lying on the ground?" Her gaze darted here and there until it rested on Homer's red face. "Isn't that *your* dog?"

"Uh-huh," Homer said.

"Thanks a lot, Homer," said Prudence, a girl from school. "The gunnysack slide was my favorite ride."

In all his years of going to the Milkydale County Fair, Homer had always had a good time. But this day was the worst ever. "It was an accident," he murmured. "Basset hounds are supposed to chase rabbits. He couldn't help it."

Mr. and Mrs. Pudding pushed their way through the crowd. "Homer, what's happened?" Mrs. Pudding asked, cherry filling on her cheeks. "Is anyone hurt?"

Gwendolyn lunged at Homer, pointing a finger in his face. "I can't believe you did this," she hissed. "I could just die of embarrassment. You're the worst brother ever!"

Mr. Crescent had an opinion, as usual, and he expressed it so the entire crowd could hear. "Those Puddings don't know how to control their animals. First the library, now this."

Mr. Pudding grabbed Homer's arm and pulled him aside. "Did you do this?" he asked, anger sizzling beneath the words. "Was it your dog that started the rabbit chase?"

"It was an accident." Homer looked at his feet. "I'm sorry, Dad. It was an accident. It's his instinct to chase rabbits. He couldn't help it."

"Maybe so, but he's your responsibility." Mr. Pudding let go of Homer's arm. "I wish I'd never let you keep that dog." Homer's thoughts flew back to three months prior, when his father had wanted to send Dog away. Panic swelled in his chest.

"Mr. Pudding," Mayor Sneed interrupted, "may I speak to you privately?"

Mr. Pudding tucked his cap into the back pocket of his overalls. Then he and Mayor Sneed spoke in hushed tones. People stopped hollering and leaned forward, trying to catch the conversation. After a few nods, the mayor spun around and waved her arms. "That's enough. This area will be roped off. Everyone go back and enjoy the rest of the day. There's nothing more to see here."

"But what about the Pudding kid and his dog?" Mr. Crescent asked. "What if they cause more trouble?"

"Homer Pudding and his dog are banned from the fair for the duration," Mayor Sneed announced, her hands planted on her ample hips.

Banned? Surely Homer hadn't heard right?

"What about my gunnysack slide?" the gunnysack man asked. "Who's gonna pay for that?"

"I'll pay for it," Mr. Pudding said. "If my boy's dog did this, then I'll pay."

Homer's stomach clenched. His father couldn't pay for the slide. Goat farmers weren't rich.

"Mr. Pudding and I will discuss compensation," Mayor Sneed said. "Now, everyone, please go and enjoy the day."

Murmuring, the crowd dispersed, including Gwendolyn's date. Mayor Sneed turned to Mr. and Mrs. Pudding. "I won't change my mind. Homer and his dog are banned, and that's final. I suggest you send them home immediately. As for the cost to replace the gunnysack slide, I will be in contact with you." She sidestepped some pigeons that were helping themselves to the spilled popcorn, then strode away, the ends of her sash flapping in her wake.

Mr. Pudding hung his head. Homer reached out to touch his father's arm but stopped midway. It was as if an invisible wall stood between them. "Dad?"

"There's nothing to be done now," Mr. Pudding said. He took his handkerchief from his back pocket and wiped sweat and frustration from his face. "I've got to get the dogs back to the dog barn. You go on home, Homer. We'll talk about this tonight." Without looking at his son, he walked off, his shoulders hunched, the farm dogs following at his heels.

Homer had seen those hunched shoulders too many times in his life, and he'd always been the cause. *Why do I always mess things up?* he asked himself.

Mrs. Pudding put her hand on Homer's back. He looked into her gold-flecked eyes. "Why does Dad have to pay for the slide? It wasn't his fault. I'll pay. Just like I did with the library. I'll figure out a way to get enough money."

"Your heart's always in the right place," Mrs. Pudding said as she hugged him. "Don't you worry about all the details. The grown-ups will sort that out. Now, I've got to stay and help the ladies clean up the pie mess. I want you and Dog to walk on home. We'll see you later, around suppertime."

"Bye, Homer," Squeak said as Mrs. Pudding took his hand and headed toward the pie tent. "Bye, Dog."

Dog, still lying on his side, barely mustered the strength to wag his tail.

"I will never live this down," Gwendolyn snarled. "And now my date's too embarrassed to be seen with me." She kicked the empty popcorn bucket, then stomped off.

A cleaning crew, dressed in white overalls, hung orange DANGER tape around the pile of rubble that used to be the gunnysack slide. Homer heaved Dog to his feet. "I know you're tired, but we have to go."

"Ur."

Clutching the end of the leash, Homer took the long walk of shame down the fair's main pathway, his feet like concrete blocks. Never in the history of the Milkydale County Fair had anyone ever been banned. Even if he became a professional treasure hunter and found Rumpold Smeller's treasure, he'd never live this day down. Opening day of the 157th Milkydale County Fair would go down in infamy.

"Don't try sneaking back in," the guy at the ticket booth said.

"I won't," Homer grumbled as he and Dog walked out the front gate. They passed the empty grandstand and trudged across the parking lot. What a cruddy day. It had begun on such a high note with the words *Your time has come.* Then it had veered off course with the warning *Treasure hunting will kill you.* Only to smash to smithereens with *You are banned.*

Homer wished he had a book for the long walk home—something to take his mind off his troubles.

"Grrrr."

The black rabbit sat just beyond the parking lot, beneath an oak tree. Dog pulled hard on the leash. "Oh no," Homer said. "You're not chasing that rabbit again. No way."

The rabbit hopped here, then there, sniffing a tree, tasting a shrub, bouncing around in a crazy freedom dance. Then it stopped and sniffed a puffball of fog that was about the size of Homer's hand. The puffball floated over the rabbit's head into a grove of trees where a larger patch of fog hovered. *Odd*, thought Homer. *What's fog doing in the woods on such a beautiful, sunny day?*

Homer took a quick breath and held it as he realized what he was looking at. It wasn't fog. It was a cloud, fallen from the sky.

And that could only mean one thing.

8

An Errand of Utmost Importance

"Zelda!" Homer cried as he ran into the grove of birch trees.

Sure enough, Zelda Wallow stood next to her cloudcopter, her head level with its roof. At eight feet two inches, she was the tallest person Homer had ever seen or known.

For those of you not familiar with a unique mode of transportation known as a cloudcopter, imagine a helicopter that has no doors and is powered by steam. Imagine a tangled mass of pipes sticking out all over the 'copter, from which soft puffballs of cloud emerge. The pilot refers to this as "cloud cover" and it can be set on minimum or maximum, depending on how much camouflage is needed. Now imagine looking up and seeing one of these things. It would look like a cloud, and even though it was moving kind of fast, you'd never suspect that someone was driving it. That would be insane. Who drives a cloud?

"Hello, Homer," she said, sliding her goggles onto her broad forehead. She bent over and gave him a hug. Then she knelt and patted Dog's head. "Hello, Dog." Dog wagged his tail.

Homer's grin pushed his cheeks so high that, for a moment, the world went blurry. Though he'd only known Zelda for a short time, he felt as if they'd been lifelong friends.

Just before he died, Uncle Drake had written a last letter to Homer telling him that Zelda could be trusted and that she'd continue Homer's treasure-hunting education. Zelda knew about Homer's secret map. She'd been the one to advise him to keep it hidden. She was a kindred spirit. But she didn't know Dog's secret, because Uncle Drake's last letter had urged Homer not to reveal Dog's secret. So Homer had never told Zelda, or anyone else. Lorelei, the girl with the lair, had figured it out on her own.

Homer peered into the 'copter. "Is Ajitabh with you?"

Ajitabh, the inventor of the cloudcopter, was another friend of Uncle Drake's who'd become Homer's friend.

"No," Zelda said. "Ajitabh is visiting his family in India. His father is ill, so he will not be joining us. So sudden, and so sad."

"Oh." Homer's smile faded for a moment. The swoosh of the fair's roller coaster and the screams of its passengers sounded in the distance. "I'm glad to see you," he said.

"The feeling is mutual." Zelda stopped petting Dog. As she stood, her legs creaked like branches in the wind. When they'd first met, she'd told Homer that she'd been born with a chromosomal abnormality that caused her to grow too much. Though she wasn't a giant in the fairy-tale way, her condition was called gigantism. "But I'm not here for a social visit. I've come to get you."

"Because of the letter?" Homer asked. "Is that why you're here? Did L.O.S.T. send you?"

"They didn't send me, but I am here because of the letter."

"Really? You mean…?" Excitement was building inside him, like the bubbles in a shaken can of soda. He was going to explode right there and then. "YOU MEAN…?"

"Calm down, Homer." Zelda motioned gently with her hand. "Yes, it's true. The membership is inviting you to join."

Homer dropped the leash. As he shouted with joy,

his feet took on a mind of their own and danced him around the 'copter. Dog focused his enthusiasm on a stick, which he gnawed and chewed as if it were a delicious piece of jerky.

"When? When can I join?"

Zelda pressed her hot-dog-size fingers together. "A special meeting of the Society of Legends, Objects, Secrets, and Treasures will be held in a few days. The membership is meeting specifically to discuss your uncle's chair."

"My uncle had a chair?"

"Yes, he had a chair. Well, not an actual chair. A symbolic chair. There are twelve chairs in L.O.S.T., and each chair is filled by a member. But now that Drake's dead, the twelfth chair is empty." She looked him up and down. "Before you claim the chair, however, we've got an errand to run. Go ask your parents if I can take you away for a couple of hours."

"Uh..." Homer fiddled with his ear. "They're at the fair. I can't go ask them because..." He looked away, too embarrassed to tell the story of an afternoon gone terribly wrong.

"Homer? What has happened?"

He fiddled with his other ear, which had started to burn. "I've been banned from the fair. Dog got banned, too. We're supposed to be walking home."

Zelda wrapped her black cloak around her arms. Then

she strode to the edge of the grove and looked over at the fairgrounds. The red roller-coaster cars flashed with sunlight as they sped over a village of striped tents. The orange arms of the octopus ride rose and fell. A massive bouquet of balloons bounced in the breeze. "No one's ever banned me from the fair, but it feels that way," Zelda said in her low voice. "I do not fit on any of the rides. Watching everyone else go round and round on the Ferris wheel always makes me feel so sad." She sighed. "So utterly sad."

Homer had figured out, from their short time together, that Zelda was the kind of person who felt sadness the way other people feel awakeness. It was always with her, carried in her slow movements, floating in her baritone voice. Sadness made her words heavy. She spoke more slowly than most other people, and it sometimes made Homer sleepy just listening to her.

Wispy tendrils of cloud filled Homer's nose with their fresh snowy scent. Dog stretched out on the grass and chewed on the stick. Zelda didn't move, lost in sad memories. Homer hadn't heard from her or from Ajitabh since his adventure in The City, three months ago. He'd worried that they'd forgotten about him.

"What kind of errand?" he asked.

As she strode back to the 'copter, Zelda swept her long silver hair behind her shoulders. "Before he was...*murdered*, your uncle registered your name with the Society as his rightful heir." She reached into the 'copter and grabbed a pair of flight goggles. Then she looked down at Homer, the ever-present furrow between her eyebrows deepening. "That should be enough to guarantee your membership; however life never goes exactly as we plan. I expect that one member will be opposed to having you join."

"Why?"

"Because I suspect that her values are not the same as ours. That is why we must present you in the very best light." She handed Homer the goggles. "You must have proper attire."

"Attire?" Homer cringed. "You mean clothes?"

"Exactly. We're going shopping."

If there was one thing Homer hated, it was shopping for clothes. For what seemed like hours, he'd stand in that dressing room in his underwear while his mother flung a constant stream of stuff over the top of the door. "Try this on, sweetie. It's such a good color on you," she'd say. Or, "Here's a packet of one hundred percent cotton briefs, so you won't get that rash again."

To Homer, who was not the least bit interested in style, one pair of jeans was just as good as another pair of jeans. Trying on clothing was so boring that one time he managed to sneak a book into the dressing room. He sat on the floor and read, pretending to try on the clothes. The next day, when he came downstairs in a new shirt that wouldn't even button around his stomach, and a pair of jeans that was two inches too short, his mother figured it out and banned books from the dressing room.

But Homer's dislike of clothes shopping went beyond the boredom factor. You see, Homer had a body type that did not fit into standard sizes, so he had to shop in the Husky Boys' section at Walker's Department Store. The word *HUSKY* hung above the department in big red letters, and even though his mother thought it was a nice word, everyone knew what it really meant—FAT, FATSO, FATOSAURUS.

"I've got enough clothes," Homer said.

Zelda looked at his blue jeans and plaid shirt and shook her head. "Unfortunately, many people judge others by their appearance. And right now you are dressed like a farm boy and not like a professional treasure hunter."

Homer raised his eyebrows. "I'm going to get professional treasure-hunting clothing?"

"Of course."

"But I don't have money," he said.

Zelda pressed her fingers together again. "It is my gift to you, Homer. Now, how can we do this without worrying your parents? You are supposed to be walking home, is that correct?"

"Yes."

"How long does it take you to walk home from here?"

Homer shrugged. "An hour. Maybe two if I stop and rest a lot."

"And where will your parents be while you are walking home?"

"They're staying at the fair. Mom said they'd be home at suppertime."

"Then I see no problem," Zelda said, reaching into the 'copter to grab a smaller pair of goggles. She knelt and placed the goggles over Dog's eyes. He dropped his stick and shook his head, trying to loosen the goggles. "Walker's Department Store is a quick trip by 'copter. I shall have you home in two hours. Your parents will be none the wiser."

Mr. Pudding's disappointed face flashed before Homer's eyes. Perhaps it wasn't the best day for Homer to disobey his parents. He'd embarrassed them at the fair and Dog's escapade would cost Mr. Pudding a small fortune. But becoming a member of L.O.S.T. was the opportunity of a lifetime. The members of the Society would help him in his search for Rumpold Smeller's treasure. And with their help he'd be successful—of this he was certain. He'd finish what his uncle had started.

"Homer?" Zelda waited for his decision.

Homer chewed on his lower lip. Though his mother had told him to walk home, she hadn't specified that he couldn't run a quick errand along the way. And she hadn't said that he couldn't catch a ride with a friend.

Furthermore, it is a fact that a professional treasure hunter does not require his mother's permission to run an errand.

Homer slid the goggles over his head. "Let's go!"

They took their places in the 'copter. With Dog draped over Homer's lap, and seat belts securely fastened, Zelda set cloud cover to maximum. A dense fog quickly formed. As the 'copter rose above the trees, Homer's stomach clenched. Though he'd ridden on a cloudcopter before, it always took a while for him to get used to the movement. He gripped the edge of the seat as Zelda took a steep turn. Dog whimpered as the 'copter tilted. He tucked his nose inside Homer's sleeve. "It's okay," Homer told him.

"Urrrr."

A few moments later, the 'copter leveled and they were on their way.

The sounds of the fair faded as Zelda, Homer, and Dog flew over Milkydale. They followed Grinning Goat Road, traveled over the Crescent farm, then the Pudding farm. Higher they rose until the goats in the pasture looked like goat droppings. The air grew cold and, as the cloud cover took hold, the world turned white. Anyone looking up would have seen a pretty little white cloud making its way across the sky, as if it had someplace to go.

"How have you been, Homer?"

"Kind of bored," he said.

"Yes. I can imagine. It's difficult to go back to an ordinary life when you've discovered that there's this huge adventure waiting for you."

"Yes," Homer said, scooting forward in the seat. "That's exactly how I feel." He stroked Dog's back. "What about you? How have you been?"

"Sad, mostly."

"Um, last time I saw you, you were going to…" He wasn't sure what to say, exactly.

"I was going to be reunited with the man I loved," she said. "And that's exactly what I did. But, you see, Homer, my situation is similar to yours. How can I accept an ordinary life, living in The City? Once you've got adventure in your life, it's like an incurable infection."

Just as Homer knew, they were kindred souls.

"Hey, Zelda," Homer said. Her black cloak and silver hair were barely visible through the thick cloud that filled the 'copter's interior. "Who doesn't want me to join L.O.S.T.?"

She didn't answer right away. Homer stroked Dog's ear and stared into the whiteness, waiting for reassurance. "Let's not worry about that right now," Zelda said. "In each day there are countless things to worry about. I find that it's best to focus on one worry at a time. Today we must focus on getting you some appropriate clothing."

Homer rested his head against the back of the seat. "Will I have to take a test or anything like that when I go to the meeting? I'm not very good at taking tests."

"I suspect there will be a lot of questions for you, Homer. They might ask you about the quest you wish to undertake. You should know as much about your quest as possible."

"I already know a lot about Rumpold Smeller. I've got a copy of his biography."

"I suggest you reread it," she said. "You should know everything about him." She reached through the cloud and patted Homer's knee. "But don't mention the map. Not yet. Keep it a secret. Keep it hidden."

"Okay."

A mere half hour later they reached the town of Plumtree. Zelda parked the 'copter behind the Plumtree Modern Art Museum. Homer helped Dog out of the 'copter, then tossed their flight goggles onto the seat. As they walked away, an elderly couple stopped to look at the 'copter. "I'll never understand this newfangled modern art," the old man said. "What ever happened to good old-fashioned paintings of flowers and fruit?"

Having been to Walker's Department Store countless times, Homer led the way, with Dog following on the end of his leash. Plumtree was a large town, but not quite a city, for it lacked skyscrapers and pigeon poop. A river snaked through the center of town, crisscrossed by a series of pedestrian bridges. On a street of outdoor cafés, townsfolk looked up from their newspapers and cups of coffee, their jaws dropping as Zelda passed by. Dog stopped to piddle thirteen times.

Walker's Department Store stood two floors tall and was painted bright yellow. "What am I going to do with Dog?" Homer asked. "He'll howl if I leave him outside."

Zelda took the leash from Homer's hand. "Do not fret. I know what to do."

As they walked up to the store's entry, Zelda's shadow fell over a uniformed doorman, who looked up and gasped. Then he froze, forgetting all about his job.

Zelda motioned for Homer to open the door, which he did. Bending so she could fit, she and Dog walked right in. Still frozen in bewilderment, the doorman never once looked at the ground, so he never noticed Dog.

No one inside the store noticed Dog, either. Not the perfume girls, or the makeup counter girls, or any of the customers. Time stood still in Walker's Department Store as each and every person tilted his or her neck and gazed upward.

Homer stepped onto the escalator. "Where are you going?" Zelda asked.

"To the Husky Boys' department," he said quietly. "That's where I get my clothes."

"But we are not going to the Husky Boys' department," she said as she walked past the escalator, Dog waddling behind.

Homer ran up the escalator, then down the other side. "Where are we going?" he asked when he'd caught up.

"We are going to visit my tailor."

Dog's nails clicked against the polished marble floor, but still no one noticed him. Zelda's black cape swished as she wound around displays of purses and fancy gloves. Homer didn't have to worry about any of the sales staff recognizing him. He might as well have been invisible.

He followed Zelda and Dog through the ladies' underwear department, through the men's shoe department, to a hallway with a sign: CHANGING ROOMS. They walked down the hallway to the very last changing room. Zelda pulled a silver key from her cape's pocket and, after inserting the key into the lock, opened the changing-room door. After they'd all squeezed inside, Zelda closed the door. She had to crouch to fit. Dog pressed against Homer's leg.

This was very odd. Surely she'd leave so he could try on the clothes. "What are we—?"

"Hang on," she said, grabbing his hand.

Homer's stomach shot into his throat as the floor gave way.

9

The Treasure
Hunter's Tailor

Homer and Dog sat in the middle of a large
feather pillow, looking equally bewildered.
Homer's bangs hung over his eyes and his
mouth was wide open in a silent scream. One of Dog's
ears was flipped inside out and his leash was draped over
his nose. They both took shallow, desperate breaths as if
they'd had the wind knocked out of them.

We just fell through the ceiling, Homer realized.

A white feather floated past Homer's face. He closed
his mouth and looked at the ceiling. The hole through

which they'd fallen had already closed. Dog moaned, then stuck his nose in Homer's sleeve. Homer, whose heart pounded in his ears, gave Dog a reassuring pat.

The room was large but cluttered. A pair of dressmaker's dummies stood in the corner. A sewing machine, surrounded by industrial-size spools of thread, sat on a long table. Rolls of fabric lay everywhere. Clothes in varying shades of tan and green hung on racks.

Homer scooted to the edge of the pillow. His legs wobbled a bit as he stood, but they steadied as the fright wore off. He'd never plummeted through a floor before. There'd been that one time when he'd tried to climb a cherry tree to snatch a bird's nest for Squeak and he'd tumbled off the branch. Both falls had left him with the same breathless feeling.

"Urrrr." Dog slid off the pillow and squeezed between Homer's shins.

Zelda, who'd recovered immediately, probably because there'd been less distance for her to plummet, stood in the center of the room talking to a man in a tweed suit. The man's dark blue cravat spilled from his neck like a waterfall. "I've got to get him home in an hour's time," she said.

"An hour's time?" the man said, throwing his hands in the air. "You expect me to work miracles. You ask too much." In a huffy manner, reminiscent of Gwendolyn, the man folded his arms and turned his back to Zelda.

"I may ask too much," Zelda said, her husky voice calm and steady. "But there is no one else who could do this work. You are the best, Victor. No one matches your skill. And we need the best."

Victor tapped his brown shoe that shone like polished chocolate. "Well, I am the best."

"The very best," Zelda said.

"That is certainly true," Victor said, examining his fingernails. "But you are not my only client. My schedule is quite full."

"Perhaps this would persuade you." Zelda reached into her black purse and pulled out a wad of cash—even bigger than the wad Homer's father carried at the annual goat auction. "Double the usual fee."

Victor spun on his heels and grabbed the cash. Then his pencil-thin eyebrows flew to the top of his forehead. "I accept the challenge. I assume this is the boy."

Homer shuffled self-consciously as Victor curled his upper lip and stared at him. He tried not to stare back, but it was hard to ignore the tailor's weird hair. Jet-black and parted down the middle, it ended at his shoulders in a perfectly upturned swoop.

"Yes," Zelda said. "This is Homer Pudding, Drake's nephew. Homer, I'd like you to meet Victor Tuffletop. Victor is the official tailor for L.O.S.T."

"Hi," Homer said.

"He's not built anything like his uncle," Victor mumbled. "Whose dog is this?"

"Mine," Homer said.

Victor curled his lip again. "I suppose he'll be accompanying you on your quests?"

"Uh, yes," Homer said. "Definitely."

"Then I'll have to take his measurements, too." He grabbed a yellow measuring tape. "Take off your shoes." While Homer untied his shoes, Victor tugged on Zelda's cape. "Look at this. One of my masterpieces and look how you've treated it. The hem is frayed and there's a discoloration on the shoulder. Did you throw this into the dryer?" His voice swelled to a screech. "The dryer?"

Zelda grimaced guiltily.

Victor threw his hands in the air again. When he did, his hair slid to the right, including the perfect part down the middle. "You have no idea what I go through to create your garments. No one else on the planet works with this fabric." He ruffled her cape. "This is one-of-a-kind, all-weather fabric handspun from shed cobra skin. You can't buy fabric like this. And you threw it into the dryer?"

Zelda opened her mouth, but Victor silenced her with a wave of his hand. "No use giving me your excuses. You all mistreat your garments. Boris was in here last week to patch up his jumpsuit. He wore it in a swamp and was attacked by leeches. Leeches! It says right on the label,

'Not Swamp Compatible.' Disrespect the label and you disrespect me." As he spat out the last statement, his hair tilted further. He marched over to a full-length mirror. Noticing his tilted hair, he set it back into place with a quick yank. Then he motioned for Homer to join him.

Homer looked worriedly at Zelda, but she nodded at him. With Dog at his heels, Homer approached the mirror.

Victor Tuffletop wrapped a tape measure around Homer's neck. "Hold still," he said. The measuring proceeded, Victor's pudgy hands flying here and there, writing each measurement in a notebook. "Fair-skinned. I think an extra-wide hat brim is suitable." More measuring. "Broad-shouldered. I'll add extra stretch to the fabric." He wrote that down. Then he measured again. "Do you always wear your pants so short?"

"Uh, no," Homer said. "I grew."

"I see. Still growing," he said, writing in his notebook. "I'll have to include an extra hem allowance." Then he tossed the tape onto a table. "What is your specialty?" he asked.

Homer wasn't sure how to answer that. He looked to Zelda for help. "Homer is a mapmaker," Zelda said.

"Indeed?" Victor Tuffletop tapped his chin with the end of his pen. "Not too many mapmakers left. It's a dying skill, much like tailoring."

Homer wasn't surprised to hear that. He'd never met any other kids who liked maps.

Zelda sat on a leather sofa. It creaked beneath her weight. "This is a momentous occasion, Homer. Your first fitting," she said, tears glistening in her eyes. "Your uncle would be so proud. He should have been the one to bring you here." She reached into her black handbag and took out a handkerchief.

"He's a bit young for membership," Victor said.

"The youngest yet." Zelda dabbed her eyes. "But he's inherited Drake's chair. This will be his first meeting, so he must look professional when he stands before the membership."

"Of course he'll look professional," Victor said. "I am incapable of producing anything less." He tapped his pen against the notebook. "What about the dog? What is his specialty?"

Homer didn't know what to say about that, either. He wasn't about to tell the tailor that Dog could smell treasure. "He doesn't have a specialty. He's just my friend."

Victor looked down at Dog. "Will he be carrying equipment? Will he be tracking? Will he be guarding the camp?"

"Uh, not really," Homer said.

Victor narrowed his eyes. "Surely he serves some purpose. No treasure hunter takes an animal on a quest unless that animal serves a purpose."

"Really?" Homer looked over at Zelda again.

"I'm sure that Dog could carry a few supplies," Zelda said. She ran her hands over a roll of fabric that lay on the couch. "This is lovely, Victor. What is it?"

"Gossamer gauze. It's made from silk and moth wings. I'm producing a new line of weightless long underwear." He slid the measuring tape around Dog's fat belly. Then he closed his notebook. "I have everything I need. The garments will be ready tomorrow. I expect you'd like them delivered?"

"Yes. To my house," Zelda said.

"Very well." He grabbed a roll of khaki-colored material from a shelf. "Sorry to hear about your uncle. He didn't take care of his clothes any better than the rest of them, but he was a good man. I always enjoyed creating his garments."

Homer wondered why his uncle had never mentioned Mr. Tuffletop. But then again, his uncle had had so many secrets.

"Go on. I've got a lot of work to do. You know the way out."

"Thank you, Victor," Zelda said.

"Thank you, Mr. Tuffletop," Homer said. After putting on his shoes, he and Dog followed Zelda to a doorway.

"Why didn't we use this door instead of falling through the ceiling?" Homer asked as they emerged into a little alley that ran behind the department store.

"Exit only," Zelda said pointing to the door. Sure enough, that's what it said: EXIT ONLY.

Just under the two-hour mark, Zelda landed the cloud-copter in the Puddings' lower pasture. She turned off the engine and, as the cloud cover dissipated, the little farm came into view. "The truck's not here," Homer said as he pulled off his goggles. "That means they're still at the fair."

"Good." Zelda handed Homer two train tickets. "These are round-trip tickets from Milkydale to Gloomy Moor for you and Dog. I will meet you at the Gloomy Moor station."

Homer read the date. "But these are for tomorrow."

Zelda reached into her purse and handed Homer an envelope. "Here is a letter that I've written to your parents inviting you to spend the week with me. You will need to persuade them to accept this invitation. It would be a shame if we missed the membership meeting."

"How will I persuade them?"

"The county fair runs for the entire week. Is that so?"

"Yes," Homer said.

"Then use that as your excuse. You need something to do while your family's at the fair. It was very resourceful of you to get yourself banned."

"I didn't do it on purpose," Homer said, and even if he had, he wasn't sure being banned would help. Mr. Pudding detested any mention of treasure hunting. He'd long resented his brother's abandonment of the goat farm for the glory of treasure, leaving him behind to take care of the place. Asking to stay with one of Uncle Drake's friends would not go over well. "What if they won't let me?" Homer asked.

"It wouldn't be the end of the world," Zelda said with a deep sigh. "But in order for a new member to claim an empty chair, a majority of the membership must be in attendance. That will happen this week. It is rare to have a majority, what with everyone usually scattered to all corners of the world. It could be years before a majority is able to meet again."

"Years?" Homer cried.

Dog stood on Homer's lap. Some of the goats had wandered up to the 'copter. One of them stuck her head into the cockpit and nibbled on Homer's shoelace. "Urrrr," Dog said, wagging his tail.

Zelda sighed. "If you miss this membership meeting, well, then you must wait for the next meeting."

"Which could be years away?"

Zelda nodded.

"I won't miss it," Homer said, pulling his pant leg out of another goat's mouth. "I'll be there. I'll figure out a way."

10

Sticks and Stones

On Sunday morning, the day after the gunnysack slide's collapse, the Milkydale newspaper
editor printed this headline:

PUDDING BOY AND HIS DOG
TRY TO DESTROY FAIR

And printed this article:

Opening day at the county fair, usually a joyous

occasion, was marred by the unfettered delinquency of local boy Homer Pudding and his dog.

Numerous witnesses report that Homer Pudding and his dog ran amuck with complete disregard for public and personal property. While no one was seriously hurt, a number of rabbits have yet to be found and the dog agility trials had to be postponed. Pies, ice cream, and lemonade were among the items destroyed. And there is the matter of the gunnysack slide, which will need to be rebuilt.

"Pudding should pay for the slide," Mr. Crescent said. Mr. Crescent, who lives next door to the Puddings, is familiar with Homer's shenanigans. "He digs holes in my yard. And that stupid dog of his is completely useless."

After surveying the damage, Mayor Sneed wisely banned Homer Pudding and his dog from attending the fair for the duration of the week. This editor applauds Mayor Sneed for taking such a strong stand against juvenile delinquency. And against dogs that don't behave.

Homer had read the article, as had everyone in the Pudding family, except for Squeak, who couldn't read.

This was not the first time Homer had made his way into the local newspaper. At the age of one he crawled into the middle of the parade route and caused a huge pileup. *Parade Ruined by Pudding Boy.* At the age of three he fell into Frog Egg Pond and nearly drowned. *Pudding Boy Swallows Pollywogs and Lives.* At the age of seven he left the lower pasture's gate open and the goats got out and ate all the flowers in Veterans' Memorial Park. *Pudding Boy's Goats Are Unpatriotic.* At the age of ten he dug a hole so deep that it freed an underground spring, which flooded the town. *Pudding Boy Is a Nuisance!* And then there was the recent library incident. *Pudding Boy and His Dog Burn Down the Library.*

Though each article had brought shame to the family, Mrs. Pudding kept copies tucked in the back sleeve of the family photo album. She believed with all her heart that one day, when her son had found his way in the world, they'd look back at those articles and laugh. But on that morning, no laughter filled the Pudding kitchen.

Mr. Pudding tossed the newspaper aside, then smacked his callused hand on the table. "Crescent's dogs were running with the pack, just like the rest of the dogs. How come the editor didn't mention that?"

A plate of steaming pancakes appeared before Homer. "Eat up," Mrs. Pudding said, planting a kiss on his head.

"Thank you," he said quietly. He didn't feel much like eating, so he poked the top pancake with his fork again and again. Dog lay wedged between Homer's feet, and, to Homer, his warm belly felt better than a pair of slippers.

Another plate was set before Squeak, who immediately drowned his pancakes in a sea of blueberry syrup. Homer hadn't mentioned Zelda's invitation. He was waiting for his father to head out to the barn. It would be best to show Zelda's letter to Mrs. Pudding. Convincing her would be easier. But the timing had to be right.

"Juvenile delinquent," Mr. Pudding grumbled, reaching for his mug of coffee. "He called my son a juvenile delinquent!"

"I could just die," Gwendolyn said, her face blotchy with emotion. She folded her arms and slid low in her chair. "I could just die from the humiliation of it all."

"Now, Gwendolyn," Mrs. Pudding said, flipping more pancakes. "It's not as bad as all that."

But it was as bad as all that, and everyone at the table knew it.

"I'll figure out how to pay," Homer said, looking up from his hole-covered pancakes. "I paid for the new library by selling my original Galileo Compass. I'm sure I can find a way to pay for the gunnysack slide."

"Maybe Homer can find some treasure," Squeak said.

Mr. Pudding scowled. Then something banged against the front door so loudly that Mrs. Pudding dropped her spatula. Out in the yard the farm dogs started barking, as did Dog, who nearly knocked over Gwendolyn's chair as he ran out from under the table.

"What in the name of sweet buttermilk is going on?" Mr. Pudding grumbled.

Squeak jumped off the bench, ran to the door, and pulled it open. "It's a rock," he announced. "It's got something on it."

"Hand it over," Mr. Pudding said. Squeak handed the rock to his father, who unwound a large rubber band and opened the note that had been attached. His face flushed red. Dropping the note onto the table, he rushed to the front door. "Who did this?' he called.

Gwendolyn's hand shot out and she grabbed the note. "It says, *Stay home, Homer. And your stupid dog, too. Or you'll both get what's coming to you.*" She smoothed out the paper. "There's a drawing."

Homer leaned across the table for a better look. The anonymous artist had barely mastered the rudimentary skills of figure drawing. In the pencil sketch Homer's body looked like a pumpkin with two stick legs. And Dog's looked like a pumpkin with four stick legs. Both figures had crossed eyes and buckteeth and the word *Loser* scrawled across their foreheads.

"Who would do this?" Mrs. Pudding cried. "Who would do such a terrible thing?"

Under normal circumstances, Homer would have been insulted by the drawing. While he'd been called a loser many times before, it sure didn't seem fair that they were picking on Dog. But on that morning, the note seemed more like a gift than a threat because its timing couldn't have been better. The worried look on Mrs. Pudding's face told Homer that success was possible.

Mr. Pudding slammed the front door. "Kids," he muttered. "They must have been on bikes." Then he grabbed his coat from its peg. "Finish your breakfast. We've got chores to do before the fair starts."

Mrs. Pudding pulled her husband aside and whispered. "Dear? What if they come back? Homer can't stay home alone all week while we're at the fair. It's too dangerous."

"We can't stay home and babysit him," Mr. Pudding said.

"Mom. Dad." Homer walked over to his parents and held out Zelda's letter. "This came in the mail yesterday. I opened it by accident."

Mr. Pudding read the letter, a short note in which Zelda introduced herself and asked if Homer and Dog could spend the week with her. "Says here she was my brother's friend," Mr. Pudding said with a frown. "You know what that means. It means she's one of those treasure hunters."

"She's very nice," Homer said. "She's the one who found the buyer for my Galileo Compass, Dad, remember? She's the reason I got all that money to pay for the new library."

Mr. Pudding read the letter again. "You think I'm going to let you stay with a person I don't even know?"

"But, dear..." Mrs. Pudding pulled her husband aside again. "You know how kids can be. Homer doesn't know how to protect himself. And you certainly don't want to miss the dog trials."

Mr. Pudding rubbed the back of his neck.

"Homer says she's very nice," Mrs. Pudding pointed out. "And any friend of Drake's is a friend of ours. I think it would be best to get Homer out of town until the fair's over. Everyone is feeling so... *hostile*."

"But that's an entire week," Mr. Pudding said.

"Yes, dear, but it will pass quickly."

As Dog licked syrup from Squeak's hand, Homer tapped his bare feet, waiting for his father to decide.

"Fine," Mr. Pudding mumbled.

"I don't believe it," Gwendolyn said, throwing her napkin onto the table. "Homer destroys the fair and what's his punishment? You send him on vacation."

Homer threw his arms around his mother. He felt bad

about lying to his parents, especially his mother, who'd never once told him to give up his treasure-hunting dreams. He wished he could tell her everything.

Once morning chores were finished, Homer packed his backpack. Mrs. Pudding made sure he had warm clothes, a toothbrush, plenty of underwear, and a box of Band-Aids, just in case. After she left the room, Homer unzipped his backpack and added his Swiss army knife, his Extra Strong Borington Binoculars, a water bottle, his night vision headlamp, and his copy of *The Biography of Rumpold Smeller.* He also added some mapmaking gear, such as mechanical pencils, a ruler, a pad of paper, a compass, and a protractor. The fake Galileo Compass was already around his neck, so there was nothing more to pack. He broke into a huge grin.

He was about to claim membership in the secret Society of L.O.S.T.!

Never mind the bad fortune from the fortune-teller. Never mind that one of the L.O.S.T. members didn't want him to join. Homer W. Pudding was about to claim his destiny, and nothing was going to stop him.

"Okay, Dog. Let's go."

PART TWO

GLOOMY MOOR

11

The Writer's Warning

The express train did not run on Sunday. The local train to Gloomy Moor took four hours, stopping at fourteen villages along the way, including Swineville, Pottyshire, and Lumpwood. Homer had settled into a window seat. Mrs. Pudding had packed a delicious farm lunch. Having eaten two ham and goat cheese sandwiches, Dog lay draped across the seat next to Homer, snoring.

Homer propped his book on his knees. He'd read through the first two chapters of *The Biography of Rumpold*

Smeller, which covered Rumpold's childhood. One of the reasons Rumpold grew to be such a ferocious pirate, the author theorized, was because he'd been so fond of fighting when he was a boy. He'd loved weaponry of all kinds—the sword in particular, which had made his father exceedingly proud. But the real reason Rumpold was destined to become a pirate, according to the author, was because he despised authority. Rules were made to be broken. Laws were for everyone but him. No one could tell him what to do.

Homer had read all this before. It was well known that Rumpold had been a devilish little boy. It made perfect sense that the meanest pirate in the world had been a horrid child. But during this reading, Homer paid extra attention. He had no idea what questions the membership would ask, so he needed to know as much as possible. He'd make Uncle Drake proud by answering all the questions correctly and by claiming the empty chair.

He'd just turned the page to begin chapter 3 when someone cleared her throat. "Is this seat taken?" A woman in doughnut-size sunglasses and an orange scarf stood in the aisle. She pointed at the window seat that faced Homer's window seat.

"No one's sitting there," Homer said.

She squeezed past Homer's knees, then sat. Her raincoat was buttoned up to her chin and she wore a pair of orange gloves. Her scarf was pulled snugly around her face and knotted at her chin, and her sunglasses were so big that all Homer could see of her face was her mouth and two slivers of cheek. She opened a briefcase and pulled out a notebook and pen. "My name is Ms. Pore, Ph.D. I'm a writer," she said. "I'm working on a very important book."

Dog snorted as he shifted position. Homer leaned forward. "What kind of book?"

"I'm calling it *The Encyclopedia of Professions*. I am in the process of rating all known professions." Ms. Pore pointed her pen at Homer. "What is your profession? Tell me and I'll tell you how it rates."

Homer closed his book. "I'm twelve," he said. "I don't have a profession."

"Yes, of course. But what is your *desired* profession?"

"My dad wants me to be a goat farmer."

She opened her notebook and flipped through the pages. "Here it is. It says here that goat farming rates very high on the happiness index. Goat farmers are some of the happiest people in the world, even happier than candy makers and puppy wranglers." She smiled. "Your father is very wise to choose that profession for you."

Homer chewed on his lip. "What profession is lowest on the happiness index?" As Ms. Pore flipped through the pages again, a shivery feeling washed over Homer.

Was this how Excelsior felt when he was about to predict the future? Because Homer knew, even before Ms. Pore opened her mouth, what her answer would be.

"Treasure hunter," she said. "Treasure hunter is the lowest profession on the happiness index, even lower than Porta Potti cleaner, poison tester, and skunk trainer. Even lower than the person who gets shot out of a cannon at the circus." She turned the page. "However, treasure hunters rank highest on the *misery* scale. And they rank highest on the *social rejection* scale. *And* they rank highest on the *likelihood of getting killed on the job* scale." She closed her notebook. "You'd have to be a real dummy to want to be a treasure hunter. You don't want to be a treasure hunter, do you?"

"No," Homer murmured as he scratched Dog's ear. "Not me."

"Good," Ms. Pore said. "I've been doing this research for many years now, and believe me, the happiest, healthiest, and longest-living people I've met have been goat farmers." The train slowed. She stuffed her notebook and pen back into her briefcase. "It's something to consider, young man. A happy, healthy, long life is much better than a short one drenched in misery, failure, and social rejection. Well, here's my stop. Lumpwood." And off she went.

Dog burped a bit of ham and goat cheese sandwich,

then slid off the seat and stretched across the floor. Homer stared out the window as Ms. Pore, Ph.D., hurried off the train and into the station. Two warnings about becoming a treasure hunter in two days. And not from family but from two strangers.

Homer opened his hand. The forked life line ran across the palm, the shorter path ending at the base of his thumb where the treasure hunter line sat. The longer path reached toward his index finger. They were lines like any other lines. Nothing more. Just lines on a hand.

Right?

12
To Zelda's Trinket Shop

Steam swirled around Homer and Dog as they stepped off the train. "You sure you want to get off here?" the conductor asked.

"This is Gloomy Moor, right?" Homer asked.

The conductor took off his black hat and scratched above his ear. "That's right. Gloomy Moor. But there's nothing around here, kid. You sure you know what you're doing?"

"I'm meeting my friend," Homer said, holding tight to Dog's leash.

"Okeydokey, kid. Just don't get stuck out here after nightfall. There's some nasty wildlife out on the moor." He set his hat back onto his head.

For the last half hour of the train ride, the terrain had been flat and seemingly lifeless. "What do you mean?" Homer asked. "What kind of nasty wildlife?"

The conductor blew his whistle and stepped onto the train. "Good luck." The train lurched a few times, then pulled away from the station, the *chugga-chugga* sound picking up its tempo.

Bears? Wolves? How nasty?

Homer checked his Quality Solar-Powered Subatomic Watch. Fortunately the battery was fully charged, so the clock's dials spun in a complex dance—eight o'clock in the morning in Shanghai, noon in Auckland, and eight o'clock at night in Gloomy Moor. Another hour to go before sunset.

As the train's chugging faded, the steam cleared. The depot was nothing more than a long concrete slab and a wooden bench. A sign nailed to a post read:

Welcome to Gloomy Moor. Population: One.

A train schedule hung on another post:

Northbound from Gloomy Moor: 9 a.m.
Southbound from Gloomy Moor: 8 p.m.

The train had arrived on time, but Zelda wasn't waiting. She'd said she'd meet him at the station, and since she'd been the one who'd purchased the tickets, she knew when to expect him. Why wasn't she there?

Homer pulled out his Borington Binoculars, and he and Dog turned in a full circle. The moor was flat as far as the eye could see. Not a hill, not a mound, not even a lump in the perfect plane of stubby marsh grass. Homer buttoned his coat all the way to his chin as mist settled on his face. A bullfrog croaked. Dog barked. Another bullfrog croaked. Dog barked again. Then a million bullfrogs joined in, their chorus filling the air.

"Zelda!" Homer hollered, cupping his hands around his mouth. "Zelda!"

Time passed. The frogs continued their monotonous melody. Homer looked at his watch again. The spring sun began to melt on the horizon, casting pink light across the glistening landscape. But no lantern appeared in any direction. "Zelda!"

Dog wandered to the edge of the slab where a muddy trail began. Being the only trail, it probably led to Zelda's house. But what if the trail forked? Zelda hadn't provided Homer with a map, so how would he know which way to go?

"I think we should stay put," Homer hollered so Dog

could hear him over the boisterous frogs. "She'll come. She's just running late."

But Dog didn't stay put. He jumped onto the trail and sniffed the ground. His movement must have disturbed the frogs because they stopped croaking. Dog walked in a tight circle, then sniffed some more. Homer took a sharp breath. There was only one reason in the world for Dog to sniff, because there was only one thing Dog could smell.

"What is it, boy?" Homer asked. "What did you find? Did you find some treasure?"

Dog flipped onto his back and started rolling on the trail, covering himself with the precious scent. Homer crouched at the edge of the concrete slab. "Good boy," he said. There was no way of knowing what Dog would dig up. The only thing Homer knew was that it would be something that someone desperately wanted—for that was the truest definition of treasure.

With a grunt, Dog struggled to his paws. He started digging. "Ur, ur, ur, ur," he said. Dirt flew. Dog dug. Homer watched from his squatting position, his legs growing numb, but he didn't move.

"Good boy," he repeated, his eyes wide with anticipation.

Then the digging stopped. Dog pressed his face into

the hole. After a flick of his head, something flew through the air and landed at Homer's feet. In the fading light, it appeared to be a nut. Not the shelled kind of nut, but the hardware store kind of nut—silver and shaped like a hexagon. Didn't look like much, but Homer knew it couldn't be an ordinary nut. It belonged to something special.

He patted Dog's head, then stuck the nut into his jean pocket. Then with his foot, he pushed the dirt back into the hole and patted it down. Still no sign of Zelda—or anyone for that matter. "Come on," he said to Dog.

Once he'd settled on the bench with Dog at his feet, the frogs resumed their serenade. *How long will we have to wait?* Homer wondered. His family was probably eating dessert around the kitchen table. The second day of the Milkydale County Fair had come and gone. Who had won the dog trials? Had Squeak gotten the chance to go on the Whirl-a-Tron? Had Mayor Sneed figured out how much it was going to cost to rebuild the gunny-sack slide?

Was everyone still mad at him?

He would find out when he returned home. For now, he'd come to Gloomy Moor to meet a group of professional treasure hunters and claim membership in a secret society. That was his focus. One worry at a time, as Zelda had said.

The frogs stopped croaking again. After such a ruckus, the silence was almost deafening. Dog's head shot up. Moving only his eyeballs, Homer looked around. Did the frogs know something? *There's some nasty wildlife out on the moor.* A coyote? A wolverine? What?

Homer nearly fell off the bench when something landed on the top of his head. He swatted at it. A frog leaped off his head and landed on Dog's head. Dog groaned and shook his head, sending the frog flying across the slab. Another frog landed on Homer's leg. Another on his hand. "Hey," Homer said, flicking them away. Dog stood and shook a frog from his back. Then Homer gasped. It was as if someone had flipped on a switch, because the air vibrated as little green critters leaped from the grass. They gathered on the slab, dozens and dozens, then hundreds. They flew past Homer's face, over his head, and under the bench. A growl rose in Dog's throat as a frog landed on the tip of his nose. "Yuck!" Homer cried, one landing on his chin. Dog turned in frantic circles but couldn't build up enough centrifugal force to dislodge the critters. Homer's eyes widened.

The concrete slab had transformed into a pulsating carpet of green.

Homer pulled Dog closer as countless pairs of bulbous eyes stared up at him.

A terrible image filled Homer's mind. His uncle Drake

had been eaten by a mutant carnivorous tortoise. Most people would say that being eaten by a tortoise is impossible. But it had happened. There'd been witnesses. Was it possible to be eaten by an army of frogs?

The sun melted into nothingness, and the frogs disappeared in a cloak of total darkness. One croaked, followed by another, and once again the chorus belted out its song. Dog nudged Homer with his nose.

"I agree. Let's get out of here," Homer said, wiping a frog off his ear. He tore open his backpack and felt around for his night vision headlamp. The elastic strap fit snugly across his forehead. When he switched the lamp on, thousands of tiny white eyes, like spilled popcorn, popped out from the darkness. A shudder ran between Homer's shoulders. He threw on his backpack, grabbed the leash, then slid his feet across the slab, pushing his way through the amphibians. They clung to his pant legs and shoes. But as soon as he stepped onto the muddy trail, the frogs abandoned him, leaping back onto the slab. After flicking one last frog from his shoulder, Homer hurried away, with Dog at his heels.

"This has to lead somewhere," he told Dog, as much to settle his friend's nerves as his own.

"Urrrr."

It certainly felt better to be on the move. Dog waddled behind Homer, his long ears swaying, his big paws plodding through the mud. "We'll probably run into Zelda along the way," Homer said hopefully. She knew he was coming. But maybe she was a forgetful kind of person, someone who got distracted by a good book or a new map.

The trail continued in a straight line. A breeze blew across the grasses, coating the travelers with mist. Dog sneezed as mist crept up his nose. Not a star appeared in the cloudy sky. Except for the beam of Homer's headlamp, blackness enveloped the moor. Homer tried to remember when he'd last replaced the headlamp's battery. This would be a really bad time for it to die.

Dog began to wheeze, which he did when he walked too fast. But Homer wasn't about to slow down. The air temperature was steadily dropping and his thin plaid raincoat wouldn't keep him warm if they ended up getting stuck out there all night. "Sorry, Dog," he said. "I know you're tired, but we've got to keep going."

Survival skills are an important part of a treasure hunter's education. A single night, stuck in the elements, can bring down the toughest of treasure hunters. Take Ridley Whip, for example, famous for discovering the Lost Mines of the Antipodes. He skipped survival training, which is why he thought nothing bad could happen from spending a balmy night, without a sleeping bag or tent, under a starry sky. He went to sleep and never awoke, for during the night the temperature plummeted and hypothermia set in, slowly freezing every cell in his body. Homer had read about it in chapter 7 of *Twentieth Century Treasure-Hunting Disasters*.

Homer had never taken any survival classes. Uncle Drake had died before teaching him how to build a fire with wet grass, or how to make a tent from a plaid raincoat, or how to make a delicious stew of green frogs.

We won't get stuck out here, he told himself.

As the distance to the train depot widened, the frog chorus faded. Other than Homer's and Dog's labored breathing and an occasional fluttering sound in the grasses, the moor was eerily quiet. "Just birds," Homer said, though he didn't really know. He was trying not to imagine the nasty wildlife he'd been warned about. When footsteps sounded in the distance, his first reaction was relief.

"Zelda?" he called. The footsteps stopped. Homer aimed the headlamp's beam approximately eight feet off the ground. "Zelda? Is that you?" No one answered and no one appeared in the beam. He started walking again. After a few minutes the footsteps resumed. Two feet, not four, he was pretty sure by the rhythm. But this time he realized that the footsteps came from behind. He and Dog spun around.

"Grrrr," Dog said.

"Zelda?" The headlamp's beam revealed nothing. "Who's there?"

No one answered.

The back of Homer's neck prickled. If someone had been out for a peaceful walk on the moor, that someone would have brought a lantern and would have called out "Hello." But this person was hiding. Or worse—*following*.

Homer wasn't exactly sure why someone would be following him, but clearly this person was up to no good. If robbery was the goal, Homer wasn't about to make it easy. No way was he going to hand over his drafting supplies, or his solar-powered watch or any of the items he'd carefully packed in his backpack.

More footsteps.

Dog needed no convincing. They took off down the trail at full speed. Homer's knees ached. The backpack rubbed against his shoulders as he desperately ran. The headlamp's beam bobbed like a drunk firefly.

It's difficult to judge distance in the dark, but Homer and Dog ran as far as they could before they stopped to catch their breaths. Homer staggered, gasping for air. Dog's tongue hung out of his mouth. Homer held his breath and listened. He put his hand over Dog's panting mouth and strained his ears. For a moment, all was quiet.

Maybe the person had given up. But Homer wasn't taking any chances. They needed to get to Zelda's.

"Come on," he whispered, tugging on the leash. "Dog, come on." But Dog wouldn't budge. He collapsed onto the trail, transforming his body into an unmovable boulder. Homer pushed Dog's rump. "This is not the time to be stubborn." He pushed again. Dog, with a moan of complaint, rose onto his paws.

The terrain changed from short, mist-covered grasses to taller grasses and windswept trees that all leaned in the same direction, as if eavesdropping on someone. Homer and Dog stopped now and then to listen, but no footsteps followed. Homer swallowed, but it didn't soothe his dry throat. His shoulders burned from the backpack straps.

"Hey, do you smell that?" he asked, sniffing the air. Of course Dog couldn't smell it, and of course Homer knew that, but Homer just wanted to hear the sound of a familiar voice, even if it was his own. "It's burning wood. Someone's made a fire." Which was a very good sign, indeed.

There, in the distance, a light twinkled.

Homer smiled. "Come on."

The trail grew steeper and the breeze saltier, blowing Homer's hair into his eyes. He held tight to Dog's leash as gravity pulled them down the sandy trail. Dog's ears flapped as he waddled, his legs splayed like a bowlegged cowboy. Waves crashed in the distance. "We're near the ocean," Homer said.

The smoky scent grew stronger. Homer's headlamp lit up a sign that hung from a gnarled arbor built of driftwood. The sign rocked in the wind. ZELDA'S TRINKET SHOP. Relief washed over Homer. "We're here."

A dirt road, which came from the opposite direction of the train station, led up to the arbor and widened into a small parking lot. The cloudcopter sat at the edge of the lot. The trinket shop, which stood a few yards past the arbor, was dark. But beyond the shop, an oil lamp lit up the front window of a cottage. Smoke rose from a chimney pipe. Homer threw himself at the cottage's enormous front door, pounding with his last surge of strength. The door flew open.

Zelda winced, shielding her eyes from the headlamp. Homer turned it off. "Homer!" she cried. "Are you here already? Where has the time gone? I was supposed to meet you at the station. I'm so sorry. Something came up. Something very important."

Dog waddled into the cottage and collapsed on the floor.

"Someone's following us," Homer said. "I heard footsteps. So did Dog."

Zelda reached out her long arm and pulled Homer

inside. "Stay here," she told him. She grabbed her cloak and wrapped it around her shoulders. Then she took a lantern from a shelf and lit it. "Bolt the door," she ordered. "Don't let anyone in unless it's me." Then she hurried off into the night.

"But Zelda..." Homer stood in the doorway, watching as her lantern disappeared beyond the arbor.

Did she know who was following him? It had to be someone dangerous, otherwise why would she want him to bolt the door? What if she needed help? He was about to step back outside when a loud crash rattled the door.

The crash came from inside the cottage.

13

Hercules Simple

Dog cocked his head and looked down Zelda's hallway, a soft growl vibrating in the depths of his wrinkly neck. Homer grabbed a black umbrella from a brass umbrella stand. The tip, plastic and blunt, was not much of a weapon, but it would have to do. Whoever had followed them along the moor might have come in through a back door.

His heart pounding, his skin clammy, he held the umbrella like a sword. If only he knew how to use a sword. According to *The Biography of Rumpold Smeller*, Rumpold had been trained in the art of sword fighting. Homer's uncle Drake had a black belt in karate. The Milkydale Community Center, however, had never offered classes in swordplay or self-defense techniques. Regrets filled Homer's mind. Why hadn't he paid more attention during those ninja movies? Why hadn't he practiced on that punching bag that his dad kept in the back of the barn or asked his uncle Drake to teach him some moves? The only person Homer ever fought was his sister, Gwendolyn, and that was always a matter of self-defense.

Homer tiptoed down the hall. Dog whined but didn't budge from his place by the front door. One step closer, two steps. Homer's hand trembled. *Stop it*, he told himself. *Be brave. Be brave like Uncle Drake.*

Light glowed at the hall's end. Homer's raincoat crinkled with each step. When he reached the end of the hallway, he took a quick breath, then darted around the corner, stabbing the air with his umbrella. "Who are you?" he cried.

"I'm Hercules," a quiet voice replied. "Hercules Simple."

Hercules sat in the middle of an enormous leather chair. At first Homer thought Hercules was a little kid because his feet didn't reach the floor. But then Homer realized that all the faded and patched furniture had been built to fit Zelda. The entire room was Zelda-size, from the tall ceilings to the massive fireplace that cast a gentle, flickering glow.

"You shouldn't point an umbrella like that," Hercules said, his face hidden in the chair's shadow. "You could gouge out someone's eye, or pierce someone's liver."

"I heard a crash," Homer said, tightening his grip on the plastic handle.

"I accidentally knocked over my first-aid kit." Hercules pointed to a coffee table—a huge slab of marble that sat atop of giant piece of driftwood. On top was a metal box with a handle. As Hercules scooted to the edge of the leather chair, the fire's glow illuminated his face.

Homer guessed, from the splotch of pimples on Hercules's forehead, that he was around Gwendolyn's age. His wiry black hair was cut short, and his nose was wide and flat. His skinny legs poked out from his green flannel bathrobe like two twigs. Homer's fear faded, and he slowly lowered the umbrella. An intruder wouldn't be sitting in bare feet, in a bathrobe, with a plate of cookies on his lap.

Hercules sneezed. "Excuse me," he said. Then he sneezed again. "There's so much pollen out here on the moor. I'm afraid I might be developing allergies." He felt the glands at the sides of his neck. "I wouldn't want to develop an allergy, because that could create a blockage of my Eustachian tubes, resulting in partial or total hearing loss. How does my throat look? Is it red?" He threw back his head and opened his mouth real wide.

"I don't know," Homer said, keeping his distance. What was a Eustachian tube anyway? His sister, Gwendolyn, would know. She'd probably come across many Eustachian tubes while practicing her taxidermy skills.

Hercules motioned Homer closer, then opened his mouth wider. From where he stood, Homer couldn't see anything but Hercules's teeth. He took a few steps closer and leaned across the coffee table. "I guess it looks kinda red."

Hercules's mouth snapped shut. "Red? What shade of red? Fire engine? Cherry? Did you see any white dots?"

"I don't know," Homer said with a shrug. He set his backpack down, then pulled off his headlamp and tucked it into one of the pockets.

"Howoooo!"

Hercules sat up straight. "Is that a dog?" he asked, wide-eyed.

"Yeah. It's my dog."

"Is it a big dog? Is it aggressive?" His lower lip quivered a bit. "I don't like dogs."

"He's a nice dog. Come on, Dog," Homer called.

Clicking nails sounded as Dog hurried down the hall, his leash dragging behind. He waddled into the sitting room and pushed between Homer's shins. Homer gave

Dog's rump a good scratch, then removed the leash. "Sorry I left you," he said.

Dog walked over to the leather chair and touched his nose to Hercules's foot. Hercules pulled up his legs and curled into the corner of the chair, trying to get as far away from Dog as possible. As he did so, the plate of cookies tumbled off his lap. "I don't like dogs," he repeated.

Dog lunged at the cookies. Crumbs sprayed here and there.

"How come you don't like dogs?"

"They bite."

Homer didn't know what to think about this Hercules person. But he didn't want anyone to freak out just because of Dog, so he pulled Dog away from the leather chair and the last two cookies. For a moment, only the crackling of the fire filled the room, but then Dog barked as the front door slammed shut. Zelda hurried into the living room, her black cape and silver hair glittering with sea spray.

"You didn't bolt the door," she said. Then she blew out her lantern and set it aside. "No matter. I didn't see signs of anyone."

"But I heard footsteps," Homer said. Momentarily distracted, he let go of Dog's collar. Dog trotted back to the cookies and inhaled them. "Dog heard them, too."

"I am not questioning you, Homer. I believe that someone was following you." She tossed her cape aside. "But whoever was out there is now gone. No one would choose to spend a night on the moor. The night air is thick with sadness. And frogs." She removed her sturdy black boots and placed them in front of the fire. "I see you two have met. Hercules arrived this evening, earlier than I'd expected. That's why I didn't get to the train station in time to meet you, Homer."

Hercules leaned over the armrest and nervously eyed Dog, who was licking crumbs off the carpet.

"Homer, take off those muddy shoes and that wet raincoat," Zelda said. "We don't need you getting sick."

While Zelda collected some towels, Homer set his muddy shoes, wet socks, and raincoat by the fire. As he dried his hair with an extra-large towel, Zelda knelt and dried Dog, rubbing him from head to tail. His back legs did a little dance as she rubbed. "We don't want you to get sick, either," she told Dog. He pressed his nose to hers, their gloomy expressions almost identical.

"Make yourselves comfortable," Zelda said. As Homer settled on the patched couch, Zelda stirred a cauldron that hung over the fire. "I like to cook this way," she explained. "Power is precious out here. There's not enough sun for solar panels. My windmill is just enough for the necessities."

She dipped a ladle into the pot and filled four bowls with stew. Famished, Homer ate almost as quickly as Dog. The little round potatoes and baby carrots melted in his mouth.

"Are there any peanut products in the stew?" Hercules asked, staring into his bowl.

"Are you allergic to peanuts?" Zelda asked.

"No. But I could be." Hercules frowned. "I'd rather not take the risk."

"There are no peanuts," Zelda said, reaching out to pat Hercules's knee. "Do not fret. Too much fretting can make a person sick."

"It can?" Hercules twitched.

Zelda went into the kitchen and brought back three cups of cocoa. Warmed by the fire and the stew, Homer relaxed, sinking into the corner of the overstuffed couch. Dog stretched in front of the fire, his white belly absorbing the heat like a crumpet in a toaster.

Hercules, however, sat very rigid and poked his spoon through his bowl. "These carrots really should be cut into smaller pieces. At this size they pose a choking hazard."

"Hercules," Zelda said as she sat on the other end of the couch. "Would you like to tell Homer why you are here?"

"Sure." Hercules glanced at Dog, who was fast asleep.

Then he stood up, reached into his pants pocket, and produced a small scroll. "I was entrusted with a top-secret message. Shall I read it again?" Zelda nodded. And so he read it aloud.

Dear members of the Society of Legends, Objects, Secrets, and Treasures,

I've been told that for some cockamamie reason, we need to have another confounded meeting to discuss some kind of gobbledygook or other.

I've been told that you all need to be there, so stop your lollygagging. It's going to be a big kerfuffle. That's all I know.

Signed,
Your current president, LM the XVIII

Postscript. It's Gertrude's turn to bring muffins.
Post-postscript. The meeting's at Zelda's shack, June 21st, 7 p.m.

Homer burst into a smile and plunked his mug of cocoa onto the marble coffee table. "Tomorrow night? Here?"

"Yes," Zelda said.

Tomorrow was, well, TOMORROW! So overcome with excitement, Homer practically yelled out the word. It was happening. It was really happening. He beamed at Zelda, then his gaze fell on the letter. Why had Hercules been entrusted to carry such an important message? "Are you a member of L.O.S.T.?" he asked.

"Yes," Hercules said. "But I'm not a treasure hunter. I'm an employee."

"L.O.S.T. has employees?" Homer asked.

"Two employees," Hercules said. "I am the official records keeper. I arrange all the meetings, transcribe the meeting logs, process and preserve documents, acquire necessary questing permits, allocate funds, et cetera." He placed his hand on his forehead. "I might be getting a headache. Have you had this room tested for black mold?"

"Hercules is fourteen years old—our youngest member," Zelda said, ignoring Hercules's health concern. "At least, he's our youngest member until you are granted membership, Homer."

"How did you get membership?" Homer asked.

"I won this year's World's Spelling Bee," Hercules replied, pulling off the lid to his first-aid kit.

"Our former records keeper was crushed by a rogue filing cabinet. We needed someone with excellent language skills," Zelda explained.

"The World's Spelling Bee?" Homer asked with astonishment. Every year, Mrs. Peepgrass held a spelling bee in the Milkydale schoolhouse. This year Gwendolyn lucked out and got *milk* as her first word. Homer got *illustrious* and didn't make it to the second round. "You're the champion of the *entire* world?"

"Yes." Hercules pulled out a thermometer and stuck it into his mouth.

Homer nodded, impressed by such an accomplishment. Someday he'd be the greatest treasure hunter in the entire world. "Who's the other employee?" he asked.

"She's called The Unpolluter," Zelda said, getting up to put another log on the fire. A sizable log, but her large hands easily scooped it up. Dog groaned and shifted position, aiming his backside for a round of toasting.

"What does The Unpolluter do?" Homer asked Zelda.

"The Unpolluter's job is very important. Let's say that one of our adventurers does something he's not supposed to do. And let's say it makes someone angry and it gets into the newspaper. The Unpolluter steps in and cleans up the problem. It's her job to make sure that our society remains a secret."

"She cleaned up after your Uncle Drake on many occasions," Hercules said, reading his thermometer. "I never met your uncle, but I know all about him because I've read all the paperwork."

Homer looked at Zelda for an explanation. "Drake didn't like rules," she told him as she returned to the couch. "And he had no patience, so he sometimes made a mess." She took a sip of her cocoa, then sighed. "Every time I mention his name the grief rushes back. I miss him so."

While Hercules arranged items in his first-aid kit, Homer finished his cocoa. As much as he missed his uncle, he didn't want to talk about sad things. Tomorrow was going to be the most exciting day of his life. "What will happen at the meeting?"

"I will present you to the membership," Zelda said. "And they will each be given the opportunity to ask you questions. Drake made it clear that he wanted you to take his place, so the transfer of membership should go smoothly."

"What about the one person?" Homer asked. "The one you think doesn't want me to join."

Zelda collected the empty cocoa mugs. "Let's not worry about that. Drake wrote a letter to the membership about you. The letter is on file. No one can dispute that."

"I filed the letter myself," Hercules said. "In triplicate."

While Zelda carried the mugs into the kitchen, Homer collected the stew bowls and spoons and followed. "I should call my parents," he said. The call was short because everyone in the Pudding household was getting ready for bed. It would be a big day tomorrow at the fair since the

Pudding dogs had made it to the second round of competition. After assuring his mother that he'd take a bath, brush his teeth, and put on clean underwear, Homer hung up the phone. Zelda handed him a folded piece of paper.

"Ajitabh sent this for you," she said. "Go on, read it."

Homer sat at the kitchen table and read Ajitabh's letter. The inventor's singsong accent rang clear in Homer's head.

Hello, Homer,

So disappointed that I can't be there for your big day and all that. Had to dash off to New Delhi to visit dear old Dad, who's having some problems with his ticker.

I've sent word to the membership that I wholeheartedly support your inheriting Drake's chair. It's sure to be an exciting meeting, by Jove, and I'm bloomin' sorry to miss it. But I know that you'll make your uncle proud.

Give my best to that hound of yours. Cheerio.

Your chum, Ajitabh

Ajitabh had been one of Drake's closest and most-trusted friends. To have his support, even if from a long distance, helped steady some of Homer's nerves.

"I think a good night's sleep is in order," Zelda said when Homer returned to the living room. "I'm afraid I don't have guest rooms. I seldom have guests in my lonely part of the world. You'll have to sleep on the couch. Or on the carpet by the fire."

"That's fine," Homer said. He was willing to sleep on the roof if need be. Just so long as he was here, tomorrow, for the meeting. He carried his backpack into the bathroom, where he changed into his pajamas.

Zelda collected blankets and pillows and set them on the couch.

"I hope it's not a feather pillow," Hercules said. "What if a feather gets loose in the middle of the night and I inhale it and die?"

"The pillows are made of foam," Zelda assured him. Then she blew out the lamps so that the only light came from the fireplace. "Good night," she said. "Be sure to keep the front door bolted."

"But you said the person who was following me is gone," Homer said.

"That is not why I want you to keep the door bolted," Zelda said, pushing a silver lock from her weary eyes. "You must keep it bolted so that the wind does not blow it open. If the wind blows it open, then the sadness of the moor will rush in and invade our dreams."

Homer was starting to get used to Zelda always being sad in much the same way that you get used to ice cream always being cold.

Slow, heavy footsteps sounded as Zelda made her way upstairs. The ceiling creaked as she walked to her bedroom. Hercules, already in his pajamas, arranged a pillow and blanket on the couch. Homer opened his backpack and pulled out his book. Hercules rifled through his first-aid kit, pulling out vitamin jars, cough drops, and tubes of various ointments. He sprayed something into his mouth, rubbed something onto his throat, and chewed a couple of orange vitamins.

"Do you get sick a lot?" Homer asked.

"I never get sick. But I worry that I might get sick." He climbed under the blanket and pulled it up to his nose. "Is your dog going to sleep in this room?"

"Uh, yeah," Homer said.

"Will you make sure he doesn't jump on me?"

"Okay."

"Do you know how to perform cardiopulmonary resuscitation? In case I stop breathing in the middle of the night?"

"No," Homer said.

"I am sorry to hear that. Well, good night." And with that, Hercules rolled onto his side, his back to Homer.

"Good night," Homer said. He felt kind of sorry for

Hercules. What kind of a person worries about choking on a feather from a feather pillow? If anyone in that room had reason to worry, it was Homer. Would he make a fool of himself at tomorrow's meeting? Would he know the answers to the questions? Would he make his uncle proud?

And would he ever find out who had followed him on the moor?

Homer arranged the pillow and blanket on the floor and lay down. Dog stretched next to him, his head on the pillow. Homer knew there'd be a big drool stain in the morning, but he'd gotten used to that. He also knew that Dog would kick while dreaming, but Homer had gotten used to that, too. Funny, but just a few months ago, Homer had never slept next to a dog, but now he couldn't imagine not having the warmth to curl up against.

He pulled another blanket over himself. Then he opened *The Biography of Rumpold Smeller* and read by firelight.

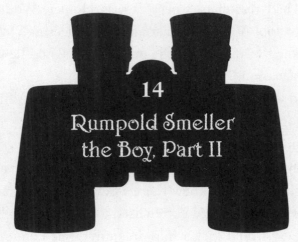

Homer didn't know this, but the book he was reading was complete rubbish. A lot of biographies are complete rubbish. Sometimes the author, in an attempt to make the subject of the biography appear to be more heroic, will mess with the facts— or will ignore the facts altogether. That is why when reading history, one must always consider who wrote the history. In the case of Homer's book, *The Biography of Rumpold Smeller*, the author was a man named Bernard Dullard, a whackadoodle who really wanted to write a bestseller. His other books, *How to Grow Pineapples* and *Where Lint Comes From*, were total flops. His biography on Rumpold, however, became a bestseller among treasure hunters and pirate aficionados, which are people who are devoted to pirates. But there is very little truth in the book. It is a story. A myth.

Here is the truth.

When Rumpold Smeller turned twelve, his father, the Duke of Estonia, called him to the armory for an important discussion. Rumpold knew it would be an important discussion because a servant had laid out his very best clothes, which consisted of some itchy trousers, a high-collared ruffled shirt that tickled his chin, and a waistcoat with shiny buttons. He also knew it would be an important discussion because his mother had been told not to interrupt them. So she waited outside the armory, her ear pressed to the wall. Eavesdropping beside her was Rumpold's twin sister, Rumpoldena.

Duke Smeller of Estonia stood before a shiny array of armor. "Hello, my son," he said as Rumpold entered.

"Hello, Father," Rumpold said, trying his best not to scratch his bottom. He couldn't wait to get out of those clothes. The day was cool but clear—a perfect day for wandering around with his sketchbook. The best things to draw were discovered when wandering—an overturned black beetle, a dew-covered rose, a napping hawk.

Duke Smeller ran his hand over a plated helmet. "This armor belonged to my father," he said. "And this set over here belonged to my father's father." Then he stared at Rumpold's ear. Rumpold reached up and removed a piece of drawing charcoal that he had tucked behind his ear. Duke Smeller frowned. "You are nearing manhood," he said. "Soon you will need to put away those childish drawings of yours. Your body will change and you will look like me."

Rumpold fidgeted. He didn't much care about growing a beard. Becoming a man meant other things he didn't much care about, such as fighting in wars and getting married.

"You will take my place as duke," his father said.

"Are you sick?" Rumpold asked. Was this why his father had called him to the armory?

"No." The duke laughed. "I do not mean that you will take my place *today*. Today I am in full robust health."

"And let us pray that you stay that way for a very long time," a voice said.

Rumpold turned around. A man had entered the armory. A head taller than the duke, and a shoulder's width wider, he stared at Rumpold with black eyes.

"Rumpold, this is Duke Vladmir."

"Hello," Rumpold said, bowing low as he'd been taught.

"Rumpold," Duke Vladmir said, "do you know why I am here?"

"No," Rumpold answered, wishing he could get away. Sunlight poured in through the windows, bouncing off the wall of swords. Rumpold squinted. He wished he could run across the manicured lawn and climb that ancient oak tree. There, in its highest branch, he could see all the way across the valley. He'd sketched the landscape many times, but each sketch revealed an entirely different world.

Duke Vladmir sat in a high-backed leather chair and motioned for Rumpold to sit on the chair next to him. Rumpold did. "Your father's dukedom is not your only inheritance," he said. "Have you ever heard of the Teutonic knights?"

"Yes," Rumpold said. He'd heard many tales from his tutor. "They used to fight to protect our land. But that was a long time ago."

"Indeed," Duke Vladmir said. "And Estonia is now at peace. But the knights are still here, still ready to protect our land if the need should arise."

Rumpold pushed his shirt's ruffle from his face. "How come I never see these knights?"

"They keep to themselves. They hide their identity."

"Why?"

Duke Smeller placed his hand gently on Rumpold's

shoulder. "Do not bombard Duke Vladmir with questions," he told his son. "Listen carefully to what he is about to tell you."

Duke Vladmir pressed his index fingers together and rested them on his bearded chin. "Membership in the Teutonic knights is a birthright. As the son of a Teutonic knight, you are expected to pledge yourself to the knighthood."

Rumpold stared at his father in disbelief. His father was a knight?

"In order to claim your birthright, your father will present you before the knighthood. Blood is not enough to guarantee your membership. You must prove yourself worthy."

"How do I do that?" Rumpold asked.

"That will be decided tomorrow."

"Tomorrow?" Rumpold said.

"Yes." Duke Vladmir nodded at Duke Smeller. "Tomorrow the knighthood shall convene in your father's dining hall. And your future will be determined."

A squeal sounded outside the door. Rumpold's mother had fainted.

Duke Smeller laid a hand on Rumpold's shoulder. "That you will follow in my footsteps is my wish for you, my son. You will make your family proud, and the name

Smeller will be forever linked to the greatest knights the world has ever known."

Rumpold couldn't ignore the itchy pants any longer. As he scratched his leg, he thought about what his father had just told him. He was to join a secret society of knights?

In all his wildest dreams, this was not the path Rumpold had imagined for himself.

15

Leech-Proof Socks

Homer looked out the kitchen window. Beyond the windswept grasses, white-tipped ocean waves crashed onto a plain of glossy, hard sand. He hadn't slept much, what with Hercules's snoring, Dog's wheezing, and all the thoughts crashing around in his head. But he didn't mind the grogginess. Today was going to be brilliant.

After a breakfast of porridge and tea, Homer read a few more chapters of the biography. Hercules kept interrupting. A mysterious red blotch had appeared on his cheek, and he was very worried about it. Homer told him that the spot was a crease from the pillowcase, but Hercules wouldn't listen. "I think your dog bit me in the middle of the night. What if I get rabies?"

"Dog doesn't have rabies," Homer said.

When Hercules strapped a helmet to his head because he was worried that he might trip over Dog and get a concussion, Homer couldn't take it any longer. Hercules's constant worrying and fussing was annoying. Not that Homer overflowed with courage, but at least he wasn't afraid of feather pillows.

"I think I'll see if Zelda needs help," Homer said, hurrying out of the living room.

Zelda was in her shop. Every nook and cranny in Zelda's Trinket Shop was crammed with things. Mechanical things, musical things, artistic things, and playful things. Rusty, shiny, painted, carved—if you desired it and had the time to look, you could probably find it there. A towering pile of scrap metal sat outside the door. Dog draped himself over a large, flat bone and proceeded to gnaw on it. "Found that on the beach," Zelda said as she dusted some shelves. "It's the fin bone from a blue whale."

Homer picked up an old clock and dusted its face. The clock read one o'clock. The meeting was still six hours away. He'd never seen such a clock. The face was an actual face, and it blinked at ten-second intervals. "It's one of a kind," Zelda said. "Created by King Ludwig's royal clockmaker. Go ahead, set the alarm and see what happens."

Homer set the alarm for twelve o'clock, then moved both hands to the number twelve. The face's mouth opened and made a cuckoo sound.

"It's missing a piece," Zelda said. "Such a shame that the clock is not whole. I could go to the hardware store and replace the missing piece, but then it wouldn't be one hundred percent authentic. I'd love to find that piece, but try finding an eighteenth-century nut in this mess."

"Oh, wait a minute," Homer said, remembering Dog's discovery on the Gloomy Moor trail. He reached into his jean pocket. "Is this it?" He dropped the nut onto the worktable. Zelda grabbed a magnifying glass and inspected it.

"Why yes, this is it, Homer. Where did you find it? I lost this five years ago!"

Homer looked over at Dog, who was still gnawing. Someday Zelda might be told the truth about Dog. But not yet. "I found it on the trail."

Though she didn't smile, her mask of sadness eased just a bit. "Thank you," she said.

"You're welcome." He smiled at Dog, who didn't seem to mind that he hadn't gotten credit.

As Homer continued to dust, his thoughts drifted to the writer with the orange scarf. "Zelda? Do you like your job?"

"I'm suited for it," she said. "Artifacts don't require conversation. They don't care how tall I am."

"Do you think most treasure hunters are unhappy?" Homer asked. "Do you think they are unhappier than most people?"

"It's possible." She set the fixed clock on a shelf. "Most treasure hunters never find what they are seeking. That can lead to a lifetime of regrets."

A bell jingled as the trinket shop's door opened. A man in a brown shirt and brown pair of shorts bustled in. "Delivery," he announced, plunking a box onto Zelda's counter.

"Hello, Peter," Zelda said. "How is the moor today?"

"Wet as usual." Peter wiped mist from his glasses. "No time to talk. I'm busy, busy, busy. See you next time." And as quickly as he'd entered, he left, a pair of muddy boot prints marking his path in and out the door.

"The package is from Victor Tuffletop," Zelda said. She handed Homer a box cutter. He smiled with excitement as he carefully cut through the thick, clear tape. Peeling back the box's flaps, he found a layer of perfectly creased white tissue paper. And nestled between the sheets—his official adventurer clothing.

"Can I go try these on?" he asked.

"Of course."

With Dog at his heels, Homer raced across Zelda's yard, through the cottage, and into the bathroom. He closed the door, then set the box on the floor. Panting, Dog stuck his nose into the box. "Careful," Homer said. "Don't drool on the clothes."

First he pulled out a long-sleeved shirt, forest green and nearly weightless. Then he unfolded a pair of khaki shorts, covered in pockets of all shapes and sizes. Something glinted between tissue layers. It was a leather belt and a silver buckle engraved with the initials *H.W.P.* "Look," Homer said proudly, showing the initials to Dog.

"Urrrr."

Homer undressed, then put on the shirt, shorts, and belt. A pair of knee-length green socks, soft but sturdy, and a pair of brown leather boots came next. The boots' spongy interior conformed to his feet. A khaki-colored vest, also covered in pockets of all shapes and sizes, fit perfectly. Last but not least, he set a wide-brimmed Panama hat on his head. Each item bore the same label: *Waterproof, Sun-proof, Blade-proof. DO NOT PUT IN THE DRYER!* Homer had to stand on his tiptoes to see into Zelda's mirror. For the briefest of moments, he thought he was looking at his uncle. Drake had worn the same kind of hat.

"I look like a real treasure hunter," he told Dog.

"Urrrr." Dog pulled something out of the box. It was another vest.

"Hey, I think that's for you." Like Homer's vest, Dog's had many pockets and fit around his middle perfectly.

"Let us see," Zelda called. After a few adjustments, and a few more minutes of staring at himself, Homer sauntered into the living room. "Oh my," Zelda said, choking back tears. "Your uncle would be so proud. So very, very proud. You look very distinguished. Victor Tuffletop did an amazing job."

"The only thing Mr. Tuffletop made me was a finger guard so I wouldn't get blisters when I take notes during meetings," Hercules said. He'd changed out of his pajamas and green bathrobe into a purple-and-black-striped rugby shirt and jeans. He was listening to his heart with a stethoscope.

Zelda pointed to the various pockets on Homer's vest and shorts. "Folded maps fit here; rolled maps, here. This pocket will carry drafting supplies, mechanical pencils, protractor, et cetera, and this pocket will hold extra pencil leads. Here you can store a compass, here a magnifying lens, here a ruler and a T square." Then she ran her hand along the back of his vest. "It's woven with titanium thread," she explained. "That makes it impenetrable to everything from thorns to swords. And those are leech-proof socks. Very practical."

"What about Dog's vest?" Homer asked.

"That pocket is for a bone; that one holds a canteen. That one is detachable and forms a dog bowl."

Dog wagged his tail as everyone looked at him. No one could possibly think Homer's dog was useless—not while wearing such an impressive vest.

"Now you are both ready," Zelda said, wiping away another tear.

"We are," Homer agreed as he patted Dog's head. "We are ready."

16
The L.O.S.T.
Membership Convenes

Just before 7 p.m., the membership began to arrive. They came by horse, Rolls Royce, scooter, motorcycle, and helicopter. One even came by a giant yacht called *Cave Woman*. Zelda told Homer to wait upstairs until she summoned him. Jittery currents ran down his legs and arms. He'd never felt so nervous. Peeking over the stairway railing, he caught a glimpse of a cowboy hat, then a head of blond curls. When the grandfather clock struck seven, Zelda came upstairs. She leaned very close to Homer and looked deeply into his eyes. "Remember," she whispered, "answer all questions honestly. Do not try to be your uncle. Be yourself."

Homer worried about that. *The real me is terribly boring*, he thought.

"And you," she said, patting Dog's head. "Be good."

Homer tugged on his Panama hat, making sure it was secure. Then he and Dog followed Zelda down the stairs and into the kitchen.

Six people sat around Zelda's long kitchen table. Six pairs of eyes stared at him. No one said a word. What had he expected? Trumpets to herald his entrance? That would have been nice. Maybe a round of applause or a great big "Hello, Homer." But they only stared. *They're disappointed*, he thought. *I'm just a kid.* Homer's knees began to shake. He felt as if he were standing in front of his school giving a presentation, only a million times worse.

Dog waddled into the kitchen. He walked right past Homer and stopped at the chair at the end of the table. He wagged his tail and stared up at the old man who sat in the chair—a man so shrunken that he had to perch on a pile of phone books. Red, pinlike eyes peered out from the man's prunish face. His black wool suit looked like funeral clothes, especially with the black top hat that rested by his elbow. The old man didn't notice Dog. Dog kept right on wagging. "Dog," Homer whispered. "Come here." But Dog didn't obey. He crawled under the old man's chair and lay down.

"Lord Mockingbird," Zelda said. She and Homer remained standing. "We're ready for you to call the meeting to order."

Lord Mockingbird? Had Homer heard right? *The* Lord Mockingbird? The author of *Marvels of Mapmaking*?

"Hmph," Lord Mockingbird said. Turned out he was the old man with the prunish face. "Let the secretary do it."

"I'm not actually a secretary," Hercules said timidly. He sat next to Lord Mockingbird, his helmet still on his head. "I'm the records keeper."

"You're a namby-pamby," Lord Mockingbird snarled. "Get on with it."

Hercules cleared his throat. "I hereby call to order the seventy-ninth meeting of the Society of Legends, Objects, Secrets, and Treasures. Four members are not present. The Unpolluter never attends. Ajitabh is in New Delhi. Sir Titus Edmund's whereabouts are still unknown. And Angus MacDoodle would rather, and I quote him directly, 'shave his bottom than attend another one of our boring meetings.'" A few people snickered. Hercules cleared his throat again. "Seven members are in attendance, however, which constitutes a quorum."

Lord Mockingbird grunted. "Keep going." He returned

his focus to a muffin from which he was picking yellow raisins.

Stacks of papers surrounded Hercules, along with file folders and notebooks. He picked up a page and read. "The first item on the agenda is to meet Homer Winslow Pudding, who has come to claim Drake Pudding's chair. The procedure, according to our bylaws, is for each member to ask Homer questions." Hercules looked up. "Zelda, will you do the introductions?"

"Of course," Zelda said.

"Hurry up!" Lord Mockingbird hollered with unexpected gusto.

Zelda took Homer's arm and stepped closer to the table. "Homer, this is His Honor, Lord Mockingbird the Eighteenth. Lord Mockingbird is the eldest member of L.O.S.T. and its current president."

Lord Mockingbird picked another raisin from his muffin. Though Homer had never met His Lordship, he knew all about him. Five of His Lordship's maps were thumbtacked to Homer's ceiling. He was considered to be the greatest mapmaker ever. Homer had thought he was long dead. But there he sat, grunting and picking and looking like he might topple off the chair. "It's nice to meet you," Homer said quietly.

Lord Mockingbird said nothing.

"Your Lordship," Hercules said, a quill perched in his hands. "It is your turn to ask a question."

Lord Mockingbird flicked a raisin across the room. "The boy looks like a nincompoop." Homer wasn't sure what a nincompoop was, but a word ending in *poop* couldn't be very good. Despite the insult, he felt overwhelmingly honored to be in the great mapmaker's presence.

"Lord Mockingbird, do you have a question?" Zelda asked.

"Hmph. How old is the nincompoop?" he grumbled.

"Twelve," Homer said. "But I'll be thirteen this fall."

"I was twelve once," Lord Mockingbird said. "And I could eat as many raisins as I wanted and they didn't give me the runs." He flicked another raisin. Hercules used a file folder as a shield, then dipped his quill into a bottle of ink and scribbled on a piece of paper.

A large woman sat in the next chair. Zelda motioned with her hand. "Homer, this is Dr. Gertrude Magnum. Gertrude earned her doctoral degree in Subterranean Worlds."

Homer imagined his bedroom ceiling and the map of the Great Crystal Cave. Dr. Magnum had discovered that cave and in turn had become the most famous subterranean explorer of all time. "I've got your book," he blurted, starstruck. "*Cavernous Realms*. I've read it twice."

Dr. Magnum smiled sweetly at Homer, two deep dimples forming on her round cheeks. She fiddled with a necklace of bright jewels. More jewels sparkled from her wrists, her fingers, her ears, and from the barrettes she wore throughout her curly blond hair. "Hello, Homer," she said, her voice squeaky.

"Hello," Homer said.

"My question for you is this: What is your opinion on caves?"

"I've never been in one," Homer said, immediately taking a liking to Gertrude Magnum. Her voice reminded him of a chipmunk, as did her face. "But I'd like to explore one."

"Is that so?" She rested her jeweled arms on the table, nearly knocking over Hercules's inkwell in the process. "Which cave would you like to explore?"

If he chose her discovery, the Great Crystal Cave, then surely she'd be flattered. But Zelda had told him to be honest.

"I would choose the Lost Cave of the Pygmies," he said.

Dr. Magnum raised her painted eyebrows. "And why would that be your choice?"

"Because no one has found it yet."

She smiled and nodded. Hercules continued to scribble.

"Move on," Lord Mockingbird grumbled while gumming a piece of muffin. "Move on, move on."

Zelda took Homer's arm and gently led him a few steps down the table. Next to Dr. Magnum sat a middle-aged man with enormous ears that poked out from a bushy head of salt-and-pepper hair. "I know who you are," Homer said. "I've got a collection of miniature plastic mummies. Your picture was on the back of the box they came in."

"Homer, this is Professor Thaddius Thick, Distinguished Professor Emeritus of Egyptology at Cairo University."

"Hello Ho...Ho...Homer." Muffin crumbs fell from Professor Thick's gray beard as he struggled through the next sentence. "So...so...so nice to meet you."

"It's nice to meet you, too," Homer said. "You've found more mummies than anyone else. I read an article at the library in *Archaeologist Monthly*, and it said that all you have to do is stick your shovel in the sand and out comes a mummy."

"Yes...yes...yes, that seems to be the case." Professor Thick pulled a pen from the pocket of his safari shirt and drew something on his paper napkin. Then he pushed the napkin toward Homer. "What is...is...is this?"

Professor Thick had drawn a rope, knotted at the ends to form a circle. Homer's mind flew to the northern

147

corner of his bedroom ceiling, to a map called "The Land of the Pharaohs." "It's a cartouche," Homer said. His shaking knees calmed down as his mind focused on the questions. "It's a symbol of protection. The rope protects whatever lies inside. If you find a cartouche on a map, it means that someone very important is buried there."

Hercules stopped scribbling and looked at Homer. Except for Dog's scratching at a flea, the kitchen fell into silence. Everyone watched and waited for the professor's reaction.

Professor Thick twisted one end of his mustache and smiled. "Ver...ver...very good."

Zelda and Homer simultaneously released a long breath. Zelda patted Homer's back. Then she motioned to a woman in a brown motorcycle jacket who sat next to Professor Thick. "Homer, this is Torch. Torch specializes in the Lost Civilization of Atlantis."

Homer had never heard of Torch. The snake tattoo that wrapped around Torch's neck might have caught Homer's attention, if it hadn't been for the live hawk that sat on her shoulder. It wore a little leather hood over its eyes and clicked its beak. Hearing the sound, Dog scooted out from under the chair to investigate.

"You don't look nothing like Drake," Torch said, glaring at Homer with icy black eyes. "How do we know you're his nephew?"

"You have my word," Zelda said.

"I'd rather have proof."

Zelda, towering over the table, lowered her voice. "Are you questioning my integrity, Torch?"

"I question your motives," Torch replied, stroking one of the hawk's talons. "You were friends with Drake. We all know you were helping him with his quest to find Smeller's treasure. Some of us think Drake found Smeller's treasure map and left it to the kid. If Homer joins the society and we finance his quest, then the two of you could become very famous."

"Unlike you, Torch, I do not desire fame," Zelda said, her tone as cold as the mist on the moor.

Torch snorted. "Everyone wants fame. Do you want fame, Homer?"

Homer couldn't honestly say that he didn't want fame. He'd often imagined all the kids from the Milkydale schoolhouse standing in line to buy tickets to the Homer W. Pudding Museum. Or tickets to a movie called *The Great Adventures of Homer W. Pudding*. "Maybe a little," he answered.

"What's the holdup?" Lord Mockingbird grumbled. "Move on, move on."

"I've got more questions," Torch snarled.

"Move on, move on."

"As procedure dictates, it is Torch's turn to ask questions," Hercules said. He opened a file folder. "I can show you the regulations if you'd like."

"Balderdash!" Lord Mockingbird cried. "Bunch of mugwumps, the whole lot of you."

Torch curled her upper lip and glared at Homer. "Why do you have that dog?"

"He's my dog," Homer said. "I'm going to take him on my quest."

"Why?" Torch asked. "What can he do?"

Dog, who didn't know that this was the most momentous day in Homer's life, began to lick raisins off the floor.

"He carries things," Homer replied.

Torch nudged the hawk until it climbed onto her wrist. "Moonwing hunts for me. I don't have to worry about running out of food. Your dog must do something else besides carry things."

Of course Dog did something else, but Homer wasn't about to spill his secret. "He just carries things," Homer said, trying to sound convincing. Torch narrowed her eyes.

"Do you have any more questions?" Zelda asked.

"Just one." Torch set Moonwing back onto her shoulder and folded her arms. "Do you have Rumpold Smeller's map?"

Zelda stiffened. Was she worried that Homer would mess up? He was supposed to be honest, after all. "No," he said, looking right into Torch's eyes. "I do not have Rumpold Smeller's map."

Torch raised her eyebrows, then slumped in her chair. *It's her*, Homer realized. *She's the one who doesn't want me to join.*

"And finally," Zelda said, "this is Jeremiah Carson. Jeremiah is a fossil hunter and an expert on excavation. He is in the process of proving that some dinosaurs had a written language."

"Ha!" Torch said. "That's hilarious."

"Almost as hilarious as your search for Atlantis," Dr. Gertrude Magnum said, which shut Torch up.

"Howdy, Homer," Mr. Carson said, nearly knocking Homer over with his booming voice. "I'm sure glad to meet ya."

"Hello, Mr. Carson," Homer said, glad to be done with Torch.

"Heck, kid, you call me Jeremiah." He reached out a weathered hand and shook Homer's so enthusiastically that Homer almost lost his balance. "I got just one question for ya. You ever been to Montana?"

"No," Homer said.

"Well, that's a dang shame. We're gonna have to get you and that doggie out there. You can't beat a buffalo steak fresh off the grill. And there's nothing like the Montana sky at night. The stars sparkle like a firefly's rump." He picked up his cowboy hat and shook it at Homer. "And we'll have to get you one of these. This here's a real hat. Not like that sissy one you've got on your head."

Homer had never heard of Mr. Carson, but he seemed real nice.

Zelda took the last seat next to Mr. Carson. The only chair remaining was empty. Uncle Drake's chair, Homer realized. He imagined his uncle sitting there, the boyish glint in his eyes, his warm laugh. "Your time has come, Homer," he heard him say. "This is your destiny."

"Do you have any questions?" Hercules asked Zelda.

"I know everything I need to know about Homer. He's first-rate." She folded her hands and looked down her long nose at Homer. "He'll make us proud. I know he will."

The kitchen fell silent as everyone turned and looked to the end of the table. Lord Mockingbird had closed his eyes. Everyone waited for him to say something else, but all that came out of his mouth were a few bits of muffin and a snore.

"Lord Mockingbird?" Hercules asked, poking the old

man in the arm with the end of his quill. "The questions have been asked. Now we move to the vote."

"Rumpledethumps."

Homer smiled. The questions had been super easy. Only Torch had asked a question about Rumpold Smeller, so all that studying had been unnecessary. It was over. Now it would become official.

"According to Inheritance Bylaw 14.5, in order for Homer to be granted full membership and claim the chair vacated by the untimely death of his blood uncle Drake Horatio Pudding a favorable majority vote must be reached," Hercules said.

"I vote yes," Jeremiah Carson said, smacking his palm on the table.

"You must make a motion to vote," Hercules said. He grabbed his quill and began scribbling again.

"Well dang it, I always forget that part. I make a motion that we vote on making Homer a member."

"I...I...I second the motion," Professor Thick said.

"I still want proof," Torch said.

Zelda sighed. "You already have proof, Torch. Drake presented his request verbally and in writing at our last meeting. It's on file."

"I wasn't at the last meeting." Torch moved her hawk to her shoulder. "I never saw no letter."

There was no doubt in Homer's mind that Torch was set against him.

"Hercules," Zelda said, "would you please show Torch the letter from Drake requesting that Homer take his place in the membership in case of his untimely passing?"

"Certainly." Hercules searched a file. "The letter is here," he said. Then he searched some more. "I filed it in triplicate, as per Filing Bylaw 8.3." He frowned, then searched a stack of papers. "It was here," he said. A pained expression spread across his face, and he looked at Zelda. His voice was barely a whisper. "The letter is missing."

"What?" Zelda stood, her knees cracking loudly. "It can't be missing."

"Look again," Dr. Gertrude Magnum said.

Hercules searched again. Zelda and Jeremiah Carson hurried to Hercules's side to help with the search. But it was of no use. The letter was gone. "Someone took it," Hercules declared.

Homer leaned against the wall, his legs wobbly.

"It doesn't matter," Zelda said, all necks craning up at her. Her face hovered above the lamp's light. "Homer's membership is indisputable. Drake told us what he wanted. He stood in front of this group and told us. The chair is Homer's right to inherit."

Then all eyes turned to Lord Mockingbird. The old man yawned. "Why is everyone looking at me?"

"Your Lordship," Hercules said, "they await your opinion."

"Well, you know my opinion. I hate yellow raisins."

"They await your opinion on Homer's right to membership."

"Fiddle-dee-dee." Lord Mockingbird pointed a gnarled finger in the air. "He may look like a ninnyhammer, but he's Drake's nephew. Give him the chair. Unless..."

Homer pushed off the wall and stood rigid. "Unless what?" he asked.

Lord Mockingbird's eyes narrowed. "Unless there is a challenge."

"I make a challenge!"

Those words had not come from anyone in the kitchen. Homer spun around. Standing in the kitchen's entryway was a girl with bright pink hair.

"Lorelei?" Homer whispered. Normally Homer would be happy to see his friend, but Lorelei had said something about a challenge. Had he heard her correctly?

She set a backpack on the floor, then walked in and plunked a gold coin onto the table. "I'm here to challenge Homer for Drake Pudding's chair."

17

The Return of a Friend

Dog waddled up to Lorelei and poked her shin with his nose. She reached down and scratched his head. Three months ago, Lorelei kidnapped Dog and took him to the evil lair of Madame la Directeur—a banished member of L.O.S.T. who had murdered Homer's uncle in an attempt to steal his precious treasure map. It had been a dark moment in Lorelei and Homer's friendship, but the way Dog's tail was wagging, he appeared to have forgiven her.

The kitchen once again fell silent as everyone stared

at the pink-haired girl who'd interrupted what was supposed to be a secret meeting. "Lorelei?" Homer's voice was hushed. "What are you doing here?"

She didn't look at him. She stuck out her chin and looked at Lord Mockingbird. "I'm here because Drake Pudding wanted me to be here."

"What's going on?" Dr. Gertrude Magnum asked, her cheeks blazing red. "How did this little girl know about our meeting? No one is supposed to know about our meetings."

"I knew about it because I'm very clever," Lorelei said, stepping closer. Her pink hair sparkled with mist and her sneakers squeaked with moor mud. "My name is Lorelei. I don't have a last name, but I'm seriously thinking about Lorelei the Great, or Lorelei the Phenomenal. Something like that."

"I like this kid," Torch said with a slight smile. The hawk clicked its beak.

Hercules peered wide-eyed over a stack of paper. "Why is your backpack moving?"

"My rat's inside," Lorelei said.

"Rat?" Hercules dropped his quill. "Rats carry the bubonic plague and have very sharp teeth."

"She's a nice rat," Lorelei said, flaring her nostrils.

Homer knew exactly how Hercules felt. Rats were disgusting. They infested barns and left their droppings everywhere. But at that moment Homer wasn't concerned about the rat. His gaze fell upon the gold coin that Lorelei had set on the table. He knew that coin. It was the membership coin that had belonged to his uncle—the very coin that had been cleverly hidden on Dog's collar. The initials *L.O.S.T.* appeared on one side, an engraving of a treasure chest on the other side. Madame la Directeur had stolen the coin. Homer thought he'd never see it again. He reached for it, but Lorelei grabbed it first.

"Drake Pudding gave me his membership coin. This is proof that he wanted me, not Homer, to take his place."

"What?" Homer nearly bit his tongue. "That's not true. Why are you lying?"

"Let the girl talk," Torch said.

"I don't see why he should let the girl talk," Zelda said. "She's not a member and she wasn't even invited to this meeting."

"I...I...I agree," Professor Thick said.

"And I happen to know that she works for Madame la Directeur." Zelda walked around the table and stood beside Homer. "We voted Madame la Directeur out of this membership because she broke her vows. Anyone who works for Madame cannot be trusted."

"I don't work for Madame anymore," Lorelei said. "How could I, anyway? After she recovered from the cobra bite, the police put her in jail. I work for myself now and I want to be a treasure hunter."

"That coin belongs to me," Homer said. "You know it does. Madame took that coin from me. You found it in her..." Homer clenched his teeth together as Lorelei looked at him for the first time since stepping into the kitchen. She narrowed her eyes. The secret waited, ready to burst out. *She found the coin in Madame's lair. It's a secret lair beneath the Museum of Natural History. Now that Madame's in jail, Lorelei lives in the lair and no one knows about it but me.*

But he couldn't spill the secret. Because he and Lorelei had made a gentleman's agreement—he kept the secret of the lair and she kept Dog's treasure-smelling secret.

"I don't know where she found the coin," Homer said. "But it belongs to me."

"I didn't find it. Drake Pudding gave it to me."

As Dog prodded Lorelei's squirming backpack, Hercules's quill flew across paper, recording the unexpected turn of events.

Homer wanted to shake Lorelei. Why was she doing this? Becoming a member of L.O.S.T. was his dream, not hers. This was his big day. "He gave it to *me*."

"Homer is telling the truth," Zelda said. "I saw the coin myself, in his possession. As did Ajitabh."

"We've been bamboozled," Lord Mockingbird said. "Hornswoggled."

"Your Lordship," Homer pleaded, "I'm telling the truth. I'm a mapmaker, just like you. Please believe me." But His Lordship stuck a finger in his ear and picked out a bit of wax.

"Hercules, can you con...con...confirm the coin?" Professor Thick asked.

Hercules opened a leather satchel that hung from the back of his chair. He pulled out a penlight and clicked on its blue beam. Then he reached out and picked up the coin. "A treasure chest on one side and the initials *L.O.S.T.* on the other side," Hercules said. "A hole has been punched into the coin."

"That's so he could put it on Dog's collar," Homer said.

"That's so I could wear it as a necklace," Lorelei lied.

Homer groaned. They wouldn't believe her, would they?

Hercules shined the light along the coin's rim. "It's a membership coin," he confirmed. "The serial number is still intact. It's Drake's number."

Lorelei smiled. "I told you it was his coin. He gave it to me."

Homer couldn't bear the lies any longer. "He did not!" he cried.

"Whoa there, kiddo," Jeremiah Carson said. "Hold your horses. We'll get to the bottom of this. Did you say that this girl used to work for Madame la Directeur?"

"Yes," Zelda said.

"We've got to shovel our way through this pile of cow dung." Jeremiah Carson slapped his palm on the table. "I know what's going on and so do the rest of y'all. Madame la Directeur is trying to weasel her way back in."

"Oh dear," Dr. Gertrude Magnum squeaked.

"Bu...bu...but Madame's in prison," Professor Thick said.

"I'm not working for Madame," Lorelei said with a stomp of her foot, spraying Homer's leech-proof socks with moor mud. "I'm here on my own. I've got the membership coin, so it's my right to claim membership."

"Makes sense to me," Torch said.

Zelda cleared her throat. "Lord Mockingbird, I assure you that this girl is trying to deceive us. Homer's right to inheritance is indisputable."

Lord Mockingbird had fallen asleep again.

Hercules stopped scribbling. "Actually," he said, then he hesitated. "Actually..." He shuffled through a stack of papers and pulled out a single sheet. Then he looked at Homer and frowned. "I'm sorry to say, Homer, but according to Inheritance Bylaw 18.2, someone in possession of a membership coin may call for a membership contest."

"Yes!" Lorelei said, stomping her foot again. "That's it. I want a contest."

"A contest?" Homer asked. "You mean, I have to compete against Lorelei?"

Everyone looked to Hercules for the answer.

Hercules held out the paper for all to see. "If you still want to claim your uncle's chair, you'll have to compete against Lorelei and you'll have to win."

18

The Making of an Enemy

Homer and Dog stood at the ocean's edge, just beyond Zelda's cottage. The hard, wet sand was like a blackboard, momentarily marked with Homer's and Dog's prints, then brushed clean by the rhythmic sweep of the waves. Tiny seabirds, too light to leave prints, poked their needlelike beaks into the sand. Dog tried to chase them, but they escaped to the sky in perfect synchronization, then landed farther down the beach. After three such romps, Dog gave up and chewed on a piece of driftwood instead.

The L.O.S.T. membership had asked Homer and Lorelei to wait while they discussed the terms of the competition. Homer had rushed out into the evening air, trying to get as far away from Lorelei as possible. He remembered the confusion he'd felt when he'd first found out that Lorelei was working for Madame la Directeur—when he'd first found out that she'd been lying to him. He remembered how the confusion had turned to disbelief, then anger.

Anger. That dark, ugly feeling once again churned inside Homer.

The sun disappeared into the sea, leaving a soft puddle like melted butter. The summer moon began its climb. Anchored offshore, the immense yacht called *Cave Woman* bobbed. Homer figured that it belonged to Dr. Gertrude Magnum, the expert on caves.

From a distance, one might think that the boy and his dog, dressed as they were in their professional adventurer clothing, were waiting for a submarine or a speedboat to whisk them away. But that wasn't going to happen. Homer stood rigid, staring out across the ocean. A mixture of ocean spray and angry tears glistened on his cheeks.

Lorelei was trying to ruin his dream.

She was supposed to be his friend. He'd forgiven her

for what she'd done in the past because her actions had been a matter of survival. Lorelei had no family. She'd been forced to take care of herself in a hostile city. She'd lived in a soup warehouse, selling soup from a cart to survive. And she'd worked for Madame la Directeur because Madame had promised to make Lorelei her partner in her treasure-hunting quests. Homer had come to understand why Lorelei had stolen a cloudcopter and why she'd kidnapped Dog. When a person has nothing, the lure of treasure can fog the mind.

Then things changed. Together they'd fought Madame la Directeur. They'd survived her attempt to kill them both. They'd made a gentleman's agreement. Lorelei had sent Homer her imitation Galileo Compass as a gift. He'd taken that as a sign of renewed friendship.

But now she was trying to take what was rightfully his. What kind of friend does that?

A delicate funnel of water spurted out of the sand, spraying Homer's knee. Dog dropped the driftwood. The funnel spurted again. Dog barked at it, then at another funnel, and another.

"Clams," Lorelei said. "They squirt when they dig."

The crashing waves had masked her approach. Homer quickly wiped his face with his hands. Lorelei set her backpack at her feet, then opened the main zipper. Out popped a large rat, Daisy by name, who sniffed the air, then jumped onto the sand. Both Homer and Dog had met this rat. She was a thief with nimble paws.

Distracted by the clams, Dog didn't notice Daisy as she headed down the beach, her rubbery tail twitching happily as she explored.

"You were the one following me," Homer said. "Last night on the moor. You followed me here." He knew it was true, so he didn't wait for her to deny it. "How did you know I was going to a L.O.S.T. meeting?"

"I figured it out," she said mysteriously.

"Why are you lying to everyone?" Homer asked. "Why are you doing this?" She flicked a piece of kelp off her shoe. Then she looked away. "Lorelei? Why are you doing this?"

"Because I need L.O.S.T."

"Why?"

"You know why." She crammed her hands into her jean pockets. "I want to be a famous treasure hunter."

"But you don't need L.O.S.T. You've got the lair and all of Madame's stuff—her treasure-hunting equipment, her speedboat, her gadgets—everything."

"Yeah, well, you've got your treasure-smelling dog. That is a million times better than any gadgets."

A clam shot water right into Dog's nose. He shook his head and sneezed.

Lorelei picked up her backpack and leaped out of the way as a wave washed over Homer's brand-new boots. Not a drop of seawater managed to seep inside.

"It doesn't matter if one of us needs L.O.S.T. more than the other. What matters is that it's my birthright, not yours." Homer clenched his fists. "That coin belongs to me. Uncle Drake's chair belongs to me. You had no right to come here."

"I can go wherever I want," she said. "It's a free country."

They looked into each other's eyes, equally determined thrusts to their chins. He remembered when he'd first met her. How she'd given him and Dog free tomato soup from her soup cart and how she'd given them a tour of The City. She'd been so nice. He tried, but he couldn't keep the words from bursting out. "I thought you were my friend!" Dog, hearing Homer's despair, pressed against his leg.

In the dusky light, Lorelei's pink hair was the brightest spot on the beach. But with Homer's words, her face turned beet red. She turned away. Homer's heart pounded in his ears. Another wave washed over his boots. Dog scampered from the wave and wandered to the dry sand, where he picked up another piece of driftwood.

Neither Homer nor Lorelei said anything for a long

while. What else could Homer say? He'd told her how he felt. And she didn't seem to care. Daisy the rat scurried along the water's edge, then crawled up Lorelei's pant leg and perched on her shoulder. The rat stared at Homer, her nose twitching. *I remember you*, Daisy seemed to say.

"Homer! Lorelei!" Zelda called from the sandy bank. "It's time."

Lorelei turned quickly. "Look, Homer, only one of us can win, so why don't we make a pact?"

Homer narrowed his eyes. "What kind of pact?"

"If I win, then you can come and stay at the lair with me. We'll have L.O.S.T. to help us *and* we'll have Dog. Imagine how much stuff we could find if we worked together. It would be the greatest partnership ever."

"Is that what you want? To be my partner?"

"It's an idea." She folded her arms. "What do you think?"

A breeze whistled across Homer's ears. He might have considered a partnership, but not now. Not after the lies she'd told to the membership. How could he trust her? "I don't want to be your partner. But if I promise to let you come on my quest with me, would you go back in there and tell them the truth?"

"Oh, you're going to *let* me come on your quest? Do I

get to carry the equipment? Do I get to make the coffee or scoop Dog's poop?"

"That's not—"

"I've never had anything, Homer. Don't you get that?" She kicked a clamshell, almost knocking Daisy the rat off her shoulder in the process. "I want everyone to know who I am. All those people who passed me in the street and never bothered to buy soup. All those people who told me to get out of their way. Who never bothered to ask if I needed any help." Her voice caught for a moment. "L.O.S.T. will help me become famous."

"But you can't tell anyone about L.O.S.T."

"I know that. But L.O.S.T. will give me a better chance of finding treasure. I'll be rich."

"You have to take a vow," he said. "If you join L.O.S.T., there's a vow that you won't use your treasure for fortune. You have to give it to a museum or a university, so everyone can enjoy it."

Lorelei chewed on her lower lip. "You'd do that?" she asked. "If you found treasure, you'd give it up?"

"Yes. That's the point. It would be for everyone."

"Homer! Lorelei!" Hercules ran across the sand, his helmet wobbling. "The meeting has resumed. You'd better get back in there before Lord Mockingbird has a stroke." He glanced nervously at Lorelei's rat, then at the ocean. "You shouldn't stand so close to the water. Rogue waves are a well-known phenomenon. They swoop right in and take you out to sea." He ran back toward Zelda's cottage.

"Are you going to tell them the truth?" Homer asked Lorelei.

She said nothing.

"Then you're not my friend anymore."

If words had a flavor, those words would taste as sour as goat milk that had been left out in the hot sun. It hurt Homer to utter such sour words, but what hurt him even more, as Lorelei stomped off, was the suspicion that she didn't much care.

Inside the kitchen they stood side by side, awaiting their fate. Homer, in his professional adventurer gear, his loyal dog at his feet. Lorelei, in her jeans, sweatshirt, and sneakers, her thieving rat on her shoulder.

The faces that looked up from the kitchen table could have been members of a firing squad. Would they shoot him down, right there and then? Did he have a chance against Lorelei? Zelda gave Homer a reassuring nod, but she nervously wrung her hands.

Lord Mockingbird, perched at the top of the phone book pile, waved a skeletal hand in the air. "Get on with it," he snarled.

Hercules cleared his throat and read from a piece of

paper. "Let it be known that during the seventy-ninth meeting of the Society of Legends, Objects, Secrets, and Treasures, two individuals, Homer Winslow Pudding and Lorelei..." Hercules paused. "Have you chosen a last name?"

"Not yet," she said.

He continued. "Homer Winslow Pudding and Lorelei have each placed a claim on Drake Pudding's chair. In accordance with Inheritance Bylaw 18.2, the current president, His Honor Lord Mockingbird the Eighteenth, has created a challenge for the competitors."

Lord Mockingbird had created the challenge? Both Homer and Lorelei shared a quick glance. Lord Mockingbird might have been a great mapmaker in his day, but now he was clearly feeble of both mind and body. Maybe that was an advantage. Maybe the challenge would be super easy.

Hercules continued. "In accordance with His Lordship's instructions, His Lordship will be the only person to know the whereabouts of the membership coin, which he will hide somewhere on the planet."

Somewhere on the planet? Homer ground his teeth. That didn't narrow things down. But he knew one thing— that if he could find the place, then Dog would take over and sniff out the coin.

"Three clues to the coin's location will be delivered to

both competitors tomorrow at noon," Hercules said. "Opening the clues before noon will result in disqualification."

Dr. Gertrude Magnum, her jewels glinting in the lamplight, smiled sweetly at Lorelei and Homer. Jeremiah Carson, however, leaned on the table and scowled. "I want to make sure this here's a fair deal. You'll give the same three clues to each kid?"

"Don't bother me with details," Lord Mockingbird said.

Lorelei stepped closer to the table. "If this is supposed to be fair, then Homer can't take his dog with him."

Homer's mouth fell open.

"Wh...wh...why can't he...he...he..." Professor Thick struggled to finish the sentence. "T...t...take the dog?"

Lorelei tapped her sneakers on the wooden floor. She pursed her lips. Was she going to tell? Surely she wouldn't, because if she told Homer's secret then he'd tell her secret. The authorities would sweep into the lair and take all the stuff that Madame la Directeur had stolen and all the stuff she'd created. A self-destruct button was a very dangerous piece of equipment that no one, especially not a twelve-year-old kid, should own.

"He shouldn't take the dog because..." Lorelei's shoulders slumped. "Because my rat can't carry as many things as his dog."

"That's a good point," Dr. Gertrude Magnum said. "We do want this to be fair."

"If the girl wants a dog, then she can go get herself a dog," Jeremiah Carson said. "Nothing's stoppin' her."

"Exactamundo," Lord Mockingbird said, pounding a withered hand on the table. "Enough blathering."

Lorelei stuffed her hands into her jean pockets. Homer smiled victoriously. He would have patted Dog's head, but Dog had once again settled beneath Lord Mockingbird's chair.

"Is the meeting adjourned?" Gertrude Magnum asked, her bracelets jingling as she raised her hand. "I would like to get home to my cave fish. They so miss me when I'm gone. I make a motion that we adjourn the meeting."

"You're a flibbertigibbet," Lord Mockingbird said. Then he smiled a toothless smile. "Membership Bylaw 30.3. Read it."

Hercules searched through a pile of papers until he found Membership Bylaw 30.3. "In the event that the competitors are under the age of sixteen, and therefore cannot legally drive or fly their own vehicle, a current member of L.O.S.T. will be chosen to act as a guardian for each competitor. This guardian will provide transportation for the competitor and will do whatever necessary to ensure the underage competitor's safety and that the underage competitor does not cheat. However, the guardian cannot supply the competitor with the answer to the challenge."

Homer looked down the table. He couldn't believe his luck. He'd choose Zelda, of course, and then he'd have access to her cloudcopter. "I choose Zelda," he cried, his hand shooting into the air.

"No way! I choose Zelda," Lorelei said.

"I said it first."

"So?"

"Zelda," Homer said confidently, "of course you'll help me, right? Not Lorelei."

Zelda opened her mouth, but Lord Mockingbird silenced her. "Quiet! Too much jibber jabber." His little legs dangled off the edge of the phone book stack. "Bylaw 50.7."

Hercules found Bylaw 50.7. "In the event that two underage competitors request the same guardian, then names will be drawn from a hat."

Lord Mockingbird held out his black top hat.

"What?" Homer and Lorelei blurted at the same time.

"I beg your pardon?" Zelda said. "Surely it makes sense that I act as Homer's guardian. I am, after all, responsible for the boy. His parents sent him to stay with me for the week."

"Bylaws," Lord Mockingbird said, pointing a shaky finger down the table. He grabbed a piece of paper, yanked the quill from Hercules's hand, and, leaning so close to the paper that his nose almost touched it, he scribbled some words. Then he tore the paper into pieces and dumped the pieces into his top hat. "Choose," he said, holding out the hat to Lorelei.

Homer was beginning to suspect that Lord Mockingbird was another person who did not want him to join L.O.S.T. Shouldn't mapmakers stick together?

Daisy the rat, still perched on Lorelei's shoulder, stopped cleaning her tail and peered curiously into the hat. Lorelei squeezed her eyes closed, then reached inside. Sweeping her fingers through the pieces of paper, she whispered, "Please oh please oh please." Then she pulled one out. Her eyes widened as she looked at the paper. A huge grin spread across her face. "Zelda!" she cried, holding the paper out so everyone could see. "I got Zelda. Fair and square."

Homer, feeling sick to his stomach, leaned against the wall. Color drained from Zelda's already pale face and her shoulders slumped. She didn't bother to push her long silver hair from her eyes. Surely she wouldn't help

Homer's enemy? Because that's what Lorelei had become. "Zelda?" Homer asked.

She sighed, pain pulling at the corners of her eyes and mouth. "I'm sorry, Homer. I am a sworn member of L.O.S.T. I must respect the bylaws."

Homer held back tears. He refused to cry. But this was a terrible turn of events.

"Well I'll be," Jeremiah Carson said quietly. "I sure feel sorry for ya, Homer. You got a bum deal, no doubt about it. But maybe you'll get my name. If you get my name, then we'll be sure to win what's rightfully yours. We won't stop till the fat lady sings."

"I beg your pardon?" Dr. Gertrude Magnum said with a snort.

"If...if...if you get my...my...my name," Professor Thick said, rubbing one of his large ears. "I'll help... help...help."

Torch said nothing.

"Get a move on." Lord Mockingbird shook his top hat, then held it out again. Lorelei stepped aside, still smirking at her piece of paper.

Everyone waited, gazes darting between the top hat and Homer. Only Dog didn't watch, his eyes closed, his chin resting on the floor. Homer closed his eyes, reached out, and stuck his hand into the hat. As his fingers shuffled through the papers, he thought about Dr. Gertrude

Magnum. She was an expert on caves, which could come in handy. One might assume that because she wore so much jewelry, she was the kind of person who didn't like getting dirty. But Homer's gaze rested on her hands. They looked kind of like a farmer's hands—stained, the nails chipped and crammed with flecks of dirt that wouldn't come out even after a good scrubbing. Clearly she'd climbed and dug her way into caves. She wasn't afraid of hard work. It might not be so bad drawing her name from the hat.

He thought about Professor Thaddius Thick, who seemed like a nice person. Homer didn't know much about Egyptology, so having Professor Thick around could also come in handy. But imagine how long it would take for the professor to explain something.

He certainly didn't want Torch. She clearly despised him. That left Jeremiah Carson, Homer's best option. Jeremiah was an outdoorsman, evidenced by his tanned and weathered skin. His broad shoulders and muscular forearms indicated strength, which Homer could use. And he seemed to genuinely like Homer.

Please oh please oh please, he thought, his fingers grasping a piece of paper. Then he opened his eyes and read the name.

And read it again.

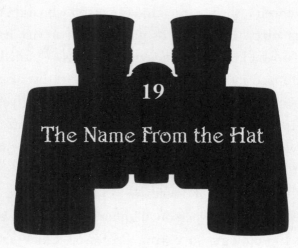

19
The Name From the Hat

Hercules?" He turned the paper to the other side, then turned it back. "Hercules?"

Hercules stopped writing. "Me?"

Lorelei's laugh ended in a snort. "You got stuck with the kid in the helmet."

"But Hercules is the records keeper," Homer said, his face scrunched in desperation. He thrust the piece of paper at Lord Mockingbird. "He's not an adventurer. And he's only fourteen."

"Me?" Hercules said again. "No, not me. I take notes."

"He takes notes," Homer said, nodding like a bobble-head doll. "Notes. That's what he does."

"What a relief," Torch said, leaning close to Professor Thick. "Last thing I want to do is help one of those sniveling brats."

"Lord Mockingbird," Zelda said, leaning across the table. "Hercules is not an adult. Surely it is better to have an adult act as Homer's guardian."

Lord Mockingbird grunted. "He's old enough. And he took the oath of membership."

Hercules sank into his chair. "I did. I took the oath."

"But he is not old enough for a driver's license," Zelda pointed out.

"He's got that butler who's always driving him everywhere," Lord Mockingbird said. "That'll do."

A dizzy sensation grabbed hold of Homer's head. He closed his eyes for a minute and steadied himself with a hand on the wall. At the speed of light it was all going terribly wrong. Hercules was scared of everything. A quivery shell filled with fear. How could he possibly do what might need to be done?

"We'll get the clues tomorrow?" Lorelei asked. "At noon?"

"Indubitably," Lord Mockingbird said.

Lorelei folded her arms. "I don't want Homer here when I get the clues. I'm real good at figuring things out and I don't want him following me."

"Me? Following you?" Homer said.

"Yeah. That's right. So you go to Hercules's house and wait for the clues there."

"Rectified!" Lord Mockingbird shouted. "Meeting adjourned."

"Tough break, kid," Jeremiah Carson said. "Well, I'd better be heading on down the trail. My doggies are plumb tired out, and it's a long way to Montana." Then he shook Homer's hand. "Take care of yourself, kid. I sure hope I'll be seeing ya at future meetings." He gave Lorelei a nod, then headed down the hallway.

"Wait," Homer called, not about to give up. He pleaded with Lord Mockingbird. "But Hercules is afraid of my dog. How can we go on a quest together?"

The remaining pieces of torn paper floated onto Lord Mockingbird's shoulders as he plunked the top hat onto his head. Then he stretched his withered legs and slid off the phone books. Standing, he only reached Homer's waist. "Toodle-loo."

"No, wait," Homer begged. Dog crawled out from under the chair and watched as the little man scurried away.

Gertrude Magnum rose from her chair. Her earrings

swayed as she squeezed herself around the table. "Best of luck to you," she said, patting Homer on the shoulder. Then to Lorelei she said, "And best of luck to you, my dear. It would be nice to have another female onboard. There are so few of us in the treasure-hunting community."

Torch walked past with only the briefest of glances. "Whatever," she said as she carried her hawk down the hall.

Professor Thick scratched his beard. "Does...does...doesn't seem right. Dray...Dray...Drake wouldn't have liked this." He got up from his chair and walked around the table, where he shook Homer's hand. He opened his mouth to say something else but changed his mind, shrugged, and headed down the hallway.

Zelda's front door closed.

For a moment, no one in the kitchen spoke. Homer leaned against the wall, Dog at his feet. Zelda sat perfectly still, her eyes focused on her fingers as she strummed them on the table. Lorelei petted her rat. Hercules read and reread the bylaws.

The weight of the evening's events pulled on Homer's legs. He wanted to curl up on the floor next to Dog. "Zelda?" he said quietly. "What do we do?"

She stood like a praying mantis unfolding itself—first her legs straightened, then her spine, then her neck, until her head, once again, floated above the lamplight. "Homer," she said, her low voice gravelly with pain, "I am responsible for you until Sunday evening. I must ask you to reconsider this challenge. You do not have your parents' permission, and I will not be able to protect you."

"What are you saying?" Homer asked. "You want me to go home?"

"It would be the safest decision."

"Hey, I think that's a great idea," Lorelei said. She set the phone books on the table, then sat in Lord Mockingbird's chair. Daisy the rat jumped onto the table and began nibbling on muffin crumbs. "I don't have parents, so I don't have to worry. I can go anywhere."

Homer ground his teeth together. His mom and dad would be worried, of course, but they didn't have to know. They thought he was at Zelda's and they expected him back on Sunday. That gave him five days to find the membership coin. He had to try. For Uncle Drake, he had to try.

"I'm not going home," he said.

Zelda nodded. Of course she understood. The same passion ran through her blood.

Hercules shuffled through the papers. "I don't want to do this. There's got to be a way out," he mumbled.

"I think you should leave now," Lorelei said. "Zelda and I have a lot to talk about." She smiled sweetly at Homer, but he knew, with all his heart, that the sweetness was a clever ploy. Not an ounce of her could be trusted.

Zelda took Homer's hand and looked down at him. "Please, never doubt me. Though I'm helping Lorelei, my heart is with you."

"I know," Homer said.

Homer, Hercules, and Dog stood beneath Zelda's driftwood arbor. The horse, Rolls Royce, scooter, motorcycle, and helicopter were gone, as was the yacht. "Good luck," Lorelei called before shutting Zelda's front door. A gentleman would have wished her good luck in return, but Homer couldn't bring himself to say those words—not after everything she'd done.

"I'm real sorry about this," Hercules said, adjusting his helmet strap. "I know you don't want to be stuck with me."

"Uh..." What could Homer say? It was true. "It's fine," he lied as he slid his arms through his backpack straps.

"It's not fine. I don't want to go on a treasure hunt.

I'm supposed to file papers." Hercules shuddered. "What if we have to climb something? Or go underwater? Or... do something dangerous?"

Homer wiped sea spray off his face. "You don't have to do any of those things," he said. "I'll do them. I'm the one who has to find the coin. You're just supposed to make sure I don't cheat. And drive me around." Homer looked around. "So, you have a butler?"

"Yes, and I scheduled a pickup."

A roaring sound filled the air. Clutching his first-aid kit and pulling a little wheeled suitcase, Hercules led Homer and Dog around Zelda's cottage to the beach. The summer moon floated above the calm sea. The seabirds had gone to bed. But there, on the hard sand, sat an airplane. The airplane's door opened and a small staircase unfurled. A man with a red mustache walked down the stairs. He removed his pilot's hat and bowed. "Good evening, Mr. Simple," he said.

Hercules dumped his suitcase at the man's feet. "Hi, Baldwin. What's the weather like?"

"No need to worry," Baldwin said. "Flying conditions are mild. The chance of crashing is one in thirty billion."

Hercules frowned. "One in thirty billion? Are you sure we won't encounter any hurricanes? It is hurricane season, you know."

"No hurricanes. The sky is perfect for a night flight."

"Okay." He adjusted his helmet. "Uh, this is Homer Pudding and his dog, Dog."

Baldwin bowed. "Good evening, Mr. Pudding. Good evening, Dog."

A renewed sense of hope wrapped itself around Homer. "Hercules, is this your plane?"

"Yep."

"Really?" A plane was so much better than a cloud-copter. They'd be able to beat Lorelei to any location. "This is great."

Baldwin picked up Hercules's suitcase. "Where to, Mr. Simple?" he asked.

"Home," Hercules said.

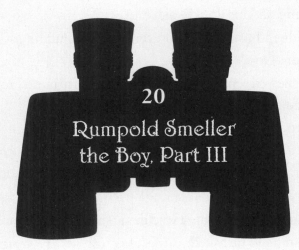

20

Rumpold Smeller the Boy, Part III

Rumpold balanced on the branch. It swayed slightly, but the base was sturdy enough to hold him. His long, skinny legs were built for climbing, and he weighed little more than he had last year.

Duke Smeller's castle had been in the family for fourteen generations. Built atop a rocky hill, it overlooked fields where peasants worked their crops, and where goats and sheep grazed. In exchange for the duke's protection and land, the peasants provided the estate with eggs, milk and cheese, cabbages, carrots, and potatoes.

The duke also employed a band of hunters who kept venison and rabbit on the supper table.

Rumpold balanced a piece of wood on his lap, onto which he set a precious piece of parchment. With a sharpened stick of charcoal, he sketched the horizon where the forest met the sky. A few minutes into the drawing, a cloud of dust caught his attention. A horse moved along the road at a fast pace. Rumpold frowned. It was another knight, come to join the others who'd been arriving throughout the day.

Rumpold rested his back against the tree's trunk as the horse and rider started up the steep road to the castle. They cut through a herd of sheep that were crossing to the other field. The knight did not wear armor but wore a long white tunic with a black cross sewn across the chest.

Why do I have to join the knighthood? Rumpold wondered. It was bad enough that he was destined to become the next Duke of Estonia. He'd be stuck in the castle, overseeing and protecting, when all he wanted to do was travel down that road, on and on, sketching everything he saw.

"It is your duty to get married and have a son," his mother often told him. "Duke Frederick's daughter would be a suitable match."

Rumpold had met Duke Frederick's daughter once, at his cousin's wedding. She'd called him ugly and had pushed him to the ground.

"Daydreaming?" The knight, having stopped his horse beneath the tree, looked up at Rumpold. His long blond hair was tied back with a cord, and his beard was neatly trimmed. "Thinking about faraway places?"

"Yes," Rumpold admitted.

"That is understandable. Faraway places can be most intriguing." The knight nudged his horse and continued up the road.

Rumpold tossed the drawing board to the ground, rolled up his parchment, then scrambled down the tree. With a long stride, he ran after the horse. "Have you been to faraway places?" he asked when he'd caught up.

"Many."

"Really?" Rumpold stumbled over a stone. The knight slowed the horse's pace so that Rumpold could walk alongside. "Where have you been?"

"I've fought in Cypress and Macedonia. I've battled in Scotland and Wales."

"Oh." The horse kicked some dust onto Rumpold's face. He wiped it away with his sleeve. "Is that why you go places? To fight?"

"In my youth I went where the money was good. If they paid, I fought. But now I stay here to protect my homeland." He reached out and rubbed the horse's neck. "Things never stay the same. Change is always in the wind, like the seasons."

"My father expects me to become a knight."

"Ah. You are Duke Smeller's son." He smiled kindly at Rumpold. Then he nodded at the rolled parchment. "You are an artist?"

"Yes," Rumpold said. "I want to go to other lands and whatever I see, I want to draw. And then I can put it all into a book so that other people can see the world, too."

"Is that so?"

"Yes. That is so."

The road grew steeper as they approached the palace. An armed guard stepped aside as Rumpold led the horse through the gates and into the courtyard, where the knight dismounted. He removed his gloves and put a hand on Rumpold's shoulder. "I only have daughters. Silly-minded creatures who spend their days needle-pointing and combing their hair. It is every father's dream to have a son who will follow in his footsteps."

Rumpold nodded, pretending to agree. This knight would never understand Rumpold's true feelings—that following in his father's footsteps was the last thing he wanted to do.

Clutching the parchment, he watched as the knight strode into the palace. Then he looked up and met his sister's gaze. Rumpoldena stood on the balcony, a piece of needlepoint in her hands, her face heavy with sadness. He waved to her. She frowned as a woman appeared and escorted her off the balcony, back to the women's chambers.

The horse snorted, then nuzzled Rumpold's arm. Rumpold looked into its gentle brown eyes. Maybe this horse didn't want to be ridden. Maybe it wanted to be free, to roam the fields, to graze in the meadow. Maybe his sister didn't want to sit around all day and do needlework. Maybe she, too, wanted freedom. But she was a girl. And he was the son of a duke.

Rumpold knew, there and then, that he'd never be a traveling artist. His future was carved like a riverbed.

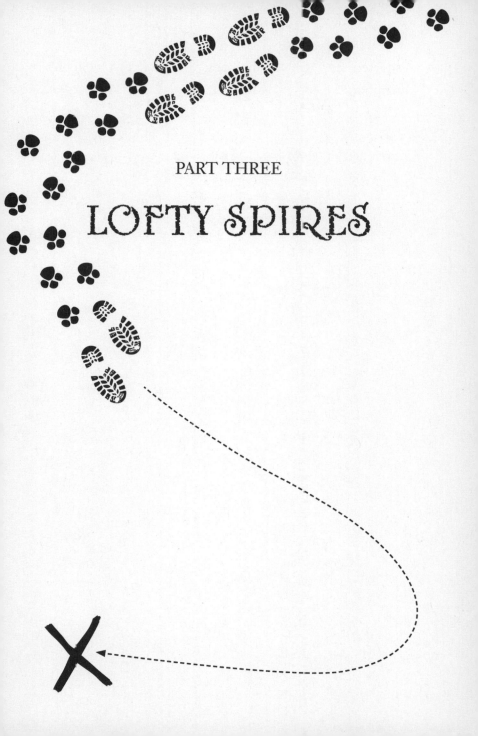

PART THREE

LOFTY SPIRES

21

The Palace of the Gods

D awn sent its rosy rays through the airplane's windows, tickling the faces of the sleeping passengers. Homer opened his eyes and rubbed away bits of crust. He'd fallen asleep in what Hercules had called a "sleeping berth"—two airplane seats that folded out to make a little bed. The night had passed quickly—at least that's how it felt to Homer, who'd slept so soundly he couldn't remember dreaming or even changing position. Not that he could have changed position. Late last night, Dog had wedged himself between Homer and the armrest. His soft brown ear was draped over Homer's arm. His white tummy rose and fell in steady breaths.

There was a moment each morning, just as Homer woke and his brain kicked into gear, when he worried that Dog wouldn't be beside him. This fear had plagued Homer ever since that horrid morning three months ago when he'd woken to find that Lorelei had kidnapped Dog. It could happen again. If the wrong person found out that Dog could smell treasure...

The thought was too much to bear. The last thing Homer wanted was to relive the panic and heartache of that day when he'd thought he'd lost Dog for good.

Homer picked a strand of dog hair from his mouth. He'd gotten used to the short strands appearing in all sorts of odd places, like in his pockets, in his cereal, and mixed in his belly button lint. They were like little invaders, those dog hairs.

He stretched his legs, then sat up. Dog, his eyes still closed, moaned his disapproval. "Don't worry, you can sleep some more," Homer whispered.

Hercules lay in the berth across the narrow aisle. With a black mask over his eyes to keep out the light, he looked like some kind of bizarre superhero. He'd taken a pill to prevent motion sickness, which apparently he'd never suffered from, but "there is always a first time," he'd said. Then he'd grabbed an orange parachute. "Just in case we get hit by lightning or a meteorite." He'd fallen asleep clutching the parachute to his chest.

While Homer had flown on a cloudcopter, he'd never flown on an airplane. The ride was much smoother, but the best part was that he didn't have to worry about being flung from his seat and falling over the side. The other benefits of airplane travel, he decided, were not having wind blowing in his face and not constantly inhaling cloud cover, which had a flavor unlike anything else. The only true description is, "It tastes like cloud."

The world outside was pinkish, thanks to the morning sun. It was also flat and composed of green squares, like the quilt that lay on Homer's bed, the one his grandmother had sewn from old pillowcases. A house sat on each square. Homer leaned over Dog to get a better look out the tiny window. At first glance they looked like houses, but as the plane descended, Homer realized that the houses were sprawling estates—some with towers, some with moats, most with Olympic-size swimming pools. One even had a Roman coliseum in the backyard. No one in Milkydale, not even Mayor Sneed, lived in a house half as large as these. The former Milkydale library couldn't even compare.

Milkydale felt a whole world away Homer sighed, remembering last night's phone call to his family, just before leaving Zelda's cottage. "Zelda and I are going camping," he'd lied to his mother. He'd regretted the lie, but there was no way he could tell her about the L.O.S.T. challenge. "So I won't be able to call you for a couple of days."

"Oh dear," Mrs. Pudding said. "You'll be sure to take your raincoat?"

"Yes." That wasn't a lie. He'd packed it into his backpack. "What happened at the fair today?"

Her voice instantly cheered. "I won first place for my lemon cream pie. But tomorrow is mincemeat day, and you know I don't like mincemeat."

"How did Dad do at the dog trials?"

"Max and Lulu both made it to the finals," she said. "But we're five points behind the Crescent dogs. Your father and Squeak are out in the barn right now giving the dogs a good rubdown."

"Tell Homer that someone threw another rock!" Gwendolyn called out.

"Another rock?" Homer asked. "Did it have a note?"

"Don't you worry about it. It was just another silly note telling you to keep away from the fair." Mrs. Pudding paused for a moment. "It's best to ignore bullies. If you ignore bullies, then they'll get bored and go away."

"Homer!" Gwendolyn must have pulled the phone out of Mrs. Pudding's hand. "I'm stuck doing your chores. You're gonna owe me big when you get home. I'm gonna make you do my chores for the rest of the summer."

"I'm sorry," Homer said. He didn't want Gwendolyn to get stuck doing his chores, but he wasn't about to rush home, no matter how miserable Gwendolyn was planning to make his life. He had to finish his quest.

"Be careful on your camping trip," Mrs. Pudding said after wrestling the phone away from Gwendolyn. "And call me as soon as you can. We all miss you very much and can't wait to see you on Sunday."

"Tell Dad that I hope he wins. And I hope you win the mincemeat contest, too."

As the conversation faded from Homer's mind, he focused on the green plaid landscape. The plane tilted slightly and turned to the south, granting him a clear view of the next mansion with its glass dome ceiling. A loudspeaker crackled. "Good morning, Mr. Pudding," Baldwin said. "Would you please wake Mr. Simple and let him know that we are landing in five minutes?"

Homer reached across the aisle and nudged Hercules's shoulder. Hercules bolted upright and tore the mask from his eyes. "What's going on?" he cried. Dog's eyes flew open. "Are we plummeting to earth?" He blinked once, twice, then looked at Homer. "Well?"

"We're landing in five minutes," Homer said.

"Oh." Hercules grabbed his helmet and stuck it on his head.

It took a great deal of nudging and then a giant shove to get Dog out of bed. He scratched his ear with his hind leg, which was an amazing feat considering the distance between his head and his back feet. Then he waddled over to the exit door and whined.

"You can go to the bathroom in five minutes," Homer told him, setting the seats upright.

"Urrrr." Dog sat, his tail thumping on the carpet, his gaze never leaving the exit door.

As the plane descended, Homer felt as if someone had stuffed cotton balls into his ears. "Hey, Hercules, where are we?" he asked.

"The gated community of Lofty Spires," Hercules said, still hugging the parachute.

The plane tilted again. "What's a gated community?" Homer asked.

"It's a fancy neighborhood with a big wall around it to keep out the riffraff." As the plane straightened, Hercules squeezed his eyes shut. "You can only get in if you're invited."

They passed over a circular lawn that glistened like a green lollipop. *What kind of people live in a gated neighborhood?* Homer wondered. *Maybe a president, or a king, or a movie star?*

The loudspeaker crackled again. "Please make sure your seat belts are fastened."

"Dog," Homer called, but Dog refused to leave his place by the door. Homer secured his seat belt, then gripped the armrests as the floor vibrated and a humming sound filled the air. "What's that?"

"Landing gear," Hercules explained, squeezing his eyes harder. "That's a good sign, but there's still the chance we could miss the runway entirely. Or explode on impact."

Those weren't reassuring words to hear, especially since Homer had never landed in an airplane before. As the black runway rose up to meet them, Homer also closed his eyes. The plane gently bounced as the wheels touched down. The engines quieted and the movement eased. Hercules released a loud sigh. Homer opened his eyes just as a sign passed by the window:

PRIVATE AIRSTRIP.
Property of Lofty Spires. No Riffraff Allowed.

"*Terra firma*," Hercules said, tossing the parachute aside. "Solid ground." The plane taxied to the end of the runway, then turned toward an enormous metal building. HANGAR 3B: THE SIMPLES. The hangar's double doors opened, and the plane taxied into the gleaming interior.

As soon as the plane was parked and the engines shut off, Baldwin emerged from the cockpit. "Our guest looks eager to leave," he said, giving Dog a pat on the head. Baldwin reached up and pulled a lever. As the exit door lifted upward, a staircase unfolded downward. Dog, his tail wagging madly, pushed past Baldwin and scrambled down the stairs.

"Ur, ur, ur," he grunted.

Homer unbuckled his seat belt and grabbed his backpack.

"You can leave your baggage," Baldwin said. "I will have it delivered to Mr. Simple's room."

"That's okay," Homer said, not wanting to leave his gear with anyone. Even if they'd landed in a place that was riffraff-free, he wasn't about to take the chance. The contents of his backpack were all he had in his quest to defeat Lorelei. That, and Dog.

Homer followed Hercules down the stairs. Dog piddled on a tuft of grass just outside the hangar's doors. "Did anyone notice my absence?" Hercules asked as Baldwin opened the door of a black stretch limousine.

"Your absence went unnoticed as usual, Mr. Simple."

Hercules frowned. Clutching his first-aid kit, he slid into the limousine's backseat.

"Come on, Dog," Homer called. Dog lifted his leg over another tuft of grass, then another. Even though

Dog couldn't smell, the instinct to leave his scent was in his blood. And once he started marking, it was always difficult to get him to stop. "Hello, over there. We're waiting."

After a heave and a push, Dog landed on the limousine's floor. Homer climbed in and smiled in wonderment. The limo was a house on wheels. A white leather couch wrapped around the interior. A sink and a refrigerator sat in the corner. Baldwin, who'd exchanged his pilot's hat and epaulettes for a shiny black driver's cap and black driving gloves, took the driver's seat and drove the limousine out of the hangar and onto a paved road. Hercules scooted to the far end of the seat, as far away from Dog as possible.

Homer's Quality Solar-Powered Subatomic Watch read 7 a.m., Tuesday morning in Lofty Spires. Five hours until noon. "How will Lord Mockingbird get the clues to me if there's a wall around the neighborhood?" he asked.

"The mailman is allowed inside, same with the hired help."

"You have hired help?" Homer asked.

"We have gardeners, cooks, butlers, pantry maids, and a laundry and cleaning staff. I'm sure there are more, but I can't keep track of them. And there's Baldwin, of course. He's my personal butler."

Homer had never known anyone with a butler. He'd seem them in movies, though.

At ground level, the mansions of Lofty Spires were as impressive as anything Homer had ever seen in history books. They drove past a hedge trimmed like a row of hearts, where two heart-shaped wrought iron gates opened onto a red driveway. A brick wall surrounded another residence. Grimacing gargoyles lined the wall and guarded its gates, as did two men in security guard uniforms. They passed one of the moats Homer had seen from the air. GUARDED BY PIRANHAS, a sign read. As Homer and Dog watched the scenery pass by, Hercules kept his distance at the far end of the limo, clutching his first-aid kit and nervously tapping his feet.

"Are my parents home?" Hercules asked, leaning toward the driver's seat.

"No, Mr. Simple. Your parents are in Saint-Tropez at a fund-raising event for children who have only one millionaire parent. But your brothers and sister have returned from college for summer vacation."

Hercules swallowed hard. "All of them?"

"Yes, Mr. Simple. All four of them."

"Crud." Hercules opened his first-aid kit. "If they're home, I'm going to need another tube of antibacterial ointment, a bag of cotton swabs, and a quart of benzoyl peroxide. Another ice pack would be good, and I should boost my immune system with vitamins C, D, A, E, B12, and B6." He closed the first-aid kit. "Are you certain no one noticed my absence?"

"I'm certain, Mr. Simple."

If Hercules lived in a house as large as the other houses in Lofty Spires, then it made perfect sense that no one had noticed his absence. His family members probably got lost just trying to get from their bedrooms to the kitchen table. *Good thing*, Homer thought, *that I brought a compass*—even if it was a fake Galileo Compass from that traitor Lorelei.

"Here we are," Hercules said as the limousine turned up a paved driveway and passed beneath a stone arch that was entwined with ivy. Broad green stripes crossed the lawn in a perfectly mowed pattern. Statues of Roman archers, gladiators, and soldiers rose from the grass like giant chess pieces posed for a game. As the limousine slowed, Homer rolled down his window and he and Dog stuck out their heads. Eight massive columns loomed over them.

"It looks just like the Pantheon," Homer said, imagining the ancient Rome map from the southwest portion of his ceiling.

"My father is a Romanophile," Hercules told him as Baldwin opened the limousine door. "He loves all things Roman."

"Is that why he named you Hercules?"

"Yep." Hercules pointed to his helmet. "I have an extra one in my room. You can wear it."

What was he worried about now? That something would fall from the sky and land on Homer's head? "I'm okay. I don't need a helmet," Homer said.

"Believe me. You do."

Up the huge stone steps they walked, then between two of the columns. A white-gloved doorman held the door as they walked into a grand room. Homer felt as if he'd shrunk. Not even Zelda, standing on a ladder, could touch the ceiling. The polished marble walls gleamed, reflecting a million shards of light from the crystal chandelier. Homer shielded his eyes with his hand. When his pupils had adjusted, he looked around.

A wall of painted portraits dominated the room, each portrait more than double life-size and each labeled with an engraved gold plate. Homer adjusted his backpack, then wandered over to the wall. He had to crane his neck to read the plates.

SENATOR SIMPLISTICUS SIMPLE. The man in the portrait wore a red suit. His gray hair was crowned with a laurel wreath.

"That's my father. He's a senator." Hercules scratched beneath his helmet. "You'd better not stand too close. If one of those fell off the wall, you'd be instantly crushed."

Homer took a step back, then moved to the next frame. SYLVANIA SIMPLE. The beautiful woman in the portrait wore a green gown and a diamond necklace.

"That's my mother. She's an elitist. She and my dad travel all over the world. They never take me with them."

"My dad and mom are goat farmers. They own the Pudding Goat Farm in Milkydale."

"Really? I've never met any goat farmers. Is it dangerous?"

"No. And supposedly, goat farming is the happiest job you can have." Homer walked farther down the wall. "Are these your brothers and sister?"

"Yep. And they are, in one word, simpletons."

ROMULUS. A guy with black smudges beneath his eyes and a football tucked under his massive arm had posed for the artist in full football gear. Homer could practically hear a growl vibrate behind Romulus's mouth guard.

TIBERIUS. He'd posed in a wrestler's singlet. His skin glistened with sweat and his muscles bulged like balloons. He held some unfortunate kid in a headlock.

CAESAR. This brother held a hockey stick and was the only person on the portrait wall who was smiling— probably to show off his two missing front teeth.

DIANA. She was the only girl on the wall, but as beefy as the boys. She'd posed in a soccer uniform, her hands on her hips, a soccer ball caught beneath her cleats. Mud covered her shin guards, as well as parts of her face and neck.

All four had the same wiry black hair as Hercules.

Beneath these portraits, on a long shelf, stood dozens of gilded trophies, each engraved with the word *champion*. Homer had never won a trophy. His sister had three from past science fairs. Last year she'd won the Golden Cup of Taxidermy.

Homer came to the end of the wall and the final portrait. HERCULES. Hercules had posed in a suit and tie, a dictionary in his hands. His portrait was smaller than the others. No trophy stood beneath. "Didn't you get a trophy when you won the World's Spelling Bee?" Homer asked.

"Yes, but someone took it," Hercules said, his voice echoing off the gleaming walls. "One of *them* took it." Then he tucked his first-aid kit under his arm and hurried toward a long hallway. "We'd better get out of here," he called. "Before they see us."

They?

And that's when the floor began to vibrate. Dog whined and pushed between Homer's shins. The portraits rattled against the wall. One of the trophies tipped over. Was a train approaching? Homer hadn't noticed a train track. Dog whined again. "Oh no," Hercules said, stopping midstride halfway down the hall. He spun around, a wild look in his eyes. "Too late."

The vibrations ran up Homer's legs to his back teeth. He'd never been in an earthquake. In Mrs. Peepgrass's class, they prepared for earthquakes by hiding under their desks. "What do we do?" he asked, looking around for something to crawl under. The vibrations turned into steady pounding, like an approaching herd of elephants.

"There's no time!" Hercules cried, flattening himself against the hallway's wall as the pounding intensified. "Save yourself!"

"How?" Homer cried.

"Get out. Get out now!"

22

A Horde of Simpletons

Romulus Simple, one of Hercules's brothers, charged up the hall, a football tucked in the crook of his arm. His arms pumping, his face gritted with determination, he ran. With each of his pounding footsteps, Dog bounced an inch off the ground.

Romulus was as wide as two men, and his elbow barely missed Hercules, who was holding his breath and pressing against the hallway wall. Homer, who still stood in the front room, grabbed Dog by the collar and pulled him out of the way just as a whoosh of air, thick with body heat and sweat, swept past them.

But there was no time for a sigh of relief because more pounding footsteps sounded in the distance.

Hercules, his helmet atilt, peeled himself off the wall and dashed up the hallway toward Homer. His eyes darting wildly, he pushed Homer and Dog behind a giant pedestal that held a bust of Senator Simplisticus Simple. Homer's backpack slipped off as he crouched next to Hercules in their hiding spot. Dog peered around the side of the pedestal. A low growl hummed in his chest.

"Shhh," Hercules whispered breathlessly.

The bust rocked back and forth as Tiberius, Caesar, and Diana Simple barreled up the hallway and into the front room. "Tackle him!" one of them hollered.

"Don't let him get to the front door!"

Just as Romulus reached for the front door's knob, Tiberius, Caesar, and Diana threw themselves on him. If Homer hadn't seen it with his own eyes, he might have thought a building was being demolished, such was the decibel level as the Simples crashed into the door. Forming a great writhing heap, they broke into a fit of laughter.

Hercules whispered to Homer. "Follow me. Be very quiet." On tiptoe, his first-aid kit hugged to his chest, he started toward the hallway. Homer grabbed his backpack, but as he stepped out from behind the pedestal, a helmet flew through the air. Hercules was lying on the floor, flat on his back. Then something flashed before Homer's eyes, and before he could react, his backpack flew from his hand and he also landed on his back. Something very large pinned him to the floor.

Sniff, sniff, sniff.

"Whatever you do, don't move," Hercules whispered as they lay shoulder to shoulder on the floor. "It's Brutus."

A wet nose poked Homer's chin. A face the size of a lion's, black as coal and surrounded by saggy folds of skin, stared down at Homer. A thick thread of drool swung back and forth as the beast panted. Pungent dog breath infiltrated every cell in Homer's body. "N...n... nice doggy," Homer said, cringing as the breath washed over him, hot and sticky.

"She's a Neapolitan mastiff," Hercules whispered. Both he and Homer were pinned—Hercules by the beast's back half, Homer by its front half. "She's our guard dog and she'll eat your face if you try to get away."

"Grrrr." Dog was doing his best to push Brutus off Homer, an impossible task because Brutus could have worn Dog as a hat. Homer flinched as the thread of drool dipped closer. No wonder Hercules didn't like dogs.

"Hey, look what Brutus caught." Tiberius, who looked exactly like his portrait, only smaller, leaned over and stuck his face next to Brutus's. They both looked down at Homer with matched satisfaction. "Brutus caught a kid. Good girl, Brutus." Brutus panted joyfully, her tail *thwapp*ing against the marble floor. She must have weighed a ton—at least that's how it felt as Homer tried to breathe beneath her bulk.

Caesar, another brother, leaned in to get a look. Homer could see right up his nose. "Hi, kid."

"Uh, hi," Homer said.

"Is this your little dog, the one trying to wrestle Brutus?"

"Uh-huh."

"That's a funny little dog." Caesar straightened and hollered, "Hey, Diana, did you see this funny little dog? It's wearing a little vest."

Homer couldn't see Dog, but he could hear the growling. "Dog," he said, wheezing beneath Brutus's weight. "Come here. Leave the nice big dog alone."

Dog had worked himself into a tizzy, growling like a rabid mongrel and head-butting Brutus with all his might. Brutus ignored Dog, her eyes focused on Homer's face. Dog had droopy skin, but Brutus's was ten times droopier, the folds framing her black face like drapes around a window. A second thread of drool emerged from the other corner of her mouth. *Please don't eat my face*, Homer thought.

"Hey, Hercules," Diana said, looking down at her

little brother. "We're heading out to the coliseum, and we need someone to scoop horse poop."

"No way," Hercules said, gasping for breath. "I'm not going to the coliseum. I just got the cast off my arm." He groaned. "Could one of you please get this dog off of us?"

"Yes, please get the dog off of us," Homer said, so drenched in dog breath that he was certain he'd never be able to smell anything else ever again. And that's when Brutus sneezed. The two threads of drool broke and fell across Homer's cheek. "Gross," he said, trying to turn away.

Dog stopped growling and collapsed onto the floor. With a frustrated groan, he rested his chin on Homer's shoulder. Homer knew Dog would faithfully stay by his side—at least until someone offered him something to eat.

"Hey, what's this?" asked Romulus, the eldest brother. He stood over the boys, dangling Homer's backpack in midair.

"That's mine," Homer said. He recognized the evil smile that spread across Romulus's face. It was the same evil smile that always appeared on Earl's face just before a game of keep-away. Earl, one of Homer's classmates, often yanked Homer's Galileo Compass off its string. He'd tossed it back and forth with a buddy while Homer bounced between them, trying to catch the compass.

They'd reenacted this humiliation countless times over the years. Homer had tried to ignore the boys—a tactic supported by Mrs. Pudding. But what Mrs. Pudding didn't understand, because she'd never been bullied, was that the very thing that angered a boy like Earl was being purposefully ignored. In fact, it enraged him. And so the one time Homer put his mother's advice into action, his book *Buried Celtic Treasures* ended up in the school toilet.

Homer grimaced as the smile on Romulus's face widened. A new game of keep-away was about to begin.

"You want your little backpack?" Romulus asked with a snicker. Homer could practically see the wheels spinning in Romulus's head. *Me got backpack. Me throw backpack. Make boy cry.*

Pinned to the floor, Homer was as helpless as a fish in a bucket. Panic shot down his limbs. "Please," he said. "That backpack contains very expensive equipment, and some of it can't be replaced."

"Oh?" Romulus tucked the backpack into the crook of his arm. "Is that so?" Then he charged toward the front door.

"Catch him," Diana yelled.

The doorman opened the front door, and Romulus charged outside. Caesar, Tiberius, and Diana took off after him.

"Ruff." Brutus heaved herself to her paws and bounded out the front door, her jowls flapping like wings, threads of drool flying through the air like streamers.

Homer wiped the drool off his face with his sleeve. Then he and Dog scrambled to their feet. Homer's chest ached as if it had been flattened, but he managed to stumble out the front door. Romulus, the backpack imprisoned beneath his muscular arm, jumped over a gardener who was weeding the pansies. The gardener looked up for a moment, then threw himself on the ground as the rest of the Simple siblings charged like a raiding horde of Vikings, bellowing and shaking their fists. More gardeners crouched fearfully as the horde trampled patches of lilies and marigolds. "Ruff!" Water sprayed as Brutus charged through a fountain like a four-legged tidal wave. One of the gardeners caught a goldfish in midair.

Homer stood at the front of the Simples' palace, trying to figure out how to get his backpack. Romulus, still on the move, toppled a wheelbarrow as well as the gardener who'd been pushing it. Then he disappeared around the garden wall, his brothers and sister close behind. Brutus leaped from the fountain and bounded after them, her skin rippling like black waves.

"What are you doing out here?" Hercules asked, quickly strapping his helmet back onto his head. "It's too dangerous. Come on."

"But I need to get my backpack. It has everything in it."

"They're heading for the coliseum. You can't go out there."

"But..."

"Do you know how dangerous it is out there?" He waved his first-aid kit in the air. "Even this can't protect you out there. You have to come inside. We'll go to my room, where we'll be safe. Don't worry. My brothers and sister have very short attention spans. They'll toss your backpack around, and then they'll forget about it. I'll tell Baldwin to get it for you."

Homer hesitated. So much of his life was in that backpack.

Hercules grabbed Homer's arm. "Listen to me. I'm supposed to keep you safe. If they come back and find us, they'll make us go to the coliseum. The last time they forced me to the coliseum, they used me as a human shield. I was in the hospital for a week."

Homer imagined himself dressed in a tunic and standing in a Roman coliseum, facing Brutus the way gladiators had faced hungry beasts. Had Hercules been forced to endure this his whole life? No wonder he was afraid of everything.

Shouting and barking filled the air. "They're coming back!" Hercules let go of Homer's arm and ran into the house. The gardeners fled in all directions, like the rabbits had fled the rabbit barn. Homer needed no convincing, nor did Dog. They followed Hercules down the hallway, the stripes of his rugby shirt their guiding light.

"You won't believe how many bones I've broken just because I live in a house filled with Neanderthals." Hercules dashed around the corner, then started up a stairway. "And don't let them tempt you with Ping-Pong. That little ball might weigh no more than a wad of cotton, but when it's hurled at you at the speed of light, well, it can get lodged in very uncomfortable places. Hurry!"

Hurrying was easier said than done. Homer wrapped an arm around Dog's middle and half-pulled, half-carried him up the stairs.

"And then there was the time they wanted me to play badminton," Hercules said. By the time Homer and Dog reached the top, Hercules was at the end of the next hallway, his voice fading around the corner. "They threw me over the net."

Two corners later, Homer lost sight of Hercules and could no longer hear his voice. "Hercules!" Homer called. He'd tried to keep a mental map of the journey, but he'd been so worried about escaping that he hadn't paid close enough attention. And he hadn't bothered to take a compass reading, either. As he skidded to a stop,

Dog bumped into his calves. A long hallway stretched before them, lined on both sides with blue doors. "What do we do now?" Homer asked Dog.

"In here, Mr. Pudding." Baldwin stepped out of a room at the very end of the hall. He'd changed out of his chauffeur's uniform and now wore a butler's black suit with a white bow tie and a striped vest. He motioned them down the hall. "Mr. Simple has ordered breakfast. He prefers to eat in his room. Do you have any special dietary requirements or requests?"

"Yes," Homer said as he caught his breath. "I mean, no, I'll eat anything. But I need my backpack. It's very important. Romulus took it."

"I see." Baldwin tapped a finger to his chin. "If Romulus took it, then it will probably end up in the coliseum." He pulled a little notebook from his vest pocket. "I'll add your backpack to the list of items that need to be retrieved." He read from his list. "A washing machine, a golf cart, a jumbo pack of toilet paper, two maids, and now, a backpack. After breakfast I will prepare for a clandestine trip to the coliseum."

"Thank you," Homer said.

"And what about your hound? What does he like to eat for breakfast?"

"He likes pancakes," Homer said. "Oh, there's something else. I'm going to get a delivery at noon."

"Very good, Mr. Pudding. I shall bring it to you."
After a little bow, Baldwin strode up the hall.

A personal butler comes in very handy, Homer realized.
Perhaps drawing Hercules's name from the top hat
hadn't been bad luck after all. Homer considered this as
he stepped into Hercules's bedroom.

The opulence of the Simples' mansion had not made its
way to Hercules's room, which was as boring as a motel
room. Just a bed, a single window, a desk, a chair, and a
bookshelf. "We're safe in here," Hercules explained. His
first-aid kit sat on his desk. "This is the servants' wing. I
moved here last year, and my stupid brothers and sister
haven't found me yet. I can get a good night's sleep without having to worry about being tackled."

Homer worried about his backpack being tackled.
Would any of his equipment survive? Uncle Drake had
given him the Borington Binoculars and the night vision
headlamp. If he'd been in his own room, he could have
distracted himself from his worries with one of his maps
or adventure books. But Hercules kept only dictionaries
on his shelf. "Is this what you read?" Homer asked, running his hand across their spines.

"Mostly. I have to study a lot to win those spelling
bees. But my brothers and sister are bound to find my
hiding place one day. When they do, I won't have a single dictionary left. They'll take them just like they took

my trophy." Hercules opened his closet door and started rooting around in a pile of clothes. "I like to memorize definitions. When everything else is spinning out of control, a word is solid. That sounds stupid, doesn't it?"

"No, it doesn't sound stupid." Homer pulled *The Complete Dictionary of the English Language* off the shelf. "I do the same thing. When I've had a really bad day at school, I read my maps. They take me someplace else."

Hercules changed into a new rugby shirt, one with orange and yellow stripes. "The other one was covered in Brutus hair," he explained. "Do you need a new shirt? I bet yours is wet with Brutus slobber."

"No, I'm good." Fortunately, Homer's clothing had proven to be slobber resistant. He'd have to tell Mr. Tuffletop about that.

Homer set the massive dictionary on the desk and fanned through its pages. "Was it hard to win the world championship?"

"Very. Do you want to know what my winning word was?"

"Okay."

"It was *honorificabilitudinity*."

"That's a word?"

"Yep. It means 'honorableness.' The ablative plural is honorificabilitudinitatibus. That's one of the longest words in the English language." He emerged from the closet holding a helmet. "Here, you can borrow this." He tossed it to Homer.

Homer caught the helmet. "Thanks." Then he set it aside. "I would like to live my life with honori…honorif…honor—whatever it was."

"Honorificabilitudinity."

Homer checked his watch again, hoping that some kind of miracle had occurred and time had flown by and it was noon. Of course it hadn't. The dials spun, revealing the time in Lofty Spires, London, and Cairo. "Wait a minute," Homer said, rotating one of the dials. "We're in a different time zone than Lorelei. She's three hours ahead of us. That means she's already seen her clues. She has a head start."

"That doesn't seem fair." Hercules sat on his bed and folded his arms.

"It isn't fair." Homer checked his watch again. Anything was possible with a three-hour head start. "What if she's already found the coin?"

"Then I won't have to go on a quest," Hercules said happily. He coughed and looked at his feet. "I mean, that would be really terrible."

"I know you don't want to go on this quest," Homer said, pacing between the bed and the closet. "But I do. Maybe I can't beat Lorelei, but I want the chance to *try* to beat her. If she's got a three-hour head start, I'm doomed."

Dog pricked up his ears as a knock sounded on the bedroom door. Homer yanked it open. "What are you doing?" Hercules cried, crawling under the bed. Homer had forgotten all about the dangerous Simple siblings. He was hoping to find a delivery with his name on it. But instead he found a little wheeled cart waiting in the hallway. Three silver domes sat on a white tablecloth. Homer pulled the cart inside. "Who is it?" Hercules asked from under the bed.

"I think it's breakfast."

Lovely, tantalizing scents filled the room as Homer lifted the first silver dome. Scrambled eggs, thick strips of maple bacon, and six pieces of buttered toast were arranged on a china plate. "That's your plate," Hercules said, getting to his feet. Homer lifted the second dome, revealing a bone-shaped bowl filled with cut-up pieces of pancake. He set the bowl on the carpet next to Dog. Dog wagged his tail and began to inhale his meal.

"What are you having?" Homer asked, grabbing a fork.

Beneath the third dome was a plate of white toast, scrambled egg whites, and a cup of hot tea. "I have a nervous stomach," Hercules explained.

Homer couldn't imagine turning down bacon. Even when he had the flu, he still loved bacon.

Piling the eggs on top of his toast, Homer ate as quickly and as loudly as Dog. He hadn't eaten anything since Zelda's, and with each swallow his mind sharpened and his energy surged. A professional treasure hunter must be grateful for each and every hot meal. The places where treasures tend to hide, like caves, tombs, and the bottom of the ocean, aren't places where bacon is readily available, or any food for that matter. Once a quest is under way, it's often a matter of feast or famine.

After breakfast, Dog slept on a pile of dirty clothes. Hercules read one of his dictionaries. And Homer stared at his watch. "One more hour," he announced.

"Forty more minutes," he said.

"Thirty more minutes." He ran to the window. No sign of a delivery truck. "Don't you think I should wait downstairs?"

"Too dangerous. Baldwin will bring the delivery the moment it arrives," Hercules said.

"Twelve minutes." Homer paced.

"Three minutes."

"One minute!" This was it. The watch's alarm buzzed, startling Dog out of his dream world.

A knock sounded on the door.

23

The Box of Clues

"S pecial delivery for Mr. Pudding," Baldwin said
after Homer had opened the door.

"Thanks," Homer said, grabbing the small box.
Baldwin turned crisply on his heels and strode up the
hall. After closing the bedroom door, Homer sank onto
Hercules's bed. Dog waddled over and sat at Homer's feet.

In wobbly handwriting, the box was addressed thusly:

TO: *That Chunky Kid in the Khaki Shorts*
CARE OF: *That Namby-Pamby Kid Who's*

Afraid of Everything
The Simpleton Palace
Lofty Spires

Trepidation held Homer in its grip. What if he couldn't do this? What if he failed?

"Aren't you going to open it?" Hercules asked.

Thick strapping tape sealed the box. Homer reached for his Swiss army knife but then remembered it was in his stolen backpack. "Do you have scissors?"

"No," Hercules said. "Scissors are very dangerous. Do you know how many people slice off their fingers every year because of scissors?"

Scissors had never frightened Homer, but the way Hercules was staring at him, his eyes blinking nervously, Homer began to tremble. It wasn't the potential danger of scissors that induced the trembling—rather, it was the fact that Homer was about to face the truth. Whatever lay inside the box was all he'd have to work with. This was the moment of reckoning. He'd figure it out or lose to Lorelei. There was no going back.

Had Uncle Drake taught him enough? Had Homer read enough treasure-hunting books, studied enough maps? Would he be smart enough to find the coin?

With a shaky hand, he grabbed a butter knife from the breakfast cart and cut through the tape.

The box's flaps popped open.

From out of the box, Homer pulled a plastic bear-shaped container of honey and two scrolls. He turned the box upside down to make sure he hadn't missed anything. Upon unrolling the first scroll, a smile burst across his face. "It's a map!" This was a huge advantage over Lorelei—because if there was anything Homer knew how to do, it was how to read a map. He knelt on the carpet and spread out the map. Hercules held down the two top corners. Dog lay on his stomach, resting his chin on one of the bottom corners.

It was a simple map, drawn by Lord Mockingbird's shaky hand. No longitude or latitude lines. No key to indicate scale. A north/south arrow sat in the upper right-hand corner. His Lordship had drawn a simple shape with an *X* marked in the shape's center. There were no other markings on the page. The title read: WHERE I HID THE DOOHICKEY.

"What's a doohickey?" Homer asked.

"It's an unspecified object. I'm guessing he means the membership coin. I don't know if you noticed, but Lord Mockingbird likes weird words."

"I noticed."

Hercules pointed to the center of the scroll. "*X* marks the spot. That should make it easier."

"Maybe," Homer said. He pushed back his bangs and

squinted at the scroll. The two lines that comprised the X were darker and thicker than any other lines on the map—meant to draw the eye. "The X could be a trick."

"Why do you think that?"

"Because Lord Mockingbird is a famous mapmaker. Well, he was famous, when he was younger. Anyway, only an amateur would mark his treasure with an X." Homer ran his finger over the X. "Everyone thinks that pirates marked their treasures this way, but they didn't. Why would they? It would give away the location. The only reason a pirate would mark an X on a map would be to misdirect someone."

"You think Lord Mockingbird is trying to misdirect you?"

"Maybe." Dog's chin held the map in place while Homer unrolled the second scroll. "It's a riddle of some sort."

Hercules smiled and leaned forward. "I love riddles. I'm really good at them." Then he frowned. "Oh, but I forgot. I can't give you any answers."

The riddle was written in the same wobbly handwriting. Homer read it out loud.

> *If ever you meet a mycologist,*
> *A spore-loving, fungal find-ologist,*
> *He'll tell you a tale,*

Blue whale in scale,
That is sure to best a biologist.

"There's no such word as *find-ologist*," Hercules said.

"What's a mycologist?" Homer asked.

"I know that." Hercules smiled proudly. "It's an easy word to break down. The prefix, *mycol*, comes from the Greek for 'fungi' and the suffix, *logy*, comes from the Greek for 'branch of knowledge.' So a mycologist is a person who studies fungi. That's plural for *fungus*."

Homer tapped his finger on the page. "A mycologist would want to find fungus. So he's a fungal find-ologist."

"I guess so. But it's still not a real word."

Homer picked up the plastic honey bear. "So what's the honey for?" He read the riddle again. "I don't get it. How does this all fit together?" He looked hopefully at Hercules. "Have you figured it out?"

Hercules shook his head. "No. But even if I had I couldn't tell you the answer. But I haven't."

This made Homer feel a bit better. If the World's Spelling Bee champion hadn't solved the riddle, then maybe Lorelei hadn't been able to solve it, either. "Maybe you should focus on the map," Hercules said. "Since that's your specialty."

"There's not a lot to go on. I'm guessing that the shape is an island," Homer said. "But I don't really know. I don't even know what part of the world it's in. I don't even know if the island is surrounded by freshwater or salt water—if it even is an island." A big rush of disappointment hit Homer hard, and he slumped against the side of the bed. He knew the symbols and codes that had been used on maps throughout history, and that could have been his big advantage on this quest. But this map was like a child's drawing. "What am I supposed to do? No one could figure this out. Lord Mockingbird is crazy."

"Torch thinks he's crazy. She called him a crazy old man at one of our meetings." Hercules lowered his voice. "I think he's crazy, too. He's the one who hired me. Look at me. I'm the last person who should be in a treasure-hunting club. I break out in a cold sweat just trying to cross the road." Dog groaned and rolled onto his side, presenting his belly to Hercules for a scratch. Hercules scooted away.

Homer's fate rested in a crazy man's scribblings. He strummed his fingers on his knees. Lorelei was very clever—she'd proven that by finding the secret L.O.S.T. meeting. She'd proven it by surviving in a soup warehouse, by kidnapping Dog, and by taking over an evil lair. She was determined.

"Determination is the treasure hunter's oxygen," Uncle Drake had once told Homer.

Gripping the second scroll, Homer sat real straight,

cleared his throat, and tried to work his brain around the limerick.

If ever you meet a mycologist,
A spore-loving, fungal find-ologist,
He'll tell you a tale,
Blue whale in scale,
That is sure to best a biologist.

"The riddle is about a person who wants to find fungus, so wherever the coin is hidden must be a place where fungus grows. Which could be—"

"Basically anywhere in the world," Hercules said.

Homer's chest deflated. "Yeah. Basically anywhere in the world." He stretched out next to Dog and read the riddle again. "I don't understand why a mycologist would tell a tale to a biologist. What tale? And what does a blue whale have to do with it?"

"Maybe blue whales swim near the island," Hercules said, then he smacked a hand over his mouth. "Crud. Was that helping too much? Did I just help you find the answer? Because if I did, I'll have to tell the membership."

"No," Homer said. "You didn't help me find the answer. But maybe you should stop talking just in case."

"That's a good idea."

A little puddle of drool had dampened the map directly

beneath Dog's chin. Homer slid the map free and held it up. He turned it sideways, then turned it upside down. Then sideways, then upside down. "Hey," he said, sitting up. "Do you think the island is shaped kinda like a mushroom?" Hercules nodded. "And a mushroom is a kind of fungus, isn't it?" Hercules nodded again. "I wonder...Do you have an atlas?"

"We had an atlas in the library downstairs, but Romulus took all the books to the coliseum for batting practice."

"What about your dictionaries? Do you have a dictionary that lists places?"

"I have a dictionary of proper nouns," Hercules said, jumping to his feet. He rushed to the bookshelf and grabbed a thick black book.

"Maybe there's a Fungus Island, or a town called Fungus." Homer searched, but nothing turned up. "What about the honey bear? Honey, honeybee, honeydew, honeymoon. Hmmmm...no Honey Island or Honey Bear Island. Are you sure this dictionary is complete?"

"Yes."

"Wait a minute." Homer's fingers flew through the dictionary. "Mush. Mushroom. MUSHROOM ISLAND!" He slammed his palm onto the page. Startled, Dog jumped to his paws and growled. Hercules scooted backward, nervously eyeing Dog. "An uninhabited island shaped like a mushroom," Homer read. "That's it. That has to be it. An island shaped like a mushroom." Homer got to his feet. "But I can't be sure. I need to see the island's shape, either a drawing or a photograph. Then I can compare it to Lord Mockingbird's drawing. I need an atlas."

At the sound of an engine, Dog waddled over to the bedroom window and stared up at the panes. Homer pulled the curtain aside. Three floors down, a gardener worked in a little side garden, planting red geraniums in a rectangular bed. It could have been a scene on a postcard, except for the army tank driving up the path. It was the kind Homer had seen in movies about World War II, and it rolled right past the gardener and stopped beneath the bedroom window. The driver's hatch opened and Baldwin, dressed in fatigues and an army helmet, popped out. He looked up and waved. Homer waved back. "What's Baldwin doing?"

Hercules peered over Homer's shoulder. "He's preparing to storm the coliseum. The safest way in and out is in an armored vehicle."

"You said the atlas is in the coliseum?"

"Uh-huh," Hercules replied.

"I have to get it. And my backpack."

"No way. You can't go out there." Hercules backed away from the window. "Baldwin can drive us to a bookstore, and we'll buy another atlas. It's only an hour's drive."

"Another hour? That's too much time. Besides, I still need my backpack." What choice did he have? Lorelei, three hours ahead, might already be flying to Mushroom Island on the cloudcopter, with all of Zelda's equipment at her disposal. Homer needed his gear.

"But Diana and my brothers are in the coliseum. If they get their hands on you, they'll toss you through the air like a Frisbee. They'll roll you across the arena like a bowling ball. They'll—"

"I want my backpack." Homer didn't want to face the Simple siblings any more than he wanted to face a pride of hungry lions, but without his binoculars and night vision lamp and all the other stuff, he was just Homer. And that didn't give him a whole lot of confidence. He opened the window and leaned out. "Baldwin!" he yelled, waving wildly. "Wait for me!"

He stuffed the scrolls and the honey bear into the clue box. Then he tucked the box under his arm. "You don't have to go. But I do. This is my quest." He looked down at Dog. Would they toss him like a Frisbee? "Maybe Dog can stay here with you."

"What?" Spit flew from Hercules's mouth. "You want me to stay alone with your dog? No way."

"Ur."

Of all the things Hercules was afraid of, his fear of Dog seemed the most ridiculous to Homer. Dog wouldn't hurt anyone. He was practically perfect. Certainly there were dogs that smelled like shampoo rather than smelling like sweaty feet, but there were no dogs with gentler, sweeter personalities. And it kind of hurt Homer's feelings that Hercules wouldn't even pet Dog.

"Fine," Homer said as he opened the bedroom door. "We'll do this without you. Come on, Dog."

Dog ambled toward Homer, and they got halfway down the hall when a voice called out. "Wait!" Hercules caught up to them. "Put these on." He handed Homer a helmet and elbow and knee pads. Then he slid pads over his own knees and up the striped sleeves of his rugby shirt.

"What are you doing?" Homer asked.

"I took a vow. I'm a sworn member of L.O.S.T." He tucked his first-aid kit under his arm. "I'm supposed to keep you safe, and if I don't do what I'm supposed to do, they might kick me out. I don't want to get kicked out. I like going to the meetings. I like having someplace to go."

"Then you're coming with us?" Homer asked.

Hercules nodded. "I've survived the coliseum. If you're

233

going to survive, you'll need my help. But I want you to promise that you won't leave the tank until I tell you. It's really important that you listen to my instructions. It's crazy out there."

"Okay," Homer said, strapping on his helmet. "I promise."

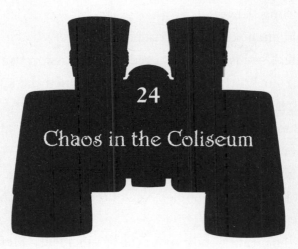

24

Chaos in the Coliseum

Sherman tanks are not designed with basset hounds in mind. Most things are not designed to be basset-hound-friendly. Homer tried heaving Dog onto the tank. "Urrr," Dog complained as Homer gripped his haunches.

"You're...too...heavy," Homer grunted.

"I'll do it," Hercules said. He wrapped an arm around Dog and then scampered onto the tank. After setting Dog onto the hull, he reached out his hand and pulled Homer up.

"Thanks," Homer said, surprised by Hercules's strength. He was obviously hiding some muscles under those long sleeves.

Baldwin poked his head out of the driver's hatch. "Mr. Simple, I've just received a radio transmission from the chef. Your brothers and sister have stormed the kitchen in search of protein shakes."

"Good," Hercules said. "That will give us a bit of time but not much. Let's go."

Baldwin frowned. "Are you certain you want to go to the coliseum, Mr. Simple? Need I remind you of the last incident?"

"I don't want to talk about the last incident," Hercules said, his voice trembling. "So you'd better go before I change my mind."

"If your brothers and sister are in the kitchen, can't we just run out to the coliseum and get the backpack?" Homer asked. Surely it would take less time than maneuvering a piece of World War II machinery around flower beds.

"Yeah, you can run out there. If you want to...DIE. Do you know how long it takes to chug a couple of protein shakes? Not long enough." Hercules lifted Dog onto the turret, then climbed up next to him. The turret was the top, roundish part of the Sherman tank that usually held a long machine gun, but on this particular tank, the gun had been removed. Hercules opened the turret's hatch, then reached into the depths of the tank and set his first-aid kit inside.

Homer climbed onto the turret and handed his clue box to Hercules, which was also placed inside the tank. Then Hercules closed the hatch. He, Homer, and Dog perched on the top of the turret as the tank began its slow trek out of the side garden. Baldwin drove around a statue of a Spartan warrior, then through an opening in the hedge. Homer's breath caught as the coliseum swelled into view.

A piece of ancient Rome had been re-created in the gated community of Lofty Spires. There, in the backyard of the Simples' palace, stood a wonder in architecture. Made of stone and three stories high, with arch-shaped windows cut along each elliptical wall, the coliseum rose from the bright green lawn. Homer had seen it from the airplane window, but at ground level it was massive. The tank rolled beneath an arch and into the coliseum's arena.

For a moment, Homer felt like he'd gone back in time. Though the coliseum's seats were empty, he could practically see and hear the screaming crowds in their togas, cheering for the gladiators. But the mirage faded as he looked around the arena. Chairs, umbrellas, televisions, and uprooted trees were just a few of the items that littered the ground. Books lay everywhere, as if a tornado had set down in the middle of a library.

Baldwin drove the tank into the arena, crushing a chair and a cutting board in the process. Then he shut off the engine. Hercules reached into the hatch and pulled out a pair of binoculars. "Here," he said, handing them to Homer. They were standard issue, not nearly as nice as the Borington Binoculars in Homer's backpack, but they'd have to do. Homer stood, carefully balancing on the edge of the turret. Squinting into the lenses, he scanned the elliptical field. *Backpack, where are you?*

"I see the washing machine," Hercules reported, pointing. "Baldwin, what else was on your list?"

Baldwin popped up from the driver's hatch and read from his list. "A golf cart, a jumbo pack of toilet paper, two maids, and Mr. Pudding's backpack."

"Don't forget about the atlas," Homer said. "We need that, too."

"I see the maids," Hercules reported, pointing over Baldwin's head. "They're being used as goalposts."

Homer aimed the binoculars. Sure enough, at the edge of the field, two maids in black-and-white dresses stood on stone pedestals, like statues, except they were trembling. "I shall retrieve them," Baldwin said as he climbed out of the tank. Then he jumped onto the dirt and ran toward the maids. Homer turned slowly on the turret, sweeping the binoculars across the dirt, then up the stone benches that rose above the field. "There it is," he said. "On the second row. My backpack."

"I'm guessing you have about ten minutes until they return," Hercules said. "Go now. As fast as you can."

The distance to the backpack seemed vast. Two football fields could have fit inside the coliseum. And Baldwin had parked the tank smack-dab in the center.

"Hold Dog," Homer said.

Hercules cringed. "I can't hold him. You know I don't like dogs. What if he bites me?"

There was no time to argue. Homer pulled Dog's leash from one of the many pockets in his shorts and tied Dog to the turret. Dog cocked his head as if to ask, *What are you up to?*

"I'll be right back," Homer told him. Then he slid off the tank and sprinted as best he could. The helmet bounced on his head as he jumped over a toilet seat and over a dresser drawer. He darted around a broken bust of some Roman guy. Needle-sharp shards of china lay in the dirt. Sunlight bounced off broken windows. The arena was like a war zone. In war movies, soldiers always kept low to the ground as they crossed a battlefield. Even with the knee pads, Homer wasn't about to crawl through this dirt. Even if his professional adventurer clothing was bladeproof, those china shards would easily pierce his hands. But if Hercules's brothers and sister returned, he'd be an open target. *Might as well paint a red dot on my back.*

"Howoooo!"

Homer glanced over his shoulder. Dog teetered on the edge of the tank. Hercules stood next to him, peering through the binoculars.

"Howoooo!"

Dog would just have to wait. He'd only be without Homer for a few minutes. Homer raced up the stone steps, passing the first row of stone benches. He turned down the second row. The backpack lay in one piece, zipped shut. A wave of relief washed over Homer as he grabbed a strap and threw it onto his back. Then he cringed as something rattled inside. Something was broken.

Dog threw his head back. "Howoooo!"

"Homer!" Hercules yelled, pointing. "The atlas. It's on the seventeenth row. It's red!"

This was turning out to be much easier than Homer had hoped. He slid his arm through the other backpack strap, then started up the steep stone steps. His thighs burned, but he pushed hard. How many minutes had passed? Empty water bottles and soda cans crunched beneath his feet as he turned down the seventeenth row. A large red book lay faceup on the bench. *The Illustrated Atlas of the Entire World.* It took both hands to lift the massive volume.

The seventeenth row offered a panoramic view of the field. Baldwin was helping the maids into the tank. Dog stood on the turret watching Homer's every move. Even though there was still no sign of the Simple siblings, Hercules jumped up and down, frantically motioning for Homer to come back. For one victorious moment, Homer smiled. He'd gotten the backpack *and* the atlas.

Clutching the heavy atlas to his chest, Homer hurried down the stone steps. The backpack thumped against his spine as he started across the arena grounds. He ran past a broken television, a lamp, and an electric fan. Sweat broke across the back of his neck. Lorelei had probably just grabbed an atlas from Zelda's sitting room. She'd probably read it in front of a comfortable fire with a plate of cookies at her side. Maybe she'd gotten a three-hour head start, but Homer wasn't defeated yet. Another smile spread across his face when he reached the tank. He handed the atlas and backpack to Hercules, then climbed onto the hull. "I did it," he said proudly.

"Just in time," Hercules said as thunder filled the air. "They're coming back."

"Prepare for departure," Baldwin said as he jumped back into the driver's seat and closed the driver's hatch.

"Quick, get in." Hercules pointed into the open hatch at the top of the turret. Homer climbed up and peered in. It would be a tight squeeze, what with the two quivering maids already stuffed inside.

"Come on, Dog," Homer said as he handed his backpack to one of the maids. He reached for the ladder. "Come on." His eyes widened as he looked around. "Where's Dog?"

"What do you mean *where's Dog?*" Hercules asked. "He's right..."

Homer's heart sank into his gut. The leash and the empty collar dangled over the side of the tank. He turned in a quick circle, desperately scanning the arena. Where was Dog? The thundering grew louder. A cloud of dirt arose at the coliseum's entrance. Then, out of the cloud, two horses emerged, their hooves kicking up debris as they charged into the arena. Each horse pulled a golden chariot. Two more horses followed, pulling two more chariots. Romulus, Caesar, Tiberius, and Diana—whips flying in their hands, the sun bouncing off their golden helmets and breastplates—shouted and laughed. Homer gasped.

Gladiators.

The horses galloped to the center of the arena, then split, two to each side of the tank, a cloud of dirt following behind like exhaust fumes. Dirt landed on Homer's face as the horses and chariots charged past. "Hey, Hercules," Diana called.

When the gladiators reached the other side of the arena, they turned and formed a line. The horses stomped their hooves. Diana held up her arm. "On your mark..." she cried. They were going to race.

"Dog!" Homer yelled, cupping his hands around his mouth. He wiped dirt from his eyes. "Dog!" Where was he?

"Do you see him?" Hercules inhaled dirt and broke into a coughing fit.

"Get set..." Diana yelled.

As the cloud settled, motion caught Homer's eye. Something moved over near the washing machine. It was Dog. But what was he doing?

Homer's heart skipped a beat.

Dog was digging!

25
The Gladiator's Treasure

Homer leaped off the tank. Pumping his arms and legs, he charged across the field. He didn't care that Dog was digging. He didn't care that Dog was about to uncover treasure. All he cared about was keeping Dog from getting crushed beneath chariot wheels.

"Go!" Diana yelled.

With the crack of the whips, the horses bolted forward, their eyes wild. Hooves tearing up the ground, manes flying, they galloped across the arena, kicking books and water bottles into the air. Dog, still digging, was apparently oblivious to the danger. Homer had learned that when Dog smelled treasure, nothing else mattered until that treasure was uncovered. Homer pumped his legs faster. The knee pads rubbed together, slowing him down. But there was no time to remove them. If the gladiators stayed on course, racing straight across the arena, then Romulus's chariot would run right over Dog.

Diana pulled in front of her brothers. "Whoopeee!" she yelled. A whoosh of hot air blew across Homer's neck and back as her chariot passed by, nearly hitting him. His heart pounded in his ears. Romulus, the red feather on his helmet waving, was closing in.

Dog was only a few yards away. "Ur, ur, ur, ur, ur," he grunted, his bottom sticking out of the hole he'd already dug. Dirt flew as he kicked his stubby legs, digging deeper.

"Dog!" Homer yelled. He took a huge breath and launched himself at the hole. But he missed by a foot and landed on the hard ground. His helmet toppled off. Sharp pain stabbed his right shoulder. Flying through the air always looked easier in the movies. Wincing, he rolled onto his side. A dirt cloud approached, swirling like a tornado. Through its haze, the beating black legs of a stallion and Romulus's golden helmet appeared.

There was no time to escape. Homer rolled into the hole and threw himself over Dog. He closed his eyes tight. This was it. One horse hoof or one wheel—that's all it would take to crush them. *Treasure hunting will kill you.* He pressed his face against Dog's warm neck and inhaled, for the last time, the sour scent of basset hound. The noise was deafening. Romulus's battle cry rang throughout the coliseum. A whoosh of air sounded. And the danger passed by.

Homer let go of his breath and raised his head. He and Dog were unhurt. The horse had veered around the hole. The race ended near the archway. Diana, the winner, laughed heartily, leaning out of her chariot to slap her brothers' hands. Hercules motioned frantically from the top of the tank. "Hurry!" he called.

As soon as Homer scrambled out of the hole, Dog started digging again. Homer reached in and grabbed Dog's back legs, but Dog wiggled free. "Oh no you don't," Homer said, leaning into the hole and clutching Dog by his vest. Dog grunted and turned his dirt-covered nose up at Homer. He blinked his red-rimmed eyes. *Why can't I dig?* he seemed to ask.

That's when something glinted at the bottom of the hole. Dog sniffed it, then pushed at it with his nose. Curiosity clouded Homer's judgment. He grabbed an edge and tried to pull the object free, but it was wedged deep.

"Woof!"

Something dripped onto Homer's face. He looked up into black eyes and a mass of black fur. "Uh-oh," he whispered as he wiped drool from his forehead. "Good girl, Brutus," he cooed. "Go away now. Go away."

Dog wagged his tail as he furiously dug. Nothing would divert him from the scent of treasure—not a rabbit, not a dozen rabbits, not even a Neapolitan mastiff twenty times his size.

Brutus stuck her face into the hole and sniffed Dog. Homer covered his face as she sniffed him. Then Brutus thrust her front half into the hole and started digging. Like the Simple siblings, she was a muscular power-house, a force of mighty strength. After only a few strokes of her paws, the treasure broke free.

It was a golden trophy. Dog wagged his tail and licked the trophy, cleaning away the dirt to reveal the engraving: SPELLING BEE CHAMPION OF THE WORLD.

"Homer!" Hercules yelled. "Hurry!" His voice echoed off the coliseum's walls.

"Come on," Homer urged. He reached in and grabbed the trophy. He expected Dog to start growling and barking at Brutus, as he'd done on their previous encounter. But Dog sat very still as Brutus sniffed him. Then he wagged his tail as she licked dirt from his nose. His saggy expression looked even dopier than usual.

"What are you doing?" Homer pleaded. "This is no time to fall in love. Come on."

The chariots had lined up again. Diana pointed her whip at the sky. Caesar, Romulus, and Tiberius held their reins, their steely gazes focused on the opposite side of the arena.

"On your mark..." she yelled.

They were going to race again. Homer pulled Dog out of the hole. The Sherman tank's engine roared to life, and the tank began a slow roll toward them. Homer couldn't carry Dog and he had no leash to pull, so he waved the trophy in Dog's face. "See the treasure?" he said to Dog. "Treasure. See it? Come on."

"Get set..." Diana yelled.

It worked. Homer ran, holding the treasure out like a carrot before a donkey. Dog followed, his loping gait sending his ears flying. The tank rolled closer.

"Go!" Diana hollered.

Hercules's helmet fell off his head and tumbled onto the dirt floor as he leaned over the side of the tank and reached out his arms. Homer tossed the trophy up onto the turret. Then, with a surge of pure panic, he heaved Dog upward. Hercules didn't complain about touching Dog. He pulled him to safety, then took Homer's hand and pulled him up, too. The tank rocked slightly as the chariots veered around it. Diana's hair waved behind her like a flag. Caesar held his whip like a lance. The wheels of Tiberius's and Romulus's chariots screeched as they almost crashed into each other.

And Brutus, who'd continued digging, emerged from the hole with a bone in her mouth.

Inside the tank, the maids clung to each other, teary-eyed. Hercules, Homer, and Dog balanced on the turret. "Hey, Hercules!" Caesar yelled. "Don't be such a wimp. Come back and play."

"You're a bunch of maniacs!" Hercules yelled at his siblings.

As they made their escape and rolled beneath the arch, Homer took a final look at the arena. Brutus happily chewed on her bone while Romulus, Diana, Caesar, and Tiberius wrestled beside the chariots.

"That was a close call," Homer said.

Hercules set his trophy in his lap. "I can't believe you found it. I thought I'd never see it again."

"Dog found it," Homer said. "He likes to dig. And sometimes he finds things."

Hercules looked at Dog. Then he took a very long breath, slowly reached out his hand, and patted Dog's head. "Thanks, Dog."

"Ur."

Once they'd reached the palace, the tank stopped at the servants' entrance, where the maids climbed out. "We quit!" they announced, stomping off.

"Sometimes I wish I could quit this family," Hercules said.

"Every family has problems," Homer told him. But admittedly, Hercules's situation was pretty bad, considering that his parents didn't even know he was alive and his siblings thought he was a piece of sporting equipment.

Then everything rushed back to him. He'd survived the coliseum, but the quest was waiting. And his opponent had a three-hour head start.

Homer reached into the tank and pulled out the atlas. Brushing dirt from its red cover, he opened to the index. "Mushroom Island," he murmured. "Where is it?" His fingers trembled as he turned the pages. "Mushroom... mushroom... here it is!"

The shape wasn't exactly like Lord Mockingbird's drawing, but it was close enough. A hand-drawn map is never perfect. "It's the right place. I just know it. This is where we'll find the membership coin. Here are the coordinates. Can Baldwin fly us there? Right now?"

"Yes," Hercules said, "but..."

"But what?"

"I know I'm not supposed to help you solve the riddle,

but I think there are still some parts of it that you haven't solved. Like the honey bear, for instance."

"I'll worry about the honey bear when I get there. There's no time to waste. Lorelei might already be there." Homer refastened Dog's collar around his neck. Then he scrambled down the ladder, collected his things from inside the tank, then climbed back up. "Here's your first-aid kit. And I've got my backpack and the clue box." *And I've got Dog.* "Are you ready?"

"No, I'm not ready. Of course I'm not ready. Do we really have to do this? Are you sure you want to be a member of L.O.S.T.?"

"Of course I'm sure," Homer said. "I promised my uncle that I'd continue his quest. I'm going to find Rumpold Smeller's treasure and I need L.O.S.T.'s help to do it."

"I wish we hadn't lost our helmets. Helmets always come in handy." Hercules grabbed his first-aid kit. "Maybe I should get some more bandages? What about insect repellent? What about ice packs? Do you think we'll need antivenom in case we run into snakes?"

"Do you think Rumpold Smeller had ice packs or antivenom when he headed out to sea?"

"Maybe?"

"No. Of course he didn't." Homer flung his backpack over his shoulder. "Rumpold Smeller didn't need bandages.

He wasn't afraid of anything. He fought cannibals, slave dealers, even the British Navy. We're going to a little island that's shaped like a mushroom. How dangerous could that be?"

Hercules opened his mouth, but Homer cut him off.

"The only other thing we need is determination," Homer said. Then he looked at his wide-eyed, terrified companion, and he looked down at his droopy, panting dog. "And maybe luck. Lots and lots of luck."

26
Rumpold Smeller
the Boy, Part IV

Seven men sat around the grand table in Duke
Smeller's dining hall, casting curious glances at
Rumpold. A bushy beard hung from each man's
face. Their cheeks and hands bore the smooth scars of
swords, the jagged scars of daggers. Each man wore the
white tunic of a Teutonic knight.

Rumpold stood in front of the table waiting for the
men to finish eating. To pass the time he counted six
missing fingers, four missing front teeth, two missing
ears, one missing leg, two eye patches, and one nose

that was made from silver. Why would his father want him to become one of these knights? Rumpold needed his fingers and eyes for drawing. He'd become fond of his legs, and his teeth were handy. If he had to choose something to lose, he supposed he could give up an ear.

Grease glistened on the knights' beards and lips, for they'd just consumed an entire stag. The bones, gnawed clean, were scattered across the table. A pair of hounds lay on the floor, gnawing on the stag's knee joints.

"Shall we commence?" Duke Vladmir asked after emptying a goblet of wine.

From the corner of his eye, Rumpold noticed a small movement. His twin sister, Rumpoldena, sat in the far corner, hidden in the shadows. Girls were not allowed to attend such a meeting. If caught, she'd be sent to her room without supper. Or worse—she'd be locked in her room with an entire tapestry to needlepoint.

"How do you intend to prove your son's bravery?" Duke Vladmir asked.

Rumpold and his father, who sat at the end of the table, exchanged a long look. The worry in his father's eyes matched his own worry. Rumpold tried to remember if he'd ever done anything brave. Nothing came to mind. The time he found a snake in his bed, one of the servants caught it. The time an angry peasant tried to kill Duke Smeller with a pitchfork, a guard threw himself in front of the pitchfork and saved the duke's life. The time a rumor reached the palace that the duke's food had been poisoned, a food taster tasted all the food before anyone in the Smeller family was allowed to eat. Each of those people had acted with bravery.

But it took no courage to be pampered each day, to be fed and clothed, and to sit in a tree and draw pictures. That is why Duke Smeller cast such a worried look at his son, fearing for his son's safety but also fearing the shame of failure.

"Shall it be the usual test?" the silver-nosed knight asked. The others replied with nods and grunts.

"It cannot be the usual test," Duke Smeller said, pushing his goblet aside. "He is not yet a master of weapons."

"My son is the same age and he is a master of weapons," a one-eared knight said. Then he glared at Rumpold. "You do not wield a sword?"

"No sir."

"What about a lance?"

"No sir."

"A crossbow?"

"No sir." Rumpold looked down at his feet as murmurs arose around the table.

"What are we supposed to do with him?" the

one-legged knight asked. "Why have we gathered? This is a waste of time. This boy is not ready."

"He is my son," Duke Smeller said, his voice tense, his eyes flashing. "He has the blood right to join our knighthood during his twelfth year. That is the law we are sworn to."

More murmurs.

The oldest knight, one with long gray hair, folded his hands and said, "But he cannot take the usual test if he does not master weaponry."

"I'll take the test!" Rumpoldena ran from the shadows. She threw herself at the table. "I'll take it. I know how to use all those weapons. Let me take it."

Some of the men laughed, while others scowled. Duke Smeller arose from his chair, took his daughter's arm, and pulled her toward the door. "What are you doing? Are you trying to humiliate me?"

"But, Father, I've been watching and learning. Rumpold doesn't even like fighting and..."

"This is not your place," he said, shoving her into the hallway, where a group of servants pretended that they hadn't been listening at the door. "Go join your mother in the women's quarters. Now!"

The frustration in his sister's eyes rolled across the room and hit Rumpold like a boulder. Why was she so angry with him? This wasn't his choice. In a heartbeat he'd gladly give up his right to become a Teutonic knight. He wanted it no more than she wanted to make another tapestry.

The chuckles died down. Duke Smeller stormed back to his son's side. "Rumpold may not be a weapons master, but he is my son," he told them forcefully. "This is his right and he shall claim it. Send him on his quest. Do it now and let him prove himself."

"Perhaps we can devise a different test," said the blond-haired knight who had found Rumpold sitting in the tree, drawing. Rumpold cringed. This knight knew that Rumpold wanted to be an artist. Would he humiliate Rumpold in front of his father? But the knight smiled gently at Rumpold. "The battlefield is not the only challenge we face."

"True," the knights said.

"The wilderness is a constant battle. How many times have you found yourself in the thick of the forest without roads or landmarks?"

"Too many times," they said.

"It is a weakness to not know our own forests. The next wave of invaders might sneak across our borders through the woods. We need a map of our land, a good map." The blond-haired knight pushed some bones onto the floor, then placed his palms on the table. Firelight glinted off his jeweled rings. He was an important man,

Rumpold realized, to have so many jewels. "Send the boy forth, into the wilderness, to draw us a map."

Into the wilderness? Rumpold's knees suddenly felt soft.

"He will face dangers in the wilderness," Duke Vladmir said. "Wild animals, starvation, criminals..."

"Father," Rumpold said, poking the duke's arm, "perhaps there is another secret society I could join?"

"Quiet," his father snarled.

The blond-haired knight continued. "The boy will return to us once he's created a map that we can use to help guard our borders. Not until then. Does he accept this challenge?"

After a sturdy shove from his father, Rumpold nodded.

"Get him what he needs," the old knight said. "Then send him off at dawn."

What I need is luck, Rumpold thought. *Lots and lots of luck.*

PART FOUR

MUSHROOM ISLAND

27

Into the Wide Blue Yonder

After studying *The Illustrated Atlas of the Entire World*, Baldwin decided that they wouldn't take the same plane that had carried them from Zelda's place. "Mushroom Island is uninhabited, so there won't be a runway. We'll have to land on the water. We'll take *Mercury*."

"Who?" Homer asked from the backseat of the limo.

"*Mercury* is the name of our floatplane," Hercules told him. "We keep it on Lake Lofty Spires."

During the limo ride, Homer checked the contents of

his backpack to see which items hadn't survived the destructive force known as Romulus Simple. He pulled out a broken magnifying lens and a broken protractor. But nothing else was broken. His jeans and raincoat had provided nice padding for the rest of the gear.

"Most everything is okay," he said, pulling out his Panama hat and sticking it on his head.

"I wish I had my helmet," Hercules mumbled.

As they pulled up to the lake, Homer grinned. A floatplane named *Mercury* waited at the end of the dock. The Simples owned a private jet, a limousine, a Sherman tank, and a coliseum. Of course they owned a floatplane.

"Does your family have a submarine?" he asked as they walked down the dock.

"No. But my dad's part owner of a rocket ship that can carry you into space and back in an hour."

"Wow. I want to do that," Homer said. "Can we do that? Will your dad take us up there?"

"Are you crazy? I'm not going into space. There's no air up there."

The flight took all afternoon. They traveled north, stopping to refuel on the coast before heading out over the string of islands that formed the San Juans. Hercules refused to look out the window. He'd strapped a para-chute to his back, just in case they encountered a hurricane or a U.F.O. Dog had taken a newfound liking to Hercules, ever since the pat of gratitude when he'd rescued the spelling bee trophy. He lay at Hercules's feet and Hercules didn't complain. Homer's shoulder ached from his fall in the coliseum, but he didn't complain, either. There were too many things on his mind to focus on something as insignificant as throbbing pain.

The floatplane was stocked with bags of pretzels and cans of soda. Dog liked the pretzels but sneezed when the carbonated drink tickled his nose.

"Is Lorelei your girlfriend?" Hercules asked suddenly.

"What?" Homer snorted so hard, some lemon-lime fizz shot up his nose. "Why would you ask that?"

"I don't know." Hercules picked the salt off a pretzel stick. "You looked so happy to see her when she walked into Zelda's kitchen."

"I was happy to see her," Homer admitted. "But that's only because she's my friend. I mean, I thought she was my friend."

"How did you meet her?"

"We met in The City. And I was stupid enough to think she was my friend—even after I found out that she'd spied on me for Madame la Directeur."

"How did Lorelei know about the L.O.S.T. meeting?"

"She followed me," Homer said, shoving his hand in the pretzel bag. "Maybe she's been watching me. I don't

263

know. But I haven't left Milkydale in three months, so she must have figured I was going somewhere important."

"I had a friend once," Hercules said. "But my brother Caesar tossed him into the neighbor's moat. After he escaped the piranhas, he never came to see me again."

"That's too bad." Homer chewed, taking only quick sideways glances at Hercules. Admitting you don't have many friends is pretty embarrassing. It didn't much matter that they both felt that way; it was still difficult to admit.

The plane began to bump across the sky as if it had landed on a gravel road covered in potholes. "We've hit a patch of turbulence," Baldwin called from the cockpit.

"I hate turbulence," Hercules said, gripping his parachute.

Homer didn't mind the movement. It felt exactly like sitting in the bed of the Puddings' red truck. The motion quickly lulled Dog into a sound sleep. The turbulence continued. While Hercules sat frozen and quiet, Homer wiped the salt off his fingers and opened the clue box.

They were flying to an island shaped like a mushroom called Mushroom Island. It was bigger than a blue whale and the *X* on the map indicated that the treasure was buried in the center of the island. The only missing ingredient was how the honey bear fit in.

Homer tapped his fingers on the armrest. Sometimes

things can seem too simple. Like the time when he'd finished his geometry test a half hour before anyone else in the class, only to find out, the next day, that there'd been more problems on the back of the page.

He turned the scrolls over to check the back. Nothing. Had he overlooked something? Or maybe Lord Mockingbird had made it super easy because Homer and Lorelei were kids. Or maybe he'd made it super easy because his brain had turned mushy with old age. Well, one thing was certain. Even with Lorelei's three-hour head start, Homer still had a chance of arriving at Mushroom Island first. The cloudcopter couldn't match the speed of *Mercury*.

"The island is in sight," Baldwin called.

Homer slipped out of his seat. He stood behind the pilot's seat and looked through the cockpit's windshield. The entire island was visible beneath the cloudless sky. Forest covered the top of the island, the part shaped like a mushroom cap. The short stem was covered in sand and driftwood. The atlas listed the island as two miles long from the tip of its stem to the top of the mushroom cap. It wouldn't take long to get to the *X*.

"Look at all those trees," Hercules said, pressing his face against his window. "How are we going to walk through all those trees? Branches fall off trees all the time, and I don't have my helmet."

"Where are we going to land?" Homer asked, wondering, exactly, how a plane lands on water.

"That appears to be a problem," Baldwin said.

"What problem?" Hercules asked, leaning into the aisle. "Is there a problem? I knew there'd be a problem."

"It appears that the island is surrounded by high reefs. See them?"

Homer grabbed his Extra Strong Borington Binoculars and peered out the passenger window. Rocky ridges stuck out of the surf. After circling the island, Baldwin said, "There are breaks in the reef that are large enough for a boat to approach the island, but not large enough for us to land this plane."

The binoculars fell against Homer's chest. "What if you land in deeper water? We could swim to the island."

"No way," Hercules said. "Do you know how cold that water is? We'll get hypothermia within minutes."

Lorelei would have no problem because the cloud-copter could land directly on the beach. Homer gripped the side of the pilot's seat. "But I have to get onto that island. Right now."

"Then you'll have to jump," Baldwin said.

Surely that was a joke.

"Huh?"

"You'll have to jump," Baldwin repeated. "If you want to get onto the island right now, you'll have to jump."

"NO WAY!" Hercules cried, just about falling out of his seat. "No way, no way, no way. That is not going to happen. Never, ever, ever am I jumping out of a plane. Not in a million years. No, no, no."

Dog moaned and sat up. He licked his lips and looked around for something to eat. A few pretzels had found their way to the floor, as had a pretzel bag. He stuck his nose into the bag and licked the salt-flecked lining.

"We have two options. I could fly low, just above the beach, and you could jump right onto the sand, but that is very risky," Baldwin explained. "We'd be traveling at more than fifty knots and you'd most likely break some bones because you wouldn't be able to control your fall."

"That doesn't sound like an option," Hercules said.

Homer agreed. "What's the second option?"

"If you jumped from a height and used a parachute, you could land with less risk of breaking anything."

Homer couldn't believe what he was hearing—less risk of breakage was the best option? "I don't want to break anything," he said. "I've got to hike to the *X*."

"How about this option?" Hercules said. "How about we forget this entire crazy quest?"

"If you are willing to delay the quest, we could go back to the mainland and hire a boat." Baldwin turned slightly in his seat and looked at Homer, waiting for a decision.

By the time they got back to the mainland it would be dark. They'd have to hang around until morning to get a boat. Lorelei would have hiked to the *X* and would have the coin in her greedy little hands.

Sometimes a decision has to be made in an instant. Like the time the famous American volcano jumper Millicent Smith ran into her burning house to save her bungee cords. She'd had no time to weigh the pros and cons of such an action, and she'd met a fiery end. Then there was the time when Sir Richard Borington, inventor of the Borington Binoculars, dropped his eyeglasses. He'd had no time to weigh the pros and cons of crawling under an elephant to retrieve the glasses, and he got squashed as a result.

Homer, like these treasure-hunting predecessors, now faced a spur-of-the-moment decision. There'd been no opportunity to take a parachuting class. No chance to say good-bye to his parents. The jump would work or it wouldn't.

Treasure hunting will kill you.

The air suddenly felt as thick as syrup and no matter how fast Homer breathed, he couldn't get a full breath. Baldwin continued to circle the island, waiting for a decision. "This is crazy," Hercules mumbled to himself. "How did I get myself into this?"

Dog removed his nose from the pretzel bag and stared expectantly at Homer.

What do I do? Homer peered out the window. The evening sun hung heavy over the western horizon. As Baldwin continued to fly the plane in a circular pattern, the eastern sky came into view, darker but clear. Except for one puffy little cloud moving steadily toward them.

Lorelei!

"I'll jump," Homer announced.

28

Rumpold Smeller
the Boy, Part V

R umpold yawned. His tutor and father had been
instructing him throughout the night, trying to
fill his head with as much information as possible. He needed to know which plants in the Estonian
forests were poisonous and which roots he could dig and
eat. Learning the intricacies of rabbit snaring, rabbit
cleaning, and rabbit cooking would keep him from starving. They tried to teach him how to make fire with a
flint, how to build a rainproof shelter, and how to stave
off insect bites with river mud. Of course, Duke Smeller

didn't know any of this stuff. Like his son, he had spent most of his life living in a castle. On the few occasions when he'd worn his Teutonic knight's armor and had guarded the borders, he'd done so with a traveling party consisting of a cook, a tent-erecter, and a groom to tend to the horses. Fortunately, Rumpold's tutor had found a book written by a monk who had spent most of his life living in the woods. "How to make soup from a rock and a leather shoe," the tutor read. "That might come in handy."

Rumpold's mother, the duchess, threw open the door and burst into the room. "Soup from a rock and a shoe?" She threw herself at her husband's feet and wrapped her arms around his shins. "Do not do this to my son, my only son. Do not send him into the wilderness alone."

"It is done," the duke said.

"Then I'll go with him."

"That is ridiculous."

The duchess tightened her grip. "Then I'll send the servants with him."

"No. He must do this on his own."

She burst into tears. "A wolf will eat him. Or he'll starve to death. Or a barbarian will enslave him." She pulled Rumpold into her arms, nearly suffocating him in her embrace. "I will never see him again. My son. My only son."

Rumpold, who'd quietly begun to accept his fate, suddenly imagined himself running from the tutor's study, taking a horse from the stables, and riding off into a world where he could be anyone but a duke's son. Where he would never have to become a knight.

"Enough," the duke said, prying his wife's arms from Rumpold. "You think I am not worried? He is my only son, too. But this must be done. It is the highest honor to be a Teutonic knight." Then Duke Smeller turned toward the doorway. Duke Vladmir stood there, his arms folded.

"The time has come," he said.

"It is dawn?" Duke Smeller asked with surprise. Duke Vladmir nodded.

Rumpold's tutor grabbed a leather satchel and filled it with parchment and writing implements. Then he stuffed the monk's book inside. His eyelids were heavy with sadness when he shook Rumpold's hand. "Good luck," he said.

The knights gathered in the courtyard. They watched silently as Rumpold said his good-byes. "Good-bye, Mother," he said, holding back his tears as best he could. Sobbing, she fled into the house, her serving women at her heels. "Good-bye, Father."

Duke Smeller leaned close to his son's ear. "Do not disappoint me. Our family honor is at stake."

Rumpold looked over at his sister, who stood off to the side, her arms folded, her eyes narrowed. "Goodbye, Sister," he called. She said nothing, but he knew what she wanted. She wanted, more than anything, to take his place. He'd give her that chance if he could.

His satchel slung over his shoulder, Rumpold walked down the castle steps into the courtyard. He took his horse's reins and led him beneath the archway and out onto the road. He was supposed to head into the forest and draw a map. But what was to keep him from simply heading down that road, and going on and on and on to wherever it took him?

When he reached his favorite tree, he dropped the reins and climbed until he could see out over the landscape. This was his father's land. His ancestors' land. To be the son of a duke meant that life came without choices. The path set before him was the one he had to follow.

"Come here," he called to the horse. The horse stopped grazing and ambled beneath the branch. Rumpold waited until the horse was in perfect position, then he scooted to the edge of the branch.

And jumped.

29

Falling Through the Sky

It is highly advisable to take a class in parachuting before jumping out of an airplane. Most experts would recommend more than one class—maybe even a college degree in parachuting, just to be on the safe side.

"You're going to jump out of the plane?" Hercules asked.

Hearing someone else say those words was like a jolt of electricity to Homer's brain. Homer Winslow Pudding, a goat farmer's son, was going to jump out of a plane? The same Homer who'd failed every school physical fitness test? While the other kids scrambled up the ropes like monkeys, Homer never got more than two feet off the ground. While the other kids ran the mile in the allotted fifteen minutes, Homer always finished five minutes behind. While the other kids flew across the sand in the long jump, Homer landed on his bottom at the three-foot mark. So what made him think he could jump out of a plane and survive?

Hercules leaped from his seat and grabbed Homer's shoulders. "Are you insane?"

Maybe Homer had lost his mind. But falling through the air didn't require any special abilities, did it? A person didn't need strength or dexterity to step into nothingness. Mrs. Peepgrass had taught her students that objects fall at the same speed. She'd proven this by dropping a book and an apple from the top of a ladder. So in this case, weight wouldn't put Homer at a disadvantage.

Homer had lived his life accepting that he'd never be as fast as the other kids in his class, that he'd never be the first chosen for a team. That he'd always come in last in a race. But at that moment, as he stared at the distant cloudcopter, a force shot down his legs and sent his heart thumping like a rabbit's back leg. This was the force that made the sprinter want to reach the finish line first, the competitive drive that propelled the swimmer down the lane. Homer wasn't going to lose this time. "I'm not insane," he said. "I'm going."

"But I'm supposed to keep you safe," Hercules said. "I won't let you go."

"Sorry, Hercules, but I'm doing this." He walked to the back of the plane and opened the EMERGENCY PARA-CHUTE compartment. With a swift tug, he pulled out an orange parachute, an exact replica of the one Hercules was already wearing.

"I'm supposed to be your guardian." Hercules looked out the window. "But Lord Mockingbird didn't say anything about jumping out of a plane." Who could blame Hercules for not wanting to jump? Why should he risk his life? He was already a member of L.O.S.T.

"You stay here," Homer said. "This is my quest and I'm the only one who should take the risk. Besides, you went to the coliseum with me. You spotted the atlas and that was a huge help. You and Dog go back to the mainland with Baldwin and get a boat. Then come and get me." He carried the parachute to the cockpit door. "How do I put this thing on?"

Baldwin showed Homer. It wasn't much different than putting on a backpack, except that the straps secured in the front. Homer's hands trembled as he clicked the safety belts into place.

"Hercules, I'll need you to open the door," Baldwin said. "I can't leave the cockpit."

"Open the door? What if I get sucked into the void?" Hercules checked his own safety belts. "It happens all the time in science-fiction movies."

"Can that happen?" Homer asked Baldwin.

"Not likely."

Dog pawed Homer's shin, then looked up at him with those red-rimmed eyes. Homer knelt and ran his hands over Dog's ears. Love, pure and true, filled the space between and around them. Dog, who'd been with him every moment for three months. Dog, who trusted and relied on him. Even though Homer needed Dog's treasure-smelling talents, he wasn't going to risk Dog's life. "I can't take you with me," he told Dog. "It's too dangerous. You stay here with Hercules."

Dog cocked his head. "Urrrr?"

"You'll be safe here." Homer kissed Dog's forehead. Then he stood and looked steely-eyed at Hercules. "You'll watch him?"

"Yeah, I'll watch him," Hercules said.

"He'll howl when I'm gone. You'll need to pet him."

Hercules frowned. "Yeah, okay. I'll pet him."

A little wave of dizziness washed over Homer. Flying around and around the island was starting to get to him. Would falling toward the island be worse?

"What do I do?" Homer asked.

"I suggest a hop and pop," Baldwin said. "You'll open the parachute immediately after leaving the plane." He pointed to a string with a handle that hung from the parachute. "You will pull that toggle, which will open the small pilot chute. The pilot chute will catch the air and open the main chute."

"What if the chute doesn't open?" Hercules asked. "Have you considered that? What if that happens?"

"There are two parachutes," Baldwin said. "If the first doesn't open, you will pull the second toggle." He pointed to the other toggle.

Homer swallowed hard. "Does that happen? Does the first chute sometimes not open?"

"Sometimes," Baldwin said.

"You see," Hercules said. "This is crazy."

"Maybe it is," Homer said. Fear was growing like a weed in his brain, trying to smother his determination. "But Lorelei would jump out of this plane in a minute, without a second thought. She'll do whatever it takes to get my coin." He pushed the fear away. "What do I do after I open the chute? I mean, how do I steer the thing?"

"Use the steering lines," Baldwin explained. "Pull the left one to turn left, pull the right one to turn right. Aim them at the landing site, which is the beach." Homer looked out the cockpit window. Wave-wrinkled sand covered the south tip of the island. "You do not want to land in the trees." The plane tilted. "We're approaching the target."

Homer opened an aft luggage compartment and pushed Dog inside. "You stay here," he told him. He closed the door. Dog scratched at it. "Don't let him out. I'm serious. He'll try to follow me."

"Okay," Hercules said. Then he grabbed his first-aid kit. "Here," he said, shoving it into Homer's backpack. "You might need this." It was a huge gesture.

Dog whined and scratched the luggage door again.

Homer made sure that the chin strap for his Panama hat was extra tight. Then he slid his arms through the backpack, wearing it across his chest. Hercules opened the exit door, then darted behind a seat. Homer stepped to the edge. The view had dramatically changed. "Why are we so high?"

"We have to be high enough for the chute to open and still have time for the reserve chute if need be."

"I can do this," Homer whispered.

"You don't have to do this," Hercules said.

"Howoooo!"

Homer inched his feet to the edge of the precipice. *I can do this. I can do this.* He wrapped an arm across the backpack, holding it protectively to his chest. His other arm stiffened, the toggle gripped in his fingers.

"Homer," Hercules said. They shared a long look. "Good luck."

"Thanks."

"We'll get a boat, Mr. Pudding, and meet you tomorrow," Baldwin called from the cockpit. "There's the beach. Best jump now."

"Okay." He closed his eyes.

And so it was that Homer Winslow Pudding, farm boy, gunnysack slide destroyer, hopeful treasure hunter, stepped into nothingness.

Skydiving had never been on Homer's list of things he wanted to do. The sensation of falling had never thrilled him, but somehow this moment didn't feel like falling. He didn't fall straight down as he'd expected. Instead, he moved forward. The air felt cushiony as it pressed against and around him like a great big pillow. Then he pulled.

His body jerked upward as the smaller chute opened. His stomach shot down to his feet, then up to his throat. His body jerked again as the larger chute opened, and the sensation changed. Homer opened his eyes and took a deep breath. The earth wasn't rushing toward him as he'd expected. Instead, he was floating steadily toward the ground. And his hat was still on his head.

"I did it," he cried. No one back home would ever believe that he'd jumped out of a plane. Uncle Drake would have been so proud. Surely this alone would prove his worthiness to the L.O.S.T. membership. "I DID IT!" he cried, hugging his backpack.

"Howoooo!"

What was that? Homer craned his neck and looked up. Something was falling through the sky.

Something shaped like an enormous vest-wearing sausage.

"DOG!" Homer screamed.

30

Beached Boys

A free-falling dog is a terrible thing to behold. Truly there are few sights that can compete on the blood-chilling, heart-stopping scale. With nothing but the heavens above and the earth below, Dog fell, and fell, and fell. With his ears sticking straight up like a rabbit's, he frantically kicked his stubby legs. His attempt to dog-paddle across the sky might have been humorous if Homer didn't believe that Dog's certain demise was mere moments away.

"DOG!" Homer screamed again. He instinctively

reached out his arms and, as he did, the backpack fell away. Homer didn't watch it plummet. Nor did he care, at that moment, that his gear was about to smash to smithereens on the reef. Paddling his own legs in a desperate attempt to reach his best friend, Homer swung from the parachute lines. Dog was supposed to be locked in the plane's luggage compartment, safe and sound. How had he gotten out? Why hadn't Hercules stopped him? Homer couldn't bear watching Dog plummet. Tears filled his eyes. "NOOOOOO!"

"DOG!" Someone other than Homer had called Dog's name.

Homer wrenched his neck. Another shape was falling through the sky. Had Homer gone mad? Was he seeing things? It couldn't be, but it was. It was Hercules. His parachute was still strapped to his back, but it wasn't open. Rather, Hercules was free-falling *headfirst*. His arms pointed straight at the earth like an Olympic diver. He was gaining on Dog. How could this be? This is not what Mrs. Peepgrass had taught her students about gravity. Homer stopped paddling and watched, openmouthed, as Hercules caught up to Dog. Hercules threw an arm around Dog's middle, then pulled his parachute's toggle. The little chute appeared and almost immediately after, the second chute popped open, blocking Homer's view. He didn't know if Dog was still in Hercules's arms. He watched over the tips of his boots as the orange chute floated to the beach and crumpled upon landing. Nothing moved beneath the chute.

Homer didn't have a moment to contemplate the amount of courage it had taken Hercules to throw himself from the plane. He'd been so distracted by the skydiving acrobatics that he'd forgotten to steer. The wind had pushed him away from the beach and he was heading out toward the ocean. He kicked his feet, trying to propel himself in the other direction. That didn't work. *What do I do, what do I do?* he asked himself, trying desperately to remember Baldwin's instructions. *How do I turn?* He grabbed the dangling lines. Pulling the right line turned his body toward the ocean. Pulling the left line turned him toward the beach. But was there enough time? He pumped his legs. *Come on, come on. I don't want to land in the water.*

Closer and closer. Waves broke against the reef. Saltwater spray drifted in the wind. Mushroom Island's only beach, shaped like a mushroom stem, spread before him. Bleached driftwood lay everywhere. He pointed his feet at a patch of gray sand. When had he last breathed? Was his heart still beating? He decided to start running through the air, so that when his feet touched down he'd already be in motion. And guess what? That technique worked brilliantly. His new boots cushioned his ankles as he hit the tide pools. He ran a few yards, the momentum pulling him forward. His boots crunched barnacle-encrusted rocks. Purple sea anemones sprayed as he ran past. *I did it*, he thought. *But I can't…slow…down.* He ran up onto the sand and straight into a log, landing in a crumpled heap on the other side. The parachute deflated and collapsed.

Homer sat up and spat sand from his mouth. He staggered to his feet. Untangling himself from the parachute's rigging, he found that his arms and legs worked. Aside from a few scrapes on his hands, he was in one piece. And his Panama hat was still on his head. He'd done it. He'd parachuted from an airplane and had lived to tell the tale.

But what about his friends?

With a yank, he released the safety harness and slid his arms free of the parachute's pack. It fell onto the sand. Homer scrambled up a large log. On tiptoe, he surveyed the beach. Where were they? If only he had his Borington Binoculars, but he had no idea where his backpack had landed.

Then he saw the puddle of orange. The compass thumped against his chest as he darted between logs.

"Dog!" he called. "Hercules!"

A lump lay beneath the shiny fabric—an unmoving lump. As Homer climbed over a massive log, he feared the worst—that the second chute hadn't had enough time to adequately slow them down. Reaching the parachute, he grabbed an edge and pulled. The lump was revealed. Hercules lay on his stomach, facedown in the sand. Homer fell to his knees. "Hercules," he said, laying his hand on Hercules's back. His hand rose and fell as Hercules took quick shallow breaths. He was alive! "Are you okay? Are you hurt?"

Hercules groaned, then slowly turned his head. "I'm too scared to find out."

"Urrrr." Dog's nose poked out from under Hercules's armpit. He was trapped beneath.

Homer gently rolled Hercules over, freeing Dog, who stood and shook sand from his fur. So many emotions competed for that moment, but it was anger that won. Homer shook a finger at Dog. "Bad boy," he said. "Bad boy for jumping out of the plane. You could have been killed. Bad boy!"

Dog stuck his wet nose into Homer's sleeve and wagged his tail.

Homer hugged Dog so fiercely that Dog moaned and farted at the same time. "Don't ever jump out of a plane again. Never again."

"I won't," Hercules said. He lay on his back, his eyes clamped shut, his face frozen in a grimace. "Never, ever again."

Homer hovered over Hercules, looking for signs of injury, like blood or bones sticking out in weird directions. "Can you sit up? Is anything broken?"

Hercules opened one eye, then the other. "Homer?" he asked, his jaw trembling. "Did I just jump out of an airplane?"

"Uh-huh," Homer said. "And you didn't even have your helmet." He grabbed Hercules's arm and helped him sit up. Then he picked a piece of dried seaweed from Hercules's hair and brushed sand off his shoulders. "It was amazing. I couldn't believe it when I saw you. It was the most amazing thing I've ever seen."

"It was?" Hercules rubbed his head. "I didn't even have my helmet." A surprised smile pushed at the corners of his mouth. "I jumped out of a plane. Me."

Homer smiled, too. "You were like a professional sky-diver. And you caught Dog with one arm. I couldn't believe it. Dog weighs a ton. How did you do that?"

"I jumped out of a plane," Hercules whispered. He ran his hands over the parachute's straps. "I jumped out of a plane." Then a smile burst across his face and he laughed. "I must be crazy."

Homer laughed, too. Not a belly laugh, like when a joke's been told. Not a snicker, like when something nasty has been said. His laughter was a hearty mixture of awe and relief, like the moment after the roller-coaster plunge when the track straightens and the ride is over.

Dog nudged Hercules's arm and Hercules stopped laughing. "I'm sorry, Homer. I was about to close the door, but the plane banked. I think Baldwin was trying to watch your fall. Anyway, the luggage compartment flew open. Dog raced after you before I could stop him."

"Why did you jump, too?"

"I didn't even think about it. I saw him falling without a parachute. I already had mine on, so I jumped. Just like that."

Homer ran his hand along Dog's back. "You saved his life. You're a hero."

Hercules unstrapped the harness and got to his feet. He strode across the beach and stopped at the water's edge. The sleeves of his rugby shirt rippled in the salty breeze. On the horizon, the sun had begun its evening melt. "My brothers and sister will never believe I did that."

"I know what you mean," Homer said as he and Dog caught up. He stuck his hands in his pockets and stared at the tangerine horizon. Though his family would never believe that he'd jumped from a plane, his uncle would have believed it. Skydiving had been one of Uncle Drake's favorite pastimes. But had his uncle ever saved a dog in midair? "I'm happy that I pulled your name from Lord Mockingbird's top hat," Homer said.

They stood side by side, Dog between them. A crazy old man had brought them together. Near-tragedy had made them friends. But as the sun disappeared and the sky darkened, their amazement faded away and reality crept into their thoughts. "So, what do we do now?" Hercules asked.

"We'll..." Homer swatted a mosquito as it whined near his ear. "We've got to find the backpack."

"What do you mean we've got to find the backpack?"

"I dropped it and I don't know where it landed."

"You what?" Hercules's chest deflated, as if all the newfound confidence that had puffed him up now suddenly leaked out of his skin. "You what? My first-aid kit was in the backpack."

"Don't freak out," Homer said. But the truth was, Homer was freaking out a little, too, because without the backpack they had nothing. No food or emergency blankets, no night vision goggles or matches—nothing. And darkness was closing in. Last night's summer moon, the one that had lit up Zelda's beach, was stuck behind a growing blanket of clouds. There was no way to tell how much distance the cloudcopter had covered since Homer had spotted it from the plane's window. "Maybe we can make a torch. Then we can start hiking."

"Hike? At night?"

"Yeah. We have to beat Lorelei to the *X*."

Dog pulled a long strand of kelp from the water and started munching on the bulbous end. "I don't know how to make a torch," Hercules said. "Do you?"

"It's easy. You take a rag and dip it in something combustible and then light it."

"Uh-huh. First of all, we don't have anything combustible. Second of all, how are we going to light it? Third of all, there are wild animals in the woods and I'm pretty sure most of them come out at night."

Homer swatted another mosquito. While most of Hercules's fears were silly, like worrying about choking on a feather from a pillow, or worrying that something might fall on his head, this latest worry made Homer look over his shoulder. "What kind of wild animals? Like bears?"

"Yes, definitely like bears. And wolves. And maybe porcupines. Porcupines can shoot their quills right into your eyes." Hercules stepped closer to Homer. "And sharks. Don't forget about sharks. A shark can leap right out of the water and grab something off the beach."

"I don't think that's true," Homer said. But not wanting to take the chance, he slid two fingers under Dog's collar and pulled him away from the water's edge. If only he'd kept his Swiss army knife in his vest pocket rather than inside the backpack. Though the blade was small, it would have been better than nothing.

Eeeeeee. A high-pitched whine filled Homer's ear. His hand flew to his neck. "Stupid mosquito."

Hercules slapped his own neck. Then his cheek. Then his neck again. "Uh-oh."

Like a symphony performed on crystal goblets, the air rang with high-pitched notes as a swarm descended. "There are too many to swat," Homer said.

Dog shook his head, trying to deflect the bloodthirsty insects with his flapping ears. It didn't work. Yelping, he ran in a circle.

"They're going to eat us alive," Hercules cried. He covered his face with his arms. "We've got to get out of here."

Like tiny aerodynamic needles, the mosquitoes pierced their targets and drew blood. "Into the water!" Homer shouted. But that's when his Panama hat made an odd whirring noise. Something dropped in front of his face. It was some kind of netting and it hung from his hat all the way to his feet, encompassing his entire body. "Mosquito netting," Homer cried. Mr. Tuffletop, the tailor, had sewn mosquito netting into the brim of Homer's Panama hat. "It must have some sort of motion detector or sound detector. Oh, I bet it's programmed to the sound of mosquitoes."

"Help!" Hercules cried as he and Dog ran in circles up the beach.

"Get in, quick!" Homer called. He ran up to them and lifted the netting. Hercules ducked beneath. Dog squeezed between Homer's shins. Homer dropped the netting. The boys froze, holding their breaths. Would it work? Though the insects continued to swarm, not a single mosquito penetrated the net. Homer and Hercules took a long, relieved breath. Dog whimpered.

"What do we do now?" Hercules asked.

"We wait for them to go away."

And so, as the sun completely disappeared, they stood shoulder to shoulder. Homer checked his watch. Five minutes passed. Then ten. "They're not going away," he said. "Why aren't they going away?"

"They can still smell our blood. Until they find someone else to eat, we're stuck."

Welts rose on Homer's neck and cheeks. Scratching didn't bring relief. Dog chewed on his legs, his own technique to deal with the itching. What would they have done without the netting? What other surprises had Mr. Tuffletop built into Homer's clothing?

"We can't just stand here," Homer said. "I've got to get to the X."

"I think I'm having an allergic reaction," Hercules said. "I'm all itchy. I need my first-aid kit."

Homer racked his brain for ideas. They couldn't hike across the island stuck together like this. "I need to sit down and think." Carefully, making sure they kept the net secure around every inch of their bodies, they sat on a log. While Homer stared up at the dark sky, wondering where Lorelei was, Dog curled at Homer's feet.

"What's going on with Dog's vest?" Hercules asked.

Homer looked down. Dog's vest glowed in the fading light. He touched the fabric. "It's made of glow-in-the-dark material." Another ingenious touch by Mr. Tuffletop. "Hey, we don't need a torch if we've got this." They could follow Dog through the dark woods. Just like having a fat furry firefly as their guide.

"You have to get rid of that vest," Hercules said.

"Why?"

"It's like a big neon sign. Here we are, wild animals, come and eat us."

"But…" Homer sighed. Hercules was right. The glowing vest was an invitation, like a highway billboard for a fast-food restaurant. Until the swarm flew away, they were stuck beneath the netting, unable to continue the quest. Homer unstrapped Dog's vest and buried it in the sand under his feet.

As the glow faded, night poured in like ink. Homer could no longer see down the beach or out over the sea. He couldn't tell if a lone cloud hovered above the island. The whine of the mosquitoes persisted. "I'm sorry I got you into this," he said, both to Dog and to Hercules.

Hercules sighed. "Baldwin will come tomorrow with a boat. We just have to make it through the night."

And so they sat, waiting for the mosquitoes to hunt elsewhere. Homer's eyelids grew heavy. Dog yawned, followed by Hercules, then Homer. "We can't all fall asleep," Hercules said. "One of us needs to keep watch."

Homer agreed. His parents thought he was on a nice camping trip with Zelda. Last thing they needed, what with the worry about rebuilding the gunnysack slide, was to learn that Homer had been eaten by a bear. "You sleep first."

Hercules yawned again. "You sure you'll stay awake?"

"Yeah. I'm sure."

🐾

Homer stretched his legs. The whine of the mosquitoes no longer rang in his ears. Seagulls called to one another as they swooped the shore. Seals barked their morning greeting. Dawn had come to Mushroom Island. Homer's Panama hat lay in the sand next to him. With the swarms' departure, the netting had retreated beneath the hat's brim.

"We made it through the night," he said with as much surprise as if he'd discovered he'd grown a tail or had turned into a toad. "We did it," he said, poking Hercules's arm.

Hercules moaned, then rolled onto his back. And that's when Homer saw the note pinned to the front of his rugby shirt.

I've got him.
You can have him back
after I get the coin.

31

The Forest of Holes

W hy did she do that?" Hercules asked as they tromped through the woods. "Why did she take your dog?"

"She hates me," Homer said. That might have been true, he wasn't exactly sure, but he couldn't tell Hercules the real, secret reason why Lorelei had taken Dog.

If anyone hated Homer Pudding at that moment, it was Homer himself. He'd volunteered for the first watch last night and he'd dozed off, right away. What kind of adventurer falls asleep when he's supposed to be guarding his two friends?

"How come Dog didn't bark when Lorelei took him?" Hercules asked, scratching a welt on his neck.

Homer pushed a branch out of his face. "For some reason I can't figure out, Dog likes Lorelei. Did you see how he was wagging his tail when she showed up at Zelda's? I guess he doesn't remember that she kidnapped him." He scrambled over a fallen tree. "And now she's done it again."

"Even so, how come we didn't hear her?"

"She's sneaky. She gets in and out of places all over The City for free. She's just like that rat of hers." Maybe that last statement was a bit harsh, but Homer felt bad about it for only a few seconds. Once Dog got close enough to smell the membership coin he'd start digging. And then Lorelei would be the winner. Homer's boots stomped the forest floor. Maybe comparing Lorelei to a rat was too nice.

Homer pulled his sleeve free of a prickly branch, then stepped in something squishy. "Gross."

"That's bear poop," Hercules said, keeping a wide berth around the large pile, which happened to be steaming.

Homer wiped his boot on a fern. "How do you know it's bear poop?"

"Of course it's bear poop. What else would make a pile that big? And it's fresh. That's not a good sign." Hercules turned in a full circle, scanning the forest. "It's a known fact that bears eat humans. They stalk them and sneak up on them and…" He stepped closer to Homer. "I'm a walking target. Look at me. Your green and khaki colors blend into the forest, but I'm in orange and yellow stripes. I might as well pour honey all over my head." He grabbed a branch. "I've got to protect myself." And just like that, he tore the branch off the tree. Then he stripped off the leaves and held the branch like a sword.

Homer cursed himself for dropping his backpack, because that Swiss army knife would have really come in handy. But maybe Hercules had the right idea. A large stick was better than nothing. If cavemen had used sticks to fend off saber-toothed tigers, then maybe they'd work against bears. Homer grabbed a branch. It bent but wouldn't tear away from the trunk. Even when he hung like a dead weight from the branch, it wouldn't pull away. How had Hercules made it look so easy?

"What if the bear is stalking us?" Hercules asked, still turning in a circle.

As Homer let go of the branch, it sprung back into place. He peered at a shadowy place between the trees, half-expecting to hear a growl. Standing still didn't seem like the best tactic. "Let's go," he said, checking his compass. Then he scratched three different bug bites. "Lorelei's probably there already. And don't forget to keep looking for my backpack. We really need to find it."

It's surprisingly easy to wander off course in a forest. The filtered light settles here and there and disrupts any directional instinct a hiker might have been blessed with. Even a straight line becomes blurred, what with the thick undergrowth and the random pattern of tree distribution. Without a compass, Homer and Hercules might have walked in circles. Even though the compass had been a gift from Lorelei, Homer was glad he had it.

After climbing over another fallen tree, Homer checked to make sure Dog's vest was still tucked into one of his pockets. He'd dug the vest out of the sand before they'd headed into the woods. Soon the vest would be back where it belonged, securely wrapped around Dog's big tummy. The last time Lorelei kidnapped Dog, Homer had thought he might never see him again. But this time was different. He'd get Dog back, no doubt about it. Lorelei wanted to use Dog, but she'd never keep or hurt him—because if she did, Homer would tell the world about her secret lair. And besides, Zelda was with Lorelei. Even though Zelda was merely there to drive the cloudcopter and to keep Lorelei safe, she'd never let Lorelei hurt Dog.

Compass in hand, Homer pushed deeper into the forest. The summer sun trickled through the canopy of cedar and alder, pooling on boulders and patches of moss. His stomach growled. Dog's stomach was probably growling, too.

"I'm thirsty," Hercules said.

Homer licked his dry lips. After working in the field, his father often said, "I got me a mighty strong thirst." That's exactly how Homer felt as a nearby stream called to him in its soft, gurgling voice. But without water-purifying pills, which were in the lost backpack, Homer didn't dare take the risk. Drinking directly from a stream was a sure way of making that fortune-teller's prediction come true.

Chapter 5 of *Twentieth Century Treasure-Hunting Disasters* told the tragic story of the Smittys, three wet-behind-the-ears brothers who'd set out for the Wild West in search of gold. They survived a bandit attack, a buffalo stampede, and some saloon girls who wanted to get married. After all that, the Smitty brothers found the largest gold vein in historical record. They didn't get to spend their fortune, however, because they celebrated by drinking from a stream without boiling the water first.

"We'll have to wait for Baldwin to bring us water." After checking his compass again, Homer veered back on course. "We should be getting close to the *X*."

"How can you be certain?" Hercules asked.

Without the atlas and Lord Mockingbird's map, which were in the backpack, Homer had to rely on his memory. "On Lord Mockingbird's map, the X was drawn in the center of the mushroom cap. That's the forested part of the island. I got a good look at the island from the float-plane's window. If I keep us on a straight course from the beach, we should get there." He slid between two sprawling ferns, stepped onto a patch of leaves and, before he could scream out, found himself sitting at the bottom of a hole.

Homer looked up to find Hercules looking down with an equally confused expression across his face.

"Hey, you just fell in a hole. Are you okay? Did you break anything?"

Pain shot through Homer's legs. He'd landed right on his tailbone. "I think I'm okay." He slowly got to his feet, his rear end aching something fierce. Once again he checked his limbs for breakage. Once again he sighed with relief. "I didn't break anything."

"This hole's really big." Hercules lay on his stomach and peered over the edge at Homer. "Do you think it's an abandoned well?"

Homer squinted up at him. "Maybe. But Mushroom Island is supposed to be uninhabited," Homer said. The hole was about as deep as two men, so it could have been a well. A mat of woven sticks lay at Homer's feet. Broken by Homer's fall, the mat had been covering up the hole. He picked it up. "Don't you think that if someone wanted to cover up an abandoned well they would have used something solid, like planks, to keep people from falling in?"

"Unless you're *supposed* to fall in."

Homer dropped the mat. "It's a booby trap."

"Hey, you know why they're called booby traps? Because the word *booby* is another way of saying *stu*—"

"Get me out of here."

"How?"

"I don't know." Homer picked his Panama hat off the ground and set it back on his head. Then he ran his hands over the walls of the hole. There was nothing to grab on to. He stood on tiptoe and stretched his arms, but Hercules couldn't reach him. He sighed. A coil of rope sat at the bottom of the lost backpack. Rope always comes in handy on a quest. "Do you know how to make rope from vines?"

"No." Hercules looked over his shoulder. "Hey, Homer, I don't like being alone up here. What if that bear comes?"

"Well, I don't like being stuck down here. Lorelei's already got a huge head start, and now I'll never catch up." He pushed his bangs from his face.

"Here, I'll use my branch." Hercules wrapped both

hands around his makeshift sword and plunged it into the hole. "Grab it and climb out."

It was the nightmare of gym class all over again as Homer held on to the end of the branch and pulled with all his might. *One hand, then the next*, he told himself. *You can do it.* He squeezed his eyes shut, forcing all his energy into his arms. *One hand, then the next.* He opened his eyes. He was only a few inches off the ground. "I can't do it," he said, letting go. "I'm not strong enough."

Hercules looked over his shoulder again. "Did you hear that?" he asked. "Something's moving around out there." He scrambled to his feet and gripped the end of the branch. "Hold on and I'll pull you out."

"You can't do that," Homer said. "I weigh—"

"Just hold on."

Homer grabbed the branch and, to his surprise, he found himself standing in forest sunlight. One moment he'd been standing at the bottom of a booby trap, the next moment he was looking into Hercules's brown eyes. "You did it. You pulled me out." He wiped dirt off his hands and looked at his friend with amazement. Hercules had caught Dog in midair with one arm. He'd ripped a branch off a tree. And he'd pulled Homer from the bottom of a very deep hole. "You're really strong."

Hercules scratched a welt on his arm, his gaze darting between the trees. "Yeah, I'm strong."

"No, I mean you're *really* strong." Homer narrowed his eyes. Hercules wasn't much taller than Homer, and he was definitely a lot lighter. No muscles bulged from beneath the rugby shirt, and yet... "You're as strong as your brothers and sister, aren't you?"

Hercules didn't respond. He turned away from Homer.

Homer thought back to his visit to the Simpleton Palace and one image stuck in his mind. "Wait a minute. Are you telling me that when Brutus was sitting on us, you could have pushed her away?"

"No, I couldn't. I mean, yes, I could. But if I'd pushed her away, then my family would know that I'm strong." Hercules's voice warbled with emotion. "You can't tell anyone I'm strong. Please, Homer. It's my secret. Dad thinks I can't do anything but spell. If he finds out, he'll make me play some dangerous sport like rugby or baseball. I hate physical contact sports. Imagine what could happen to my brain if I got a concussion. I'd never be the first person to win the World's Spelling Bee twice in a row."

"You want to win twice in a row?"

"More than anything."

If Homer understood one thing, it was the feeling of wanting something with one's entire heart. Surrounded by the deep greens of the forest and the morning chatter of birds, he promised to keep the secret—for what was one more secret in the trove of secrets he already held? And who better to keep such a secret than Homer W. Pudding, the boy from Milkydale whose very bedroom held one of the greatest secrets of all time?

Homer checked his compass again. "We've got to keep going." Hercules took a step, but Homer grabbed his arm. "Don't step there."

A discolored patch of ground waited a few feet from Hercules. "It's another booby trap," Homer said. "If you know what to look for, you can see the woven mats. There's another one. And another," he said, pointing. "Someone has set booby traps all over this place. It's kinda like the Temple of the Reptile King."

"What do you mean?" Hercules squeezed Homer's arm. "Are there reptiles around here? Bears *and* reptiles?"

One of the maps from Homer's ceiling filled his mind. "The Temple of the Reptile King was protected by viper-filled pits. After Wilma von Weiner found the temple and got rid of all the vipers, she decided to keep the traps. She didn't want anyone to get an early peek at her discovery, so she covered the traps with mats. I guess she caught a few sneaky thieves and reporters." Homer poked another booby trap with the stick. The mat gave way. "Lord Mockingbird must have had someone dig these holes to test my skills."

"Lord Mockingbird was good friends with Wilma

von Weiner," Hercules said. "I had to organize L.O.S.T.'s photo collection, and there are lots of pictures of them together when they were young."

"Really?" A tickling sensation crept up Homer's neck, and it wasn't caused by a bug. Wilma von Weiner had founded L.O.S.T. She'd been highly respected by the treasure-hunting community. She'd died a long time ago. "Zelda told me that someone in L.O.S.T. doesn't want me to join. What if it's Lord Mockingbird? If he was good friends with Wilma von Weiner, then he probably wants her daughter, Madame la Directeur, to have my uncle's chair when she gets out of jail. What if Lord Mockingbird put these booby traps here, not as a test, but as a way to..."

"To get rid of you," Hercules said.

A bird screeched from a nearby branch.

Homer took a deep breath. He'd fallen into one booby trap, but he wasn't going to fall into any more. "Let me have that branch." Hercules handed it over. "Let's go."

"No way," Hercules said. "If I fall into a hole, you'll never be able to pull me out."

"I'll go first," Homer assured him. "Follow my footsteps exactly. If one of us falls, it will be me." Homer checked his compass, then scanned the forest floor for a way between the traps. "I thought Torch was the one who didn't want me to join," he said as he poked the ground with the branch. "Remember how she kept questioning my honesty, like she was trying to prove that I wasn't Drake's nephew?"

"Don't take it personally. Torch is rude to everyone," Hercules said. "And she's always in a bad mood. According to the files, she's the only member of L.O.S.T. who's never found anything. Think about it. Her specialty is Atlantis. That place is just a story."

"It could have been a real place."

"Then why hasn't she found anything?"

That had to be frustrating. Uncle Drake's specialty had been Rumpold Smeller the Pirate, and everyone knew he'd existed. Eyewitnesses had written lengthy accounts of his dastardly deeds. But Torch had no proof. No wonder she was so grumpy.

Maneuvering around the booby traps proved to be a slow process. The only consolation was that Lorelei had probably had trouble, too. But what if Dog had fallen into a trap? He could have broken one of his little legs. *I'm starting to think like Hercules,* Homer told himself. *Focus on one worry at a time.*

The trees thickened and soon there was barely any space between them. With no more room for holes, the traps also disappeared. Homer squeezed between the trees, checking his compass again and again. He pushed between a pair of cedars. "Whoa." He stopped in his tracks. Right in front of him, a rat sat on a moss-covered log, holding a granola bar in her claws. "Daisy," he whispered.

Hercules bumped right into Homer. "Hey, what—"

Homer put a finger to his lips, then pointed. Hercules peered around the tree's trunk.

Daisy the rat stared at Homer with her beadlike eyes. Wiggling her nose, she sniffed the air. Then she turned the granola bar in her little hands and continued eating. Homer took a cautious step forward. She sat up straight and hugged the granola bar to her chest, her little eyes saying, *You can't have this. It's mine.* Homer was hungry enough to eat anything, even a granola bar covered in rat slobber, but he had something else on his mind.

"Daisy," he cooed. "Where's Lorelei?" He took another step toward her.

Daisy the rat darted beneath a fern. "There she goes," Hercules said, pointing. They followed, squeezing between more trees. Just when they thought they'd lost sight of her, the rubbery tail popped out from behind a rock, then disappeared around a tree.

Homer followed, then froze. A patch of pink had caught his eye.

Lorelei stood in a small clearing, just a few yards away. She wore no professional adventurer clothing, just a pair of jeans, a black-and-white-striped shirt and her usual sneakers. Homer sighed with relief. Dog stood at Lorelei's feet, at the end of a blue leash. The leash was too large for a rat, so clearly Lorelei had brought it, intending to steal Dog. Homer wanted to kick himself for feeling surprised. Of course she'd intended to steal Dog. She was in this to win.

But where was Zelda?

Homer cleared his throat, but neither Lorelei nor Dog turned to look at him. Hercules caught up and peered over Homer's shoulder. "What's she—?"

"Don't move," Lorelei said, still not turning around. A soft growl rose from Dog's chest.

That's when Homer's gaze traveled beyond Lorelei to the other end of the clearing. And that's when Hercules fainted.

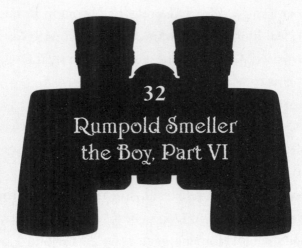

32

Rumpold Smeller
the Boy, Part VI

It didn't take long for Rumpold to settle into the horse's pace. The steady clip-clopping eased his thoughts, pushing away the images of his teary mother and his frowning father. As the morning passed, the landscape changed from fields dotted with peasants and livestock to hills covered in young alder and oak. The geometry of a fern caught his eye, as did the perfect blackness of a raven perched on a branch, but Rumpold fought his urge to draw these things. The forest waited.

The task assigned to him was far better than he could

have imagined. Though he'd never drawn a map before, at least he'd get to use his charcoal and parchment. There was that little matter of survival, however. All the last-minute instructions would help, but there'd been so many. "Don't let your kindling get wet." "Stock the fire before going to sleep." "Always skin a rabbit downwind."

"I'll do my best," he'd told his father.

By midday he'd arrived at the forest's edge. A trail, trampled by deer hooves, proved wide enough for the horse. The afternoon passed quickly and pleasantly, and they stopped every so often so Rumpold could take notes about the landscape. It was on such a break that he spied an ants' nest. While the horse grazed nearby, Rumpold sat on a log and watched the ants go about their daily chores. Could he possibly capture the depth and complexity of the nest? What about the texture of the twigs, piled one atop the other in a mysterious labyrinth? He couldn't deny himself the artistic challenge. Gripping a thin piece of charcoal, his hand moved in a hypnotic rhythm, his gaze shifting from nest to parchment.

It was the shadows on his paper that woke him from his daze. The sun was setting and darkness lingered at the edges of the trees. A chill pierced the air. Rumpold whistled for the horse, who obediently appeared. He tucked his parchment and charcoal into his travel bag, then wrapped a blanket around his shoulders and wondered what to do next. Should he build a fire, or make a shelter the way his tutor said to do? His stomach growled, so he drank water from the sheep's bladder his father had given him. He chewed a piece of dried venison that his tutor had tucked into his pocket.

Perhaps, Rumpold thought, *my current predicament isn't so bad*. If he used his time wisely, he could travel in the morning, draw the map, then use the entire afternoon to work on his own drawings.

As night crept in, the forest filled with odd sounds. Rumpold reached into his bag for the flint. Fumbling, he grabbed it, but it flew from his fingers and landed somewhere on the dark forest floor. There'd be no fire that night. The horse trampled some undergrowth, then lay down with a satisfied snort. Rumpold settled against the horse's belly, which was plenty warm. He wrapped the blanket over his body and laid his head on the horse's side.

He thought of his family back at the palace. If only he could tell his worried mother that he was fine. His father would be worried, too, but more for his reputation. It would be better to die in the forest than to return home without a map and break his father's heart.

Rumpold's eyelids grew heavy and the horse's steady breathing lulled him into a shallow sleep. But a rustling from the nearby shrubs perked the horse's ears and Rumpold's, too. The rustling grew closer and was accompanied by heavy breathing. Rumpold's eyes flew open. "Who's there?"

The horse bolted to its feet and neighed with fear. Rumpold shot to his feet and grabbed the horse's reins. He squinted into the darkness. A stench crept up his nose as the breathing grew louder. Panicking, the horse kicked its back legs, then bolted forward, ripping the reins from Rumpold's grasp. Trying to escape in the darkness, the horse stumbled and bumped into a tree.

Rumpold took a few steps back. The breathing was close enough that it blew hot across his face. A dark mass loomed before him. "Please don't hurt me," Rumpold pleaded. Then something knocked against the side of his head and he fell over backward.

He was standing at an easel, painting a vase of flowers. His canvas was the purest white that money could buy. His brush was made from the finest camel hair. His palette was covered with colors he'd never imagined. A smile of pure happiness spread across his face.

Then darkness swept over him.

33

The Scent of Honey

There are bears and there are BEARS. There are little stuffed bears that children keep on their beds and cuddle at night. There are black-and-white panda bears that coax smiles and laughter from even the most evil-minded scoundrels. There are the black bears that like to eat berries and honey and that are so shy that if you say "boo" to them, they run away. But then there are the grizzly bears. If you say "boo" to a grizzly bear, it will eat your face.

That's why Lorelei and Dog stood frozen—because

that's what stood at the edge of the clearing, the face-eating variety of bear. Zelda would have been impressed by the bear's grandeur. It balanced on its back legs like a monolith. Its eyes were so black, they looked like holes punched into its face. Homer's entire body broke into a quiver. Hercules moaned and sat up. "What happened? I think I fainted."

"Don't move," Lorelei said from the corner of her clenched mouth.

"Don't move," Homer whispered to Hercules. Then he thought about this "not moving" idea, and it didn't seem so good. "Maybe we should run."

"No," Lorelei said. "They attack if you run."

How would she know that? Lorelei had spent her life living in The City, selling soup from a soup cart and sneaking into movie theaters and museums. What made her an expert on bears? But, on the other hand, Lorelei had proven to have a keen instinct for survival.

Sticks and moss hung from the bear's dense fur. Its nose glistened like a wet river rock. Having never stood face-to-face with the king of the forest, Homer was unprepared for the stench that wafted his way. If a perfumer were to describe the odor, he might say, "The base is wet dog with undertones of decay and high notes of rotten fish gut." In other words—super stink.

Dog growled louder. His feet splayed, he pointed his

long body at the bear like an arrow. Homer wanted to reach for the leash but didn't dare. "What do we do?" Hercules whispered.

"I think we should walk away," Homer whispered back. "Very, very slowly."

"Are you crazy? I'm not leaving," Lorelei said. Someone looking on might have thought that Lorelei and Homer were practicing to be ventriloquists the way they held their faces in a frozen grimace, their words slipping out between unmoving lips. "This is the spot. *X* marks the spot. The membership coin is here somewhere."

The hairs on Dog's neck bristled as he growled louder.

Homer tightened his jaw to stop the quivering. "But we have to get out of here."

"You're going to give up membership just because of a bear?"

Was she crazy? "I'm not giving up membership," Homer said, so afraid to move that he barely breathed. "I just think that our lives are more important than the coin."

"I want that coin," she said, balling her fists with determination. "And no stupid bear's gonna stop me."

"But, Lorelei—"

Hercules, still sitting on the ground, tapped Homer's shin. "Could you two debate this later? We're about to be eaten."

The bear opened its mouth. Teeth, lots and lots of teeth, dripping with saliva, protruded from a vacuous hole as the mouth opened wider. A roar, deep as a bass drum and loud as a fighter jet, filled the clearing. The bear's fur rippled as the magnificent roar reached its crescendo. Homer's heart thumped in his throat. Lorelei took a quick step back, then another, pulling Dog along with her. "Okay, I've changed my mind," she said. "We need to get out of here."

That's when Daisy the rat scurried into the scene, her long, rubbery tail held high. Carrying the granola bar in her teeth, she darted left and right as if incapable of walking in a straight line. She stopped at one of the bear's front paws. Entranced by the new odor, she dropped her precious granola bar and sniffed the paw. The bear closed its mouth, dropped onto all fours, and licked the granola bar.

Food, Homer thought. "Lorelei, do you have any more granola bars?"

"Maybe, but I need them. They're the only food I brought."

She *was* completely crazy. "That bear is hungry," Homer said. "Give it all the granola bars and we can get out of here."

"Fine," Lorelei said. "But they're in my backpack."

"Be careful," Hercules whispered.

317

As the bear ate the granola bar, Homer crept forward. Lorelei's backpack hung on her back. As Homer unzipped the main compartment, Dog stuck his head between Homer's shins. His trembling could be felt through Homer's leech-proof socks. "It's okay," Homer whispered. Slowly reaching into the backpack, Homer found the clue box, identical to his own, the two scrolls and the plastic honey bear. "Hey, what about this?" He grabbed the honey bear. As the grizzly licked its lips, Homer stepped in front of Lorelei and Dog. "Get ready to run," he said. Hercules got to his feet. Lorelei clutched Dog's leash.

"One," Homer said as he pulled open the honey bear's lid. He squeezed its plastic belly. The sticky syrup oozed out. The grizzly sniffed, catching the sweet scent. "Two," Homer said as he held out the honey bear like an offering. The grizzly raised its head. "Three!" Homer tossed the honey bear. The grizzly caught the little plastic version of itself between its slipper-size paws. It licked the lid and a soft purring sound came from its throat. "Now," Homer said.

They ran out of the clearing, back into the dense forest. Homer expected any moment to be swatted from behind. Struggling to keep up with the others, he bashed his shoulder on a tree and lost his Panama hat to a low-hanging branch. But there was no time to stop. The only thing on his mind was getting as far away from the bear as possible. And that's why he forgot all about the booby traps.

And why he landed in a hole, right on top of Hercules and Dog.

"Get off me!" Lorelei cried from the bottom of the pile. Pushing Dog away, she pulled herself free and shot to her feet. "I can't believe we fell into one of these stupid traps!" She kicked the dirt wall. "I can't believe it!"

Dog licked Homer's face. Homer slid off Hercules. His shoulder throbbed and his tailbone still hurt. He ran his hands over Dog to make sure he was okay. While happy to once again scratch his best friend's rump, he wanted to kick the dirt wall, too. So he did. He scrambled to his feet and gave it a huge kick. Falling into a booby trap one time was bad enough. But twice?

"I can't believe I'm in another stupid hole," he cried.

"It's all your fault," Lorelei said, pointing her finger right in Homer's face. Her freckles were smudged with dirt.

"My fault?" He pointed right back. "I was following *you.*"

"Yeah? Well don't follow me."

"Don't take my dog and I won't follow you."

Hercules moaned and grabbed his ankle. "I landed on this tree root. I think my ankle's broken."

"What?" Homer's arm fell to his side. "Broken?"

"You've got to be kidding," Lorelei said. "Well, I guess that means you two won't be getting out of here."

"We'll get out of here," Homer said, pointing his finger again. "Believe me, we'll get out of here and we'll get out of here before you get out of here."

"Oh really?" She stuck out her lower lip. "I wouldn't be in this stupid predicament if you hadn't told me to run."

"What are you talking about? I saved your life," Homer said. "You should be saying, 'Thanks, Homer, thanks for saving my life.'"

Lorelei narrowed her eyes. For the briefest of moments he thought she might actually thank him. But then she folded her arms. "I should have stayed up there. While that bear was eating the honey, I could have been searching for the coin."

"Then you should have stayed there." He folded his arm. "Why don't you go back there? I don't care."

"I will. I will go back there. Because I'm going to get that coin. You'll see."

"Urrr." Dog poked Homer's shin with his nose.

"Hello?" Hercules said, cradling his leg in his hands. "Broken ankle, remember?"

Homer and Lorelei knelt beside Hercules. After rolling up his pant leg and inspecting his ankle, which had turned red and was beginning to swell, everyone agreed that it was, indeed, broken. Dog watched worriedly, his chin resting on Hercules's knee. "What are we going to do?" Homer asked.

A clump of dirt tumbled off the dirt wall. Everyone looked up. Daisy the rat peered over the edge of the booby trap. Then, nose first, she scurried down the wall, her little claws clinging to the dirt as if she were weightless. Lorelei picked her up and set her on her shoulder. Then she looked long and hard at the boys. "You guys are a mess."

It was true. Hercules's rugby shirt was torn in two places. Strands of dried seaweed, from the night on the beach, clung to both their shirts, along with clumps of moss. Scratches from the forest covered their necks, hands, and faces, along with the welts from the mosquito attack.

Lorelei ran her hand over her hair. A bunch of leaves and twigs fell out. "Guess I'm a mess, too." She smiled.

A flash of memory hit Homer. The first time he'd met Lorelei on the streets of The City, she'd smiled at him just like that. She'd shared her tomato soup and crackers from her soup cart. She'd shown him her secret room in the back of the soup warehouse. They'd been friends. That's what he'd thought.

Hercules moaned again. "It's throbbing with pain," he said. "I need to get to a hospital."

"Hey?" Homer leaped to his feet with a sudden flash of hope. "Where's Zelda? She'll get us out of here. ZELDA!" he called.

"ZELDA!" Hercules cried. "HELP! ZELDA!"

"She's not here," Lorelei said. She stuck her hands in her pockets and looked away.

"Of course she's here. I saw the cloudcopter." Homer cupped his hands around his mouth. "ZELDA!"

"HOWOOOO!"

"I left her in Gloomy Moor."

"What?" Hercules winced. "But she's supposed to be on the quest with you. I went with Homer. She's supposed to go with you. That's the deal."

"She was supposed to provide me with transportation. I took the cloudcopter when she wasn't looking." Lorelei slid her backpack off her shoulders. "Zelda is loyal to Homer. I don't trust her for a minute."

"But she took an oath to follow the rules of L.O.S.T.," Homer said. "She wouldn't break it. Zelda would never do that."

"Do you really believe that?" Lorelei searched the side pocket of her backpack. "The moment Zelda saw you in trouble, she'd break her oath. If your life was ever in danger, she'd abandon me in a heartbeat. Oaths are ridiculous. You only keep them as long as they're easy."

Homer frowned. Lorelei didn't know Zelda the way

he did. "Everyone who joins L.O.S.T. has to take an oath, Lorelei. And they have to stick to it."

"You don't have to stick to anything you don't want to stick to."

"Maybe you don't, but you shouldn't break an oath if you want to live your life with hon...hon..." Homer tried to remember the word.

"Honorificabilitudinity," Hercules said.

Lorelei snorted. "I want to live my life the way I want to live it. And no oath is going to get in my way." She pulled a rope from the side pocket. "Here's what we do. I'm the lightest one here. If I stand on Homer's shoulders, I'll be able to reach the top and pull myself out of the hole. Then I'll tie this rope to a tree and you can climb out." Homer and Hercules shared a knowing look. "What? You don't trust me? Do you have a better idea?"

Even if he did trust her, which he didn't, Homer had yet to master the skill of rope climbing. But Hercules was incredibly strong. "Do you think you can do it?" Homer asked him. "Even with the broken ankle? Do you think you could pull yourself out, then me and Dog?" Hercules nodded. "Okay, Lorelei, we'll try it. But you can't leave us here. Hercules has to get to a hospital."

"I know that." Lorelei threw the rope over her shoulder.

Dog, who'd been walking around the perimeter of the

trap, dragging his blue leash behind him, began to sniff the ground. Hercules didn't take notice, for what is unusual about a dog sniffing the ground? Sniffing the ground is an incredibly ordinary thing for a dog to do. Except, of course, if the dog can't smell.

Both Homer and Lorelei inhaled a quick, excited breath. Daisy scampered down Lorelei's arm and jumped onto the ground. She sat on her hind legs and watched, her whiskers alert.

Dog snuffled, then rubbed his back against the wall. Lorelei reached for Dog's leash, but Homer grabbed it first, flashing a quick, triumphant smile. Dirt flew as Dog furiously dug into the wall.

"Hey," Hercules said, turning away from the flying dirt. "Don't let him do that. That wall might cave in."

But Homer wasn't about to stop Dog, nor was Lorelei. "He's found it," she whispered, her eyes sparkling. "It's behind this wall."

34

Tunnel to Nowhere

The ferocity with which Dog dug treasure always amazed Homer. How could those stubby legs move so quickly?

"Ur, ur, ur, ur, ur," Dog grunted, digging as if his life depended upon it—as if he were starving and about to uncover the world's juiciest mammoth bone.

"The wall's crumbling," Hercules cried, scooting as far away as he could, which, in the tight space, was only a few inches. "We'll get buried alive. Why don't you make him stop?"

"Stop being such a chicken," Lorelei said. She stepped back as a section of wall landed at her feet. A gap appeared in the wall. Dog stuck his head into the gap, then dug until he could fit his entire body through. As soon as he was all the way through, Daisy followed. Clutching the leash, Homer got on his knees and reached his arm after Dog. "I think there's a tunnel back there."

"A tunnel?" Lorelei opened her backpack and pulled out a flashlight. She tried to push past Homer, but he blocked the way.

"No, you don't. He's my dog. I'm going first."

"Oh really?" Lorelei said. "Then where's *your* flashlight?"

"It's in my backpack."

Lorelei smirked. "So where's your backpack?"

"I dropped it when I jumped out of the plane."

"Right. You jumped out of a plane."

"He did," Hercules said. "He jumped out of a plane. We all did."

Lorelei's eyes widened. "Really? I've always wanted to jump out of a plane." She looked at her flashlight, then shrugged and handed it to Homer. He switched it on and stuck his head through the wall.

"Yep, there's a tunnel, tall enough to stand in," he reported. Dog, desperate to get down the tunnel, made little choking sounds as he pulled on the leash.

"Where does it go?" Lorelei asked, pushing on Homer's shoulder as she tried to get a view. "Can you see?"

"I can't see very far, but it must go somewhere. Maybe it's the way out. Come on."

"No way," Hercules said. "I'm not going into a tunnel. What if the ceiling caves in? I don't have my helmet."

Homer thought about his Panama hat, now swinging from the end of a branch. Mr. Tuffletop had probably lined the hat with some sort of protective shield or maybe a motion detector that would warn him of an imminent cave-in. "You stay with Hercules," he told Lorelei. "I'll go in."

"Why should I stay with him?" she asked. "You stay with him. He's your friend."

Homer looked back at Hercules. Hercules hadn't wanted to go on this quest. He could have stayed in the safety of his bedroom with his dictionaries and little carts of food. But he'd come with Homer out of a sense of honor. Many a friendship had been built on far less than that.

And he'd saved Dog's life! He was his friend.

Hercules groaned and grabbed his leg.

Homer tightened his grip on the flashlight. "We need to get Hercules out of here. We don't know where this tunnel leads, so let's use the rope like we planned. We can get Hercules to the beach to meet his butler. Then you and I can come back here with Dog."

"Leave and then come back?" Lorelei shook her head. "No, we can't do that. We're so close. Look how Dog's tugging on the leash. *He smells it.*" She whispered those last three words right in Homer's ear.

"We're helping Hercules first," Homer said.

Lorelei opened her mouth and was about to say something when a honey bear landed at her feet. Mangled and torn open, the plastic bear had been licked clean. The stench of rotten fish descended into the hole, along with a gust of hot air.

Hercules whimpered.

The grizzly lay at the top of the booby trap, licking the last remnants of honey from its lips. It reached into the hole, swiping its paw at Lorelei's backpack. Lorelei squealed and squeezed through the gap in the wall. Hercules needed no further convincing. Dragging his leg, he scooted toward the gap. The grizzly hung its head into the hole and growled.

Homer crawled through the gap. With the leash's handle wrapped around his wrist, he dropped the flashlight, reached out, grabbed Hercules by the arms, and pulled. With a push of his good foot, Hercules propelled himself through the gap and landed on his back inside the tunnel.

"You okay?" Homer asked.

"I'm alive," Hercules said. He sat up. "Where are we now?"

Lorelei picked up the flashlight and ran its beam over the stone walls, which glistened and dripped with water. "Whoever dug the booby traps didn't dig this place," she said.

"Might be some kind of cave system," Homer said. Light filtered in through the gap in the wall, which turned out to be a hollow spot between two enormous tree roots.

Lorelei pointed the beam up the tunnel, where it bounced off a slab of granite. "Dead end."

"Ack." Dog choked as he pulled on the leash. Lorelei swung around and pointed the flashlight beam at Dog. Straining at the edge of his collar, he pumped his front legs and pointed his nose down the tunnel. "Ack, ack, ack."

"Why is Dog acting like that?" Hercules asked.

Homer held fast to the leash. "He probably needs to piddle."

"Yeah, piddle." Lorelei squeezed past Homer. "Let's go."

"What if this leads to the bear's cave?" Hercules asked. "And what if the bear has cubs?"

Lorelei pointed the flashlight in Hercules's face. "What makes you think the bear has cubs? Did you see a cub?"

"No."

She groaned. "Jeez, you scared me." She dropped the beam. "Stop worrying about everything. You're making me start to worry."

A frustrated growl shot through the gap as the bear stuck its head deeper into the booby trap.

"We've got to get out of here. Can you walk?" Homer asked as Hercules struggled onto his good foot.

"I think I can limp." He took a step, then cried out. "No. That won't work. I can't walk."

"You can piggyback him," Lorelei said. "I'll take Dog."

"No way. You're not taking Dog."

"Just give me the leash."

"NO! I'm not giving you the leash."

"Ack, ack, ack."

"Why are you guys always fighting over Dog?" Hercules asked, leaning against the wall. "He's Homer's dog, Lorelei. You can't keep taking him."

"I'll piggyback him *and* I'll hold the leash," Homer said.

Another growl shot through the gap.

"Forget it," Lorelei said, shoving the flashlight into Homer's hand. "I'll piggyback him." She took off her backpack and slid it over Homer's shoulder.

"You're going to piggyback me?" Hercules said.

"Why not? I used to push a soup cart all over The City. I can piggyback a scrawny guy like you."

While Lorelei staggered beneath Hercules's weight, Dog led the way, pulling Homer as if they were competing in the Iditarod. It took all of Homer's strength to slow Dog's pace so Lorelei could keep up. With Lorelei's backpack hanging from a shoulder, and with the leash in one hand and the flashlight in the other, Homer stumbled down the tunnel. Dank walls shimmered in the flashlight's beam. The tunnel twisted and turned. Homer's heart pounded with fear and excitement, for how often in a person's life does one path lead to a man-eating bear while the other path leads to treasure? It was just like the lines on his hand. One led to a long life, the other to a dead end.

"Whoa," Homer cried, nearly tripping as something darted into the flashlight's beam. A rat scurried down the tunnel and disappeared into the shadows. "I hope that was Daisy," he said with a shudder.

"Ahhh," Hercules cried out. "You just bumped my foot on the wall."

"Sorry," Lorelei said. "Don't hold on so tight. You're choking me."

"Are you getting tired? Do you want me to piggyback him?" Homer asked.

"I'm fine," Lorelei said, gasping for breath. "Just. Keep. Moving."

Dog grunted and pulled harder. "He's picking up speed," Homer said. "I can barely hold him back. Something's definitely down there."

"How does Dog know something is down there?" Hercules asked. "Does he hear something?"

"Yeah, that's it," Lorelei said. "He *hears* something."

Please let it be some treasure other than the membership coin, Homer wished. Because he knew how tricky Lorelei was. She'd try to grab the coin before Homer, and she'd very likely succeed. *Please let it be something else.* But his wishing wouldn't change the facts. Of course Dog was leading them to the membership coin. That's what the quest was about. That's what Lord Mockingbird had sent them to find.

Except for the flashlight's beam, pitch-blackness coated the tunnel like tar. No sunlight beckoned from the tunnel's end, which would have been a relief. Homer had lost all sense of direction and couldn't even guess where they were headed. A few steps later, the flashlight's beam flickered, then died.

"Crud!" Lorelei said as she bumped into Homer.

"Ouch!" Hercules cried. "Watch out for my foot!"

"Lorelei? Do you have extra batteries in your backpack?" Homer asked.

She was silent for a moment. "Oops."

Dog's paws scratched at the ground as he tried to pull

Homer down the tunnel. "Hold on," Homer called to him. "I know what to do." He dropped the backpack and flashlight, then reached into his vest pocket and pulled out the little folded vest that belonged to Dog. Eerie green light radiated from the vest, casting an alien glow on everyone's face. Homer wrapped the vest around Dog's middle, then collected the backpack. Following the waddling light, they continued down the tunnel.

"What if this tunnel doesn't go anywhere?" Hercules asked. "What if it goes nowhere?"

"Of course it goes somewhere," Lorelei said. "Why would it be here if it didn't go somewhere?"

Homer stopped. "What's that sound?"

A single musical note, clear and bright, chimed in the distance. It grew louder, as if moving up the tunnel. Daisy the rat scurried into the vest's glow. Dog turned to sniff as she passed by. "Urrrr."

"Ouch," Hercules said as Lorelei let go of his legs. He caught his balance and leaned against the wall.

The musical note accompanied Daisy as she passed Homer. Lorelei reached down. "Whatcha got there, Daisy?"

Got? Homer dropped the backpack and whipped around. Daisy climbed up Lorelei's arm and settled on her shoulder. Something glinted from the rat's mouth.

"What is it? Give it here, Daisy," Lorelei cooed. She plucked the something from Daisy's mouth. The musical note chimed again. "I think it's a crystal."

Homer expelled a long, relieved breath. The membership coin was still his to claim. But what had Daisy found?

Dog walked up to Lorelei's feet and sniffed. The glow from his vest revealed a clear, grape-size crystal in Lorelei's palm. Hercules peered over Lorelei's shoulder. "Is it a diamond?" he asked.

"If it is, then I claim it," Lorelei said. "My rat found it." She patted Daisy's head. "Good girl, Daisy."

Dog sniffed and whined. Then he rose onto his hind legs and balanced his front paws on Lorelei's pant leg, his nose pointed up at the crystal. He sniffed and whined again. Was this the treasure he'd smelled?

Daisy the rat blinked at Homer, then climbed down Lorelei's torso and leaped back onto the tunnel floor. Her little claws scritch-scratched as she scurried into the darkness. And then the tunnel fell silent.

A memory stirred in Homer's mind. His thoughts flew to the maps on his bedroom ceiling. "Shake it," he said. "Shake the crystal." Lorelei did and the musical note once again filled the tunnel with its clear, bright tone.

"Wow," Lorelei said. "How does it do that?"

"It's a harmonic crystal," Homer said with awe. "An

actual harmonic crystal. This is amazing. They've only been found in one place—the Great Crystal Cave. I've always wanted to go there and see them." Was it possible that another crystal cave existed? If so, it would be an amazing find.

"Is it worth a lot of money?" she asked.

"Anything rare is worth a lot of money," Homer said. "Can I hold it?"

Lorelei closed her fingers around the crystal. "You'll give it back to me?"

"Yes, I'll give it back to you." Homer frowned. "I've never lied to you, Lorelei."

She narrowed her eyes. Then slowly, her fingers opened. Homer plucked the crystal from her palm and held it close. The crystal sang softly as he turned it. Imagine an entire cave filled with such wondrous inventions of nature.

"Um, the crystal is pretty, but we've got a bear after us, remember?" Hercules said. "And this broken ankle isn't getting any better."

"Right," Homer said. "Sorry." He handed the crystal back to Lorelei.

Dog dropped onto all fours and tugged at the end of the leash, trying to pull Homer farther down the tunnel. Another musical note sounded. And then another and another. Homer's and Lorelei's eyes locked.

"There're more," she said.

35

The Cave of
Crystal Music

Lorelei grabbed her backpack and took off, stumbling into the darkness.

"Hurry," Homer told Hercules. "Get on."

With Hercules on his back and Dog at the end of the leash, Homer struggled down the tunnel. If his teacher, Mrs. Peepgrass, could see him, she'd surely change his grade in physical fitness from a C-minus to at least a B.

The music grew louder, joined by more notes, each one sweet and clear, ringing like water-filled crystal goblets. Dog barked. The loud music was probably hurting his ears, Homer realized. But Dog continued to lead the way until they turned a corner and Dog's vest lit up a large space.

A cave.

Homer set Hercules against the wall. They both covered their ears with their hands. Where was the music coming from? "That music is too loud!" Lorelei yelled. She stood in the cave, her fingers in her ears.

Dog ran in a circle and as he did, the green glow of his vest revealed two lanterns and some matches sitting on the floor. Homer hurried across the cave. He struck a match and lit each of the lantern's thick wicks. The wicks ignited and a soft white glow spread throughout the cave.

Homer's first reaction was relief to find no bear cubs napping and no bear droppings, either. He'd expected the cave walls to sparkle, just like the illustration of the Great Crystal Cave on his map. But they were boring old cave walls, dripping with water, nothing else. "Look!" Lorelei cried.

A wooden crate sat in the center of the cave, filled to the top with crystals. Daisy the rat was digging through the pile, the way rats do to make a nest. She was the cause of the ear-splitting music, for the crystals were reacting to each of her movements. Lorelei scooped her up and the music immediately faded. Dog stopped barking. All was quiet.

"Wow," Lorelei said, kneeling next to the crate. "There must be hundreds of them." Dog sniffed the crate and wagged his tail.

"Good boy," Homer said, scratching Dog's rump. "You found treasure," he whispered. "Yes, you did. You found treasure."

"Urrrr." Having done his job, Dog yawned, then lay next to the crate. His tongue hung out the side of his mouth as he panted. He closed his eyes.

Lorelei leaned close to Homer. "He's going to sleep. The coin must not be here," she whispered.

So where was it? The question clung to Homer as he helped Hercules sit against the side of the cave. Lorelei carefully lifted a crystal from the crate and laid it on the floor. She made a little line of crystals. "Watch this," she said. Gently, she tapped each one and a long stream of notes ascended. Then she tapped them in a different order and an entirely different stream of notes rose toward the ceiling. "Isn't that pretty?"

Hercules moaned as he stretched out his injured leg. The ankle had turned purple and was double its normal size. "We need to get you to a doctor," Homer said, running his gaze along the cave walls. "There's got to be a way out of here."

"I don't see a way out," Hercules said. He grimaced as he tried to move his leg to a more comfortable position.

"We can't go back up the tunnel. Not with that bear waiting for more honey."

Lorelei reached into her backpack and pulled out a small blue packet. She snapped the packet then handed it to Hercules. "Instant Ice," she said. "I used to burn myself all the time when I worked the soup cart. Oh, and I've also got some aspirin in my first-aid kit."

"You have a first-aid kit?" Hercules managed a small smile. "That's great news."

Lorelei wrapped an Ace bandage around Hercules's ankle, securing the Instant Ice in place. Homer watched, relief filling him like a mug of his mother's warm cocoa. This was the Lorelei he remembered, the girl who had helped him when he was lost in The City. The girl who cared about other people.

"This is a very nice first-aid kit," Hercules said as he shuffled through its contents. He opened a tube of anti-bacterial ointment and dabbed it onto his cuts and scrapes. He insisted Homer do the same. Lorelei reached into her backpack again and pulled out a box of granola bars.

"I was saving these in case I needed them, but I think we all need them." She tore open the box and divided up the bars—two for each of the boys, two for herself, one for Daisy, and one for Dog. Sitting on the cold cave floor, his entire body aching from bumps and bruises, Homer could have eaten a hundred granola bars. He ate the first and split the second with Dog so they'd each have one and a half. Then Lorelei handed around a water bottle, which they all shared, including Dog, until the last drops were gone.

"So," Lorelei said, wrapping her arms around her knees, "you're the one who knows all about treasure hunting. What are these crystals doing here?" She flared her nostrils, waiting for Homer's response.

It was a question Homer had been struggling with. "Harmonic crystals have only been found in one place, and that's the Great Crystal Cave."

"Who found the Great Crystal Cave?" Lorelei asked.

"Dr. Gertrude Magnum," Homer said. He picked up one of the crystals and slowly turned it over. It whispered its little song.

"That fat lady at the L.O.S.T. meeting? The one with those tiny little eyes?"

"I read her paperwork," Hercules said as he unwrapped a Band-Aid. "After she found the cave, Lord Mockingbird invited her to join L.O.S.T. That was more than twenty years ago."

"So when she found the cave, what did she do with all the crystals?" Lorelei asked.

Hercules explained. "Because the crystals were considered a natural phenomenon, she couldn't lay claim to them. The government sold some to the Museum of Musicology in The City, and the rest of the crystals were left in the cave so that people could enjoy them."

"It's a tourist attraction," Homer said. "You can ride this little train deep into the cave and watch a music and light show. It's supposed to be really cool."

"Well, I think it's obvious that she took some of the crystals for herself," Lorelei said as she stroked Daisy's tail. Daisy had stuck her head into one of the granola bar wrappers and was cleaning it of every single crumb. "We just found her secret hiding spot."

"But that's against the rules of L.O.S.T.," Homer said.

"She wasn't a member of L.O.S.T. when she found the Great Crystal Cave," Hercules pointed out. "So she wasn't actually breaking L.O.S.T. rules."

"The only reason to put stuff in a cave is because you want to hide it," Lorelei said. "Dr. Magnum doesn't want L.O.S.T. to know. It would make her look bad. She's probably selling these crystals to pay for things. I saw those jewels on her fingers."

Homer remembered the giant yacht anchored off Zelda's shore—*Cave Woman*. A yacht must cost a lot of money. "Even if Dr. Magnum took the crystals before she took her membership vow, keeping the crystals still goes against the beliefs of L.O.S.T. Those crystals could be given to more museums, so more people could enjoy them."

"I bet I could sell these for a lot of money," Lorelei said. She pulled her clue box out of her backpack. Then she began gently filling it with crystals.

"What are you doing?" Homer asked.

"Finders keepers, isn't that the motto of treasure hunting?"

"Maybe some treasure hunters believe that, like pirates," Homer said. "But not everyone. Treasure found is for the greater good."

Lorelei closed the clue box, now filled with crystals. Muffled music sounded as she shoved the box into her backpack. "I need money, Homer. I'm taking care of myself, remember?"

"I'm sure my parents could give you a job," Hercules said. "We just lost two maids."

"No, thanks," Lorelei said. She picked up a crystal and held it out. "Homer? Aren't you going to take some?"

Homer looked at the crate, temptation tickling his fingertips. He wasn't an official member of L.O.S.T., so he wouldn't be breaking any rules. It would be so easy to pocket a few crystals. His professional adventurer clothing certainly had enough pockets to carry as many crystals as he wanted. And perhaps Mr. Tuffletop's special fabric was soundproof as well as bladeproof, sunproof, and waterproof. A few of those crystals could certainly pay for a new gunnysack slide. It would be so easy.

"The lure of limitless wealth can eat at the soul the way cancer eats at the body," Uncle Drake had once told Homer.

Hercules, a half-opened Band-Aid in his hand, sat very still, watching Homer. *Don't do it*, his eyes seemed to say. Even Dog raised his chin off the cave floor and thumped his tail, looking at Homer with his heavy eyes. Homer folded his arms. "I'm not like you," he told Lorelei.

"Well, that's your loss." She picked up one of the lanterns and walked around the cave. "Since the tunnel dead-ends back there, how does what's-her-name get into this cave?"

Homer picked up the other lantern. He crept along the cave's edge, holding the light close to the wall. "Hey," he said. Lorelei hurried to his side. The wall receded, forming a nook that had been hidden in the shadows. All sorts of stuff littered the nook—another lantern, a dozen or so empty paper muffin cups, and a whole bunch of brochures. Homer picked one up.

Terry Tour's Great Crystal Cave Family Special.
Hold on tight! Our tram will whisk you deep

343

underground, where you'll be dazzled by the crystal music and laser show. Then enjoy a barbecue under the stars with all the fixin's.

"She's got a bunch of brochures for fancy cruises and luxury spas," Lorelei said. "I bet that's how she's spending her money." Then Lorelei grabbed a box. "What's in here?" She opened the box and pulled out a white beard and mustache, along with a pair of white eyebrows and a puffy black hat.

Homer picked up the hat. Excelsior, the fortune-teller from the fair, had worn the exact same hat and beard. *Treasure hunting will kill you.*

Homer looked at his palm. Excelsior's voice had been high and squeaky, just like Dr. Magnum's. And they'd both worn a big gemstone ring. Dr. Gertrude Magnum had come to the fair to scare Homer.

Homer reached into the box and pulled out an orange scarf and orange gloves. *Treasure hunters rank highest on the misery scale.* Ms. Pore, Ph.D., hadn't been a writer at all. Dr. Gertrude Magnum had tried to scare Homer with false statistics.

It wasn't Lord Mockingbird or Torch after all. Gertrude Magnum was the one who didn't want Homer to join L.O.S.T. But why?

344

Lorelei rummaged through some more brochures, then wandered back to her backpack and sat on the floor with a *humph*. "I don't get it. We found the place on the map that was marked with an *X*, but the coin wasn't there." She looked over at Homer. "Maybe you read the map wrong."

"Huh?" Homer tossed the scarf and gloves aside. "What do you mean I read it wrong? You read the map exactly the same way."

"No, I didn't." She folded her arms and stuck her chin out. "I couldn't make any sense of that stupid drawing, so I decided that since you're the map expert I'd let you figure it out. I followed you here."

"You followed me here?"

"Uh-huh."

Hercules screwed the cap off a tube of anti-itch cream and began applying it to his welts.

"Wait a minute." Homer pointed at Lorelei. "You followed me that night on the moor. How did you know where I was? You didn't get off at the train depot. There was only one train. How did you...?" He was starting to understand. Uncle Drake always said, "All that sparkles is not splendid." A gift from Lorelei wasn't a gift at all. He reached under his shirt and pulled out the compass. "You've been tracking me. That's how you found me on the moor. And that's how you followed me to Mushroom

Island. You didn't solve the riddle." Homer pulled the compass from around his neck and threw it onto the ground. "You're a cheater."

Lorelei's cheeks turned red. Daisy shook the granola wrapper off her head, then scurried over to the compass and claimed it for herself.

"Hey, you guys," Hercules said, his voice quiet. "I'm not feeling so good." He rested his head against the cave wall. "My ankle's burning."

"Okay," Homer called as he continued to scan the edge of the cave. "I'm looking. There's got to be a way out of here."

With a grunt, Dog got to his feet and waddled over to the side of the cave. He scratched at the wall and whined. "What's he doing?" Lorelei asked, leaping to her feet. "Is he digging? Does he smell something?"

Dog wasn't sniffing or rolling—just whining and scratching. "He does that when he wants to go outside and piddle."

Go outside? Homer rushed to Dog's side. "I don't believe it," Homer said as he gripped a knob that was the same color and texture as the cave wall. Fresh air and sunlight poured in as Homer opened the cave door. With a little kick of his legs, Dog scampered outside and down an embankment, his leash trailing over the rocks. He lifted his leg on a shrub.

"Hercules, we found a way out," Homer called.

The door had been built into a stone cliff. There was no beach at the base of the cliff. Instead, it gradually dipped into deep water. Homer walked to the water's edge. A metal post had been pounded between two large stones. A sign attached to the post read: GRIZZLY SANCTUARY. NO HUMANS ALLOWED. A white buoy floated in the water. "This is where she moors a boat. She probably anchors her yacht, then rows to the cave," Homer said as Lorelei joined him at the water's edge. "This is how Dr. Magnum gets to her crystals. She posted that sign to keep people away."

"Grizzly sanctuary?" Lorelei folded her arms. "What I want to know is, what's a grizzly bear doing on an island in the San Juans?"

"Bears live in caves, right? She probably found it during one of her expeditions and brought it here to protect her loot."

"Oh." Lorelei nodded. "Very clever. Maybe I should get a grizzly to protect my lair."

A horn honked. Homer squinted into the sunlight. "Mr. Pudding!" a voice called.

"Baldwin!" Homer waved ecstatically.

Water lapped over Homer's boots as a motorboat pulled up with Baldwin at the wheel, a ship captain's hat on his head. "I motored around the island twice looking for you. I rented this boat for the trip back to the mainland. Where is Mr. Simple?"

"I'm up here," Hercules called, leaning in the stone doorway.

"It appears that you've broken another bone," Baldwin said as he turned off the motor. "We shall get you to the hospital straight away." While Baldwin held the boat in place, Lorelei and Homer helped Hercules hobble down the slope and into the boat. "I'm sorry to say that I don't have a helmet for you, Mr. Simple. The best I could manage was this hat from a gift shop on the mainland." Baldwin held out a baseball hat with the words I VISITED THE HUMONGOUS FUNGUS WITH TERRY TOUR.

"I don't need a helmet," Hercules said as he stretched his leg on the boat's bench seat. "I jumped out of a plane and survived a grizzly bear without one. I'm beginning to doubt the necessity of helmets."

"Very good, Mr. Simple." Baldwin started the engine. "Have you finished your quest, Mr. Pudding? Are you ready to go home?"

"No," Homer said, a prickly feeling breaking out on his arms. He stared at the baseball cap. "I haven't finished my quest."

"Then you intend to stay here?" Baldwin asked.

Homer expected Hercules to insist that they leave together. But, instead, Hercules leaned over the side of the boat and motioned for Homer to step closer. "I know I'm supposed to look after you, Homer, but you can't give up. You have to find that coin." He wiped dirt off his mosquito-bitten face, then smiled at Homer. "It's your dream. Don't give it up."

"I'm staying," Homer told Baldwin.

"What about you, miss? Do you need a ride to the mainland?"

"No, thanks," Lorelei said. "I've got my own ride."

"Very good." Baldwin tipped his hat. "As soon as Mr. Simple's leg is tended to, I shall return for you, Mr. Pudding." He sat in the driver's seat and turned the wheel. The boat pulled away.

Hercules waved, then shouted, "Honorificabilitudini-tatibus!" Homer waved back, but he didn't try to repeat the word. It would take more practice. Dog barked his good-bye as the motorboat sped off toward the mainland.

Lorelei stood at the water's edge, a spaced-out look on her face. She ran a hand over her pink hair. "What's a humongous fungus?" she asked.

Homer had been trying to figure out the same thing. "Sounds like a really big mushroom."

"It does sound like a really big mushroom." Her eyes nearly popped out of her freckled face. "A really, really big mushroom. Maybe even as big as a—"

"As a blue whale," Homer said.

"How did the riddle go?"

Homer recited, "If ever you meet a mycologist, a spore-loving, fungal find-ologist, he'll tell you a tale, blue whale in scale, that is sure to best a biologist."

Lorelei laughed and grabbed Homer's arm. "I get it. Do you get it? A fungus is a living thing, right? So if there was a fungus as big as a blue whale—"

"Then a mycologist would have a better tale to tell than a biologist." Homer also laughed. They'd solved the riddle. The Humongous Fungus was the answer.

Lorelei stopped laughing and let go of Homer's arm. "But where is it? We went to the X. X marks the spot. Isn't that the rule? X is supposed to mark the spot."

But Homer knew that wasn't true. And Lord Mockingbird, a lifelong mapmaker, would also know that wasn't true. X was a deliberate decoy. Lord Mockingbird had wanted them to find Gertrude's stash of crystals: But why? And why had he hidden the coin in a different place? "Come on, Dog," he said as he picked up the end of Dog's leash.

"Where are you going?"

"I'm going to look for a very big mushroom, and you're not following me this time." He pointed to the cave's doorway where Daisy the rat was rolling the compass around like a toy. "I'm no longer wearing your tracking device."

"But you have Dog. That's not fair," Lorelei called as Homer and Dog climbed along the rocky ridge. "Can't we do this together? We make such a good team."

"I don't trust you," Homer said. "I'll never trust you again."

Another horn sounded out on the water and a large boat appeared. Crammed with people in flowered shirts and sunglasses, the boat rocked side to side as it puttered past. Big letters across the stern read: TERRY TOUR'S TOURS. A voice boomed over the boat's loudspeaker. "Ladies and gentlemen, we hope you are enjoying your Terry Tour's Tour today. The third stop on our tour is only a few minutes away. While gigantic fungi can be found in other locations throughout the world, this one is currently the largest on record." The boat disappeared around the island.

Homer and Lorelei broke into a run.

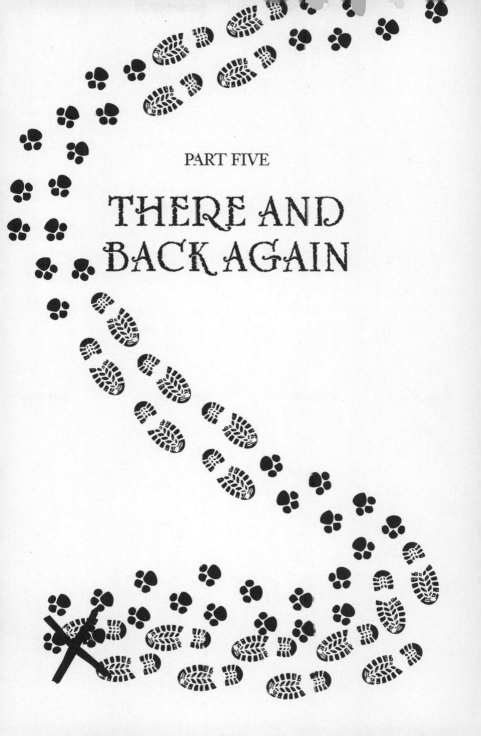

PART FIVE

THERE AND
BACK AGAIN

36

Rumpold Smeller
the Boy, Part VII

Rumpoldena sat outside her brother's bedroom
door.

She held a piece of parchment and gazed at it
with wonder. The delicate lines and shadows of the anthill were more beautiful than any pillow she'd ever
embroidered. How many pillows had she made in her
twelve years? How many would she make if she lived to
be an old woman? If she lined all those pillows up on her
ninetieth birthday, would they stretch all the way to
the sea?

Two months had passed since her brother had been sent into the forest to draw a map. Two days after his departure, his horse had returned to the castle. Wild-eyed and foaming at the mouth, the horse's flank bore ominous claw marks. The horse had escaped a bear attack, but it had returned without its rider.

Duke Smeller had sent his hunters out to track Rumpold. They found the bear prints in the soft forest floor. They found the signs of the horse's escape. But they found no signs of Rumpold. No signs that he'd been killed, but also no signs that he'd survived.

And so they feared the worst. "I will never forgive you!" the duchess had screamed at her husband. "My son is gone and it is your fault."

"The shame is mine to endure," the duke had said, hanging his head. "My only son will never be a Teutonic knight. The dreams I had for him will never come true."

But then, after two long months of grief, Rumpoldena sat at her bedroom window and heard someone call her name. She looked down into the courtyard. There stood her brother, waving. She rubbed her eyes. Had his ghost come for a visit? "Rumpold?" she called.

"I did it," he said, holding up a bundle of papers. "I did it." And then he crumpled into a heap on the cobblestones.

Though half-starved, he'd survived. His clothing in

tatters, his body gaunt and weak, he'd survived. Duke Smeller had never looked so proud. He strode the hallways of the castle. "He did it!" he told everyone. He sent messages to the other knights. "My son finished his quest. He's drawn a map of our forest." Not only that, but he'd drawn pictures of rabbits and sparrows, wild honeysuckle and buttercups. Bubbling brooks and weeping willows.

No one was supposed to disturb Rumpold while he recovered. Those were the orders of the physician and the duchess. But Rumpoldena was sick of orders. She sat outside the bedroom, looking at the drawing of the anthill, waiting for her parents and the physician to leave her brother's room.

Her parents emerged first. The duchess stood and faced her husband, her hands planted on her hips. "My son has done what you asked. But do not think that I will allow you to force him into that secret society of yours. He will never become a Teutonic knight. Never! And I will never allow you to send him away again."

"Allow?" the duke said with a sputter.

She wagged a finger in his face. "Do not forget that the royal bloodline comes from my side of the family. Cross me on this, and I shall write to my father!"

"But, my dear," the duke said, his voice softening.

"What about the honor of this family? How can I have a son who is not a member of the knighthood? What will he do?"

"He'll draw," she said. "That's what he'll do. He'll draw whatever he likes, and you won't say one word about it." And she turned on her heels and stomped off toward the women's quarters. The duke, his shoulders hunched, headed in the opposite direction. Neither had noticed their daughter.

After the physician had left, Rumpoldena crept into her brother's room and stood by his bed. A tray of cookies and pastries sat on his nightstand, ready to fatten him up. His face was as pale as moonlight. "Hi," he said, smiling weakly

"Hi." She held out the parchment. "I like your drawing." Then she sat on the bed. "How did you survive the bear?"

"I climbed a tree," he said, his voice raspy. "The bear followed the horse, and I never saw it again."

"We thought you were dead."

"I'm sorry." He closed his eyes for a moment. "I'm still pretty tired. The physician says I need to stay in bed a few more days."

"You don't have to be a knight," she said. "I heard Mother and Father talking about it."

His eyes flew open. "Really?" She told him what she'd

heard. With much effort, Rumpold sat up. "I don't have to be a Teutonic knight? That's great news. And I can draw?" His sister nodded. "You know," he said, leaning back against his pillows, "except for having to survive on my own, I kind of liked drawing that map. Maybe I'll make more maps."

Rumpoldena walked to the window and looked out over the castle wall. "Father will leave you alone now. He won't expect anything of you."

The door flew open. "There you are," a maidservant said. "Your mother is looking for you. She wants you in the women's quarters right away. You have work to do on your pillow."

"I'll be right there," Rumpoldena snapped. "Leave us."

The maidservant left.

If Rumpoldena had learned one thing while living in the shadows and pushing the needle into the fabric over and over, it was this—that life could be just like a piece of needlepoint. That the girl with the needle could fit the little stitches tidily inside the lines that had already been drawn onto the fabric, or she could ignore the lines altogether, turn the fabric over and create her own pattern.

Rumpoldena returned to her brother's bed. She knelt beside it and leaned close to his face. "I want to leave this place," she whispered. "I can't stand it here."

He turned his head. "Leave?"

"I don't want to sit in the women's quarters for the rest of my life. I'll go crazy. I want to do something else."

"Like what?"

"I don't know." She fiddled with her hair ribbon. "Maybe I'll hike up a mountain. Or maybe I'll ride a camel across the desert. Or maybe I'll sail the seven seas."

"Like a pirate?"

"Yes. Like a pirate. Maybe I'll become a pirate and then I can go wherever I want to go and do whatever I want to do." She reached into her bodice and pulled out a small bag. "I stole these coins from Father's desk. I can use these to buy myself a ship and a crew."

Rumpold nodded. "I almost ran away." Then he reached out slowly and took his sister's hand. His grip was weak, but the look in his eyes was steely. "In my charcoal case."

The case sat in the corner. Rumpoldena opened it and found another bag, heavy with coins. "Take it," Rumpold said. His eyelids fluttered.

As her brother drifted back into a deep sleep, Rumpoldena sat at the mirror and pulled the ribbon from her hair. Then she began to cut. Clump after blond clump fell away. She changed into her brother's best clothes—a long-sleeved white shirt, a vest, and a gold-buttoned jacket. The britches fit after she'd tied the waist with a

cord, and the boots fit once she'd tucked a few handker-
chiefs inside. She found a small knife that Rumpold
never used. She tucked it, along with the two bags of
coins, into a leather satchel. She rolled up the anthill
drawing and tucked it into the leather satchel as well.
"Good-bye. I'll never forget you." Then she kissed her
brother's damp forehead. "And if I ever need a treasure
map, I'll let you know."

Down the stairs she ran, past servants who gasped and
said, "Rumpold's recovered." She didn't say good-bye to
anyone else. She didn't look over her shoulder or shed
a tear.

What she did shed, however, was her old self.

37

The Membership Coin

It made no sense for Lorelei to try to outrun Homer. What could she do without Dog? A gold coin stuck somewhere in a mushroom bigger than a blue whale could take days to find. That's why Lorelei trotted alongside Homer, her backpack bouncing with each step, the crystals singing from inside the clue box. Daisy soon caught up, then scampered ahead.

Homer could see Lorelei's beaming smile from the corner of his eye, but he didn't look at her. If he looked directly at her, she might detect his fear. And he feared more than anything that he would lose the quest. She was faster, nimbler, more athletic in every way. If she grabbed the coin first, Homer would disappoint Zelda and Ajitabh, his uncle's dearest friends. But most of all, he'd disappoint himself.

Terry Tour's tour boat dropped anchor in a small cove. Harbor seals poked their gray heads from the calm water, watching the boat with aloof curiosity. The tourists, binoculars in hand, gathered on the shore side of the boat, which tipped precariously close to the water.

"Ladies and gentlemen, welcome to the Humongous Fungus," the loudspeaker voice said.

"Where is it? Where is it?" the tourists shouted, pointing their binoculars toward a large clearing where no trees grew. Kids jumped up and down with excitement.

"The Humongous Fungus grows on this side of Mushroom Island beneath the forest floor, so it is not visible to the eye," the loudspeaker voice said.

A deep groan filled the air as the tourists let the binoculars fall to their sides.

The loudspeaker voice cleared his throat. "But even though you can't see the fungus, we guarantee that it is there."

The tourists looked at one another and shrugged.

"Ladies and gentlemen, the next stop on our tour is the Magical White Rock of Bird Island, a rock covered with so much seagull poop that it has actually turned white."

"Oooh," the tourists said, applauding excitedly as the tour boat turned around and puttered out of the cove.

Homer and Lorelei crept from their hiding place behind a tree, where Dog had been going berserk. Sniffing the air, he eagerly pumped his back legs, but Homer held him firmly in place, waiting for the boat to drive out of sight. No one needed to witness the treasure-smelling dog in action. Lorelei dropped her backpack and rolled up her striped sleeves. "Watch my stuff," she told Daisy. The rat obediently settled on top of the backpack and began to groom her tail.

Dog grunted and pulled. "Ur, ur, ur, ur." He strained against the collar as Homer took slow steps forward. Lorelei matched each of his steps.

"You might as well give up," she said. "You can't beat me. I'm faster than you."

He knew her strategy—it was to freak him out and thus weaken him. He'd been on the receiving end of this strategy many times in his life. Earl, the boy at school, used the strategy every time he wanted to get something from Homer. "See this muscle in my arm, Homer?" he'd say. "I've been practicing on a punching bag. I'm getting real good. Oops, you dropped your doughnut. Guess it belongs to me now."

"There's no way you'll grab the coin before I grab it," Lorelei said. "So just give up and save yourself the embarrassment."

"Just watch," Homer said, gritting his teeth. He held tight to the leash as they inched across the clearing. "You'll be the one who's embarrassed." Then he stumbled backward as the leash suddenly went limp. "DOG!" he yelled. Dog had pulled so hard that the collar had snapped. Free, he galloped across the open space, his tongue hanging out of his mouth, rolls of skin undulating like a belly dancer's stomach.

The coin is mine! Homer regained his balance, but just as he took a step forward, Lorelei stuck out her leg and tripped him. Nothing Lorelei did shocked Homer, not anymore. That's why, before he landed face-first on the ground, he reached out and grabbed her pant leg, pulling her down with him.

"Ow!" Lorelei cried, landing on her shoulder. Homer spat out some pine needles. Then he threw himself across Lorelei's back, pinning her like a wiggling insect to a science board. "Get off me! You're killing me!" Lorelei kicked her legs.

"No. You can't have the coin."

As Homer sat on Lorelei, Dog skidded to a stop in the center of the clearing. He flipped onto his back and began to roll. *This is it*, Homer thought. *The end of the quest.* He blocked one of Lorelei's flailing legs. He and Dog hadn't survived the coliseum, a jump from an airplane, a mosquito attack, and a hungry grizzly bear for nothing. This was the final measure of his strength and character. Could he outmaneuver his opponent? Could he outwit her? Maybe not, but he certainly outweighed her, and he wasn't going to let her get one inch closer to Dog.

Dog would find the coin and faithfully bring it to him. Homer's fingers twitched as he imagined holding the coin once again. The first time he'd held it had been the day Dog arrived at Pudding Goat Farm. Homer had found the coin hanging from Dog's collar. Today, he'd hold it up to the sky, the sunlight dancing along its face, and proclaim, "I am Homer Winslow Pudding, and this is my membership coin."

"Let me go!" Lorelei cried, trying to twist around and punch him.

"No. That's my coin, Lorelei, and you know it."

Dog rubbed his back against the soft ground, groaning happily as he covered himself with the scent of treasure. Being the only scent he knew, it appeared to have a hypnotic power over him—in much the same way that a single color in a world of black and white would be difficult, if not impossible, to ignore.

Dog rolled onto his feet and began to dig. "Good

boy," Homer called, blocking Lorelei's jabbing elbow. "Stop it, Lorelei. I'm not letting you go until I have the coin."

Lying in his room at night, staring at the maps on his ceiling, Homer had long imagined the moment when he would uncover a great treasure. He'd wanted it to be exactly like the moment when Gustav Gustavson had found Aphrodite's toothbrush. The moment had been captured in a grainy black-and-white photo. Gustav had stood in his adventurer clothes next to the ruins of an ancient temple. His feet wide-set, his chin jutting proudly, he'd held the artifact above his head as if offering it to the universe. The words he'd spoken were known by treasure hunters worldwide—as significant as those words spoken when man first stepped on the moon. "I have unearthed a treasure, and even though I don't yet know what it is, I'm fairly confident that it's important."

Homer wanted to say something just as memorable— something that would be quoted for generations. And he'd always imagined himself in the same bold stance, in his adventure gear, holding his treasure above his head.

Not sitting on a girl.

"I...can't...breathe," Lorelei gasped.

"If you're talking, then you're breathing," Homer said. Quick movement caught his eye as Daisy hopped off the backpack and scampered across the clearing. A thief by nature, she circled around Dog as he dug, her nose wiggling excitedly. "Get away, Daisy!" Homer yelled. How was he supposed to keep both Lorelei and Daisy away from the coin?

Dirt flew as Dog broke through the top layer of soil. How far down did the Humongous Fungus grow? His tail wagging, Dog worked his stubby front legs like a speed skater.

"I...can't...breathe," Lorelei whispered. "Get..." And then she stopped squirming and went limp.

Homer folded his arms. "I'm not falling for your tricks." But Lorelei lay perfectly still. Her chest didn't rise or fall. Homer narrowed his eyes. He couldn't squish a person to death, could he? "Lorelei," he said, sliding off her back. "Are you okay?"

In a blur of jeans and stripes, Lorelei shot up and raced toward Dog before Homer had blinked. "Sucker!" she cried, halfway to Dog as Homer struggled to his feet.

It was a race of life or death—at least that's how it felt to Homer. Forcing his legs to move the way they'd never moved before, summoning strength from muscles he didn't even know existed, he dashed after Lorelei. She reached Dog's side and fell on her knees. Her hands flying alongside Dog, she dug. Homer grabbed her by the sneaker and pulled her a few feet away from the hole.

She kicked him in the chest, then crawled back to the hole. "Where is it?" she cried. "Daisy, help me find it."

Homer grabbed her by the shoe again and just as she kicked, the shoe slid off and he tumbled backward. Fury burned through his entire body. Lorelei kept digging, her pink hair coated with bits of forest floor, her face streaked with dirt, her eyes wild.

Homer tossed the shoe aside, clenched his jaw, balled up his fist, and...

And froze, his fist hovering just above Lorelei's back.

38

Cave Woman

Homer Winslow Pudding unclenched his fist and stepped back. Shame, hot and prickly, stung his cheeks. His uncle's voice spoke clearly in his mind.

Even the most noble treasure hunter can go bad.

"What am I doing?" he whispered. He'd almost hurt another person just to get to a treasure. And that other person was a girl, which made it worse. There was nothing courageous, or noble, or justifiable, about hitting a girl.

He walked away.

He walked away from the digging and sat on the crest of the beach, where the rocky shore turned sandy. His arms wrapped around his knees, he looked out at the quiet cove. A harbor seal popped its head out of the water. A seagull flew past and dropped a clam, which burst open on a rock. The afternoon sun warmed Homer's face and arms. The Humongous Fungus had chosen a beautiful place to grow.

"He found it!" Lorelei cried from the clearing. "He found the coin."

Though the temptation was great, Homer didn't turn around. He wasn't going to fight her. He'd made his decision.

"Give it here!" she yelled.

As Lorelei chased after Dog, the seagull landed and ate the yellow clam meat. Homer picked up a rock and tossed it into the shallows. It had all come down to this— wanting something wasn't enough. How he went about getting the thing he wanted, well, that was everything.

A shriek pierced Homer's ears. "No! Oh no! He ate it!" Lorelei stomped over to Homer and looked down at him, her hands on her hips. "Did you hear me? He ate it."

"Urrrr." Dog pushed his way onto Homer's lap, his tail wagging.

"What?"

Lorelei's face erupted as every pore turned bright red.

"He ate it." She grimaced, her nostrils flaring to twice their size. "I'm telling you, your dog ate the coin."

"He ate the coin?"

Dog's tail whapped against the sand. Then he burped. Homer opened Dog's mouth and looked inside. "You ate the coin?" he asked. Dog licked Homer's hand.

That was a turn of events most unexpected. Laughter burst out of Homer. For the first time ever, he was grateful that Dog liked to eat weird things. "He ate it," he said, belly laughing as he lay back onto the sand. Dog scooted close to Homer's face. "You ate it. You ate it!"

"It's not funny, Homer." Lorelei stomped her foot. "It's not one bit funny."

Dog licked Homer's face, then rested his chin on Homer's chest. Homer wrapped his arms over Dog's back and squeezed. "He ate it," he said, snorting with laughter.

Then a very odd thing happened, even more unexpected than Dog eating the membership coin. A quiet snicker crept out of Lorelei's mouth. Then another snicker, and another, until she was laughing, too.

She sank onto the sand next to Homer, then onto her back. And there they lay, side by side, laughing. A boy in a green shirt, khaki shorts, leech-proof socks, and boots. A girl in jeans, a black-and-white-striped shirt, and one sneaker. Just a couple of kids with a droopy dog stretched between them. They let the laughter work its way through their bodies, expelling all the emotion of the day's adventure. Then quiet fell over them.

"You know what you're going to have to do to get that coin," Lorelei said.

"Yeah, I know," Homer said. But picking through dog poop was nothing compared with what he'd been through. Down the beach, another seagull dropped a clam. "But *you* know what? I might not fight you for treasure, but I won't let you take Dog. Not ever again."

"I know that," she said. "Just so you know, I didn't take him. I borrowed him. There's a difference."

"Yeah, well, if you *borrow* him again, our gentleman's agreement is over." Homer sat up. "You get that? I will break my promise to you and tell the world about your secret lair."

Lorelei also sat up. "I thought you believed in promises and oaths and stuff like that."

"I do. But you're the one who said you don't have to stick to anything you don't want to stick to, remember?"

Lorelei nodded. A shoelace in her teeth, Daisy dragged the tennis shoe to Lorelei's side. "So what's next?" Lorelei asked as she pulled the shoe onto her foot.

"What do you mean?"

"I mean, you got the coin. You won the challenge. Now that you are a member of L.O.S.T., what are you going to do?"

"I'm going to go home and go back to school," Homer said.

"That's it?"

"That's it for now. But that's not it forever." He scratched Dog behind an ear. "I'm still going to look for Rumpold Smeller's treasure, just like my uncle did. But I'll probably have to wait a few years."

"Why would you have to wait a few years? You'll have L.O.S.T. to help you."

Homer shrugged. "Maybe I won't have to wait. I'm not sure what will happen."

"Well, I'm going back to the lair and I'm making some big plans. I'm gonna sell those harmonic crystals right away and buy a few things."

"What kind of things?"

"I'm not telling you that. If I told you, then you'd have too many secrets on me." She tied her laces. "But I did decide something important."

"What?"

"I'm not going to make up a last name for myself. Just because I'm an orphan doesn't mean I'm nobody. I came from somebody and one day I'm going to find out who, and then I'll have a last name."

Dog turned his face toward the horizon. The sound of a motor skipped into the cove. The seals darted underwater. Lorelei jumped to her feet and shielded her eyes with her hand. "It's a yacht. A huge yacht."

An enormous white boat turned into the cove. But it was not a Terry Tour's tour boat, and no tourists hung over the railing. Homer pushed Dog from his lap and stood. The name *Cave Woman II* was painted on the boat's stern. "Dr. Magnum's got another yacht," Homer said.

"Uh-oh," Lorelei said. She scooped Daisy into her hand, then ran across the clearing and grabbed her backpack. "I'm not giving these crystals back." She shoved her arms through the straps. The crystals played a muted song from deep inside the backpack. "I'm not leaving this stupid island empty-handed."

As the boat neared, the figure of a large woman in a floppy hat came into focus. She stood on deck. A smallish man in a black top hat stood next to her. "Lord Mockingbird," Homer whispered. Standing along the rail was a man in a cowboy hat, a man with a gray beard and mustache, and a young woman with a hawk on her shoulder. "Jeremiah Carson, Professor Thaddius Thick, and Torch," Homer said. Zelda stood at the bow like a silver masthead. They'd come to see who had won the quest.

Homer hurried across the clearing to Lorelei's side. Then he pushed her toward the woods. "You'd better go. If Dr. Magnum hears the crystals inside your backpack, I don't know what will happen."

Lorelei looked at Homer and smiled. "You're not going to tell on me?"

His chest still ached from where she'd kicked him. But the fight was over. Lorelei hadn't won the quest, but she'd have enough money to buy the things she wanted. Maybe that would make her happy. Maybe she would feel the same kind of happiness that Homer felt knowing that his uncle's coin was his, once and for all. "I won't tell on you."

Before he turned away, she wrapped her arms around his waist and squeezed. It may have been the quickest hug in the history of the world, but it was a hug nonetheless. "See ya, Homer," she said. "See ya, Dog." Then she ran off, her rat clinging to her shoulder.

Homer watched as her pink hair disappeared into the greens and browns of the forest.

"Urrrr." Dog pushed against Homer's shin.

"You're gonna miss her, aren't you?" Homer said. Dog wagged his tail. "Well, I'm not." But Homer turned one last time, hoping to catch sight of the pink hair and freckled face.

Lord Mockingbird's top hat bobbed as a rowboat approached the shore. Dr. Gertrude Magnum dropped the oars, then stepped out of the boat and into the shallows. "Hello, Homer," she said with a friendly smile. The hem of her white nautical dress soaked up the salt water as, with a heave, she pulled the boat onto the beach. Diamonds sparkled from around her neck. Emeralds glinted on her fingers. "His Lordship ordered the others to stay on the yacht," she explained. "He wanted to speak to you in private."

Dog loped to the side of the rowboat. Gertrude bent to pat his head. Dog pointed his nose at Lord Mockingbird, his tail wagging. Lord Mockingbird paid him no mind. He sat on the boat's bench seat, picking at a muffin and mumbling incoherently.

"I've never been to this island," Gertrude said, adjusting her floppy hat. Everything she wore sparkled, even her eye shadow. Homer now understood why her hands were stained. How long had it taken her to dig all those booby traps around her cave? "It looks like a nice island." She blinked quickly. "Was that the girl, just now, running off into the woods? Did she find the coin?"

"I found the coin," Homer said.

A scowl passed across Gertrude's face, but she quickly replaced it with a sickly sweet smile. "Congratulations. Did you hear that, Lord Mockingbird? Drake's nephew is triumphant." She tapped her soggy shoe on a rock. "My, my, aren't you a lucky boy?" She reached out to pat Homer's head, but he stepped away. "A *very* lucky boy."

"I've been bamboozled," His Lordship said, shaking the muffin in the air. "Hornswoggled! These muffins are polluted with raisins."

Gertrude looked in the direction of her cave. "Since I've never been to this island, I think I'll take a little walk." She grabbed her purse from the rowboat. "You two have much to discuss. I'll be back before you can even miss me." And off she went, down the beach, her purse swinging from her wrist.

Lord Mockingbird dropped the muffin onto the rowboat floor, then screwed up his face as if he were about to have a stroke, or maybe it was gas from the raisins. "Are you okay?" Homer asked.

His Lordship's bloodshot eyes darted right, then left. He sat so hunched, his shoulders were practically in his lap. "Is that nincompoop gone?"

"Who?" Homer asked.

"The cave woman. Is she gone?"

Dr. Magnum, who had power-walked her way to the end of the cove, darted around its bend. "Yes, she's gone."

Lord Mockingbird cleared his throat, then sat up straight. He reached into his waistcoat pocket and pulled out a set of teeth, which he popped into his mouth. As he set his top hat aside, a little smile pushed up his wrinkled cheeks. He patted the other rowboat bench, and when he next spoke, it was not in a feeble, confused voice but in a voice of strength and clarity. "Get in, young man. We have much to discuss."

39
Lord Mockingbird's Secret

With a grunt, Homer heaved Dog into the rowboat, then climbed in after. The boat rocked back and forth on the shore as Homer settled onto the bench facing Lord Mocking-bird. Dog immediately ate the muffin, paper cup and all. Then he poked His Lordship's leg with his nose, his tail wagging as if he'd found another piece of treasure. Lord Mockingbird stretched out his hand. "Good boy," he said, rubbing Dog's nose. "I've missed you."

Homer thought that an odd thing to say, seeing as His

Lordship had only met Dog the one time at the membership meeting in Zelda's kitchen.

"How is he doing?" Lord Mockingbird asked, his voice still crisp and understandable. "Are you making certain he doesn't eat anything strange or poisonous? Are you keeping his secret? You haven't told anyone, have you?"

Homer blinked, then blinked again as he reworked the questions in his mind. It was odd enough that His Lordship was no longer spitting out those strange little words, but now he was acting as if he knew all about Dog. "I'm not sure what you mean."

"Of course you're sure what I mean." His Lordship stopped petting Dog and pointed a withered finger at Homer. "Have you told anyone that your dog can smell treasure?"

Homer stifled a gasp. Trying to hold back his surprise, he folded his arms. "I still don't know what you mean. My dog can't smell anything."

"Your dog can smell treasure. I know this to be true because your dog used to be my dog."

"He did?" Homer's arms dropped to his sides. He'd often wondered about Dog's past. Dog and Lord Mockingbird knew each other? Is that why Dog had been so happy to see the old man when they were in Zelda's kitchen? "Are you the one who gave him to my uncle?"

Dog circled twice, then lay on the floor between their feet. Lord Mockingbird glanced down the beach in the direction of Dr. Magnum's secret cave. She was nowhere to be seen. He leaned closer to Homer. "One day when I was out for a morning stroll, I came upon a man on the sidewalk. He'd set up one of those guessing games with three overturned cups. He placed a gold coin beneath one of the cups, then shuffled the cups quickly. The object of the game was to find the coin with one guess. A correct guess won the coin beneath the cup plus the coin it cost to play the game. A bad guess forfeited both coins."

"I've seen that game," Homer said.

"The man had a dog by his side, a very droopy, very sad-looking dog that hadn't been bathed in quite some time and was suffering from a flea infestation. The dog, with nothing better to do, scratched himself and watched the game. Each time someone guessed incorrectly, the dog would sniff at the correct cup. The man, a dreadful creature with a sloping brow and rotten teeth, did not notice the amazing ability of his dog, but instead grew annoyed by the dog's behavior and pushed him away." Lord Mockingbird pressed his fingertips together and smiled. "But I noticed. So I bought the dog for a fair sum, took him home, cleaned him up, and made my plans for my next quest."

Though the story sounded plausible, Homer still did not admit to Dog's talent. "What happened then?"

Lord Mockingbird's smile faded. "I fell ill. I didn't leave my bed for many long months." He pulled up the sleeves on his black jacket and held out his forearms. "Do you see these? Do you see how thin they are? I may be clear-headed, but my body is as brittle as a dried twig. It is a tragedy when a man's age catches up with him." He pulled his sleeves back into place. "I realized that my treasure-hunting days had come to an end, as had my plans for the dog. So I gave him to the person I trusted most in our organization. Your uncle. And now I ask you again, Homer. Have you told anyone Dog's secret?"

"No," Homer said. "I haven't told anyone. But one person guessed."

"The girl?"

Homer nodded.

Lord Mockingbird sighed. A clamshell dropped from the sky and landed a few feet away. Dog darted to his feet and looked around. Lord Mockingbird narrowed his small eyes. "You must keep the secret. Dog must not fall into the wrong hands."

"I know," Homer said. "I am keeping the secret." He pulled Dog close. "I won't let anyone take him." *Not ever again.*

This seemed to satisfy Lord Mockingbird because he

clapped his hands together and smiled again. "Good. And you've chosen a fine name for him. Funny, but I never got around to naming him. I was so sick and all that." He shifted on the seat. "Now, let us get to the business at hand before the rest of them swim to shore to congratulate you."

Homer looked over Lord Mockingbird's shoulder. Torch lounged in a deck chair sipping a drink. Professor Thick and Jeremiah Carson sat at a table, playing cards. But Zelda stood like a statue, watching the rowboat.

"And before that horrid woman returns from her cave."

"You know about her cave?" Homer asked.

"Yes, of course I know. I may be over-the-hill, but these eyes can still see and these ears can still hear. And the mind knows what the mind knows."

"Your Lordship," Homer said. "Why do you pretend to be . . . confused?"

"I pretend to be feebleminded, young man, because people expect someone of my advanced years to be feebleminded and, therefore, believing I am a fool, they tend to talk about all sorts of things in my presence. And I've learned many things." He tapped his temple. "Many things. That's how I knew about the cave. And about the grizzly. Did the honey bear come in handy?"

"Yes," Homer said. "Thank you." Then he wondered

if His Lordship deserved a thank-you. It's nice to give someone a honey bear so that someone can fend off a grizzly. On the other hand, it's not so nice to send someone into a situation where that someone is going to have to FEND OFF A GRIZZLY!

Lord Mockingbird folded his arms. "Dr. Magnum is insufferably greedy."

"If you know that Dr. Magnum is bad, why don't you kick her out?"

"She hasn't broken her oath. She hoarded those harmonic crystals before she joined our secret organization. But one day she will break her oath, mark my words. She will show her true self to the world. It always happens that way. One's true self cannot be hidden forever. It will fight to be set free."

Slowly, Homer began to understand. "You wanted me to find the cave. That's why you marked the spot with an *X*."

"Indeed. And you passed the test."

The *X* had been a test. The cave itself had been a test. "You wanted to see if I'd take the crystals," Homer said. Lord Mockingbird nodded. "I didn't take any."

"I know that. You'd be making music if you'd taken any crystals."

Homer continued to put the pieces together. "You marked the cave on the map so I would find it. But you and I both know that 'X marks the spot' isn't usually true. So how did you know that I'd go to the X?"

"I figured that because you knew that I knew that you knew that 'X marks the spot' isn't usually true, you'd think I put it there to confuse you and so you'd have to check it out."

"Oh." Homer screwed up his face, trying to follow that logic. "So you marked the cave so I would find it, but you didn't mark the coin's hiding place because you knew that Dog would find it."

"Correct. Speaking of the coin, where is it?"

Homer looked down at Dog, who was once again lying on the floor of the boat. "He ate it."

Lord Mockingbird grunted. "That's going to prove a bit of a mess for you, but I am not concerned. As long as the coin is in your possession, which it is since Dog belongs to you, then I proclaim you the winner of this quest and the rightful inheritor of Drake Pudding's chair."

Homer wanted to live in that moment forever. He wanted to hug Lord Mockingbird, but he didn't, afraid that the old man might break into pieces. So he reached out and shook his hand. "Thank you," he said. "Thank you so much."

"You're most welcome."

Homer leaned forward, resting his elbows on his knees.

"Dr. Magnum tried to scare me," he told His Lordship. "She dressed up as a fortune-teller and told me that treasure hunting would kill me."

"It might kill you," His Lordship said. "That's a risk you'll have to take."

"And then she pretended to be a writer and told me that treasure hunting would make me miserable."

"It might. Look at Torch. She's unequivocally miserable."

"Why was she trying to scare me? Why doesn't she want me to join L.O.S.T.?"

Lord Mockingbird raised his eyebrows. "Because Dr. Gertrude Magnum wants to take my place as the president of L.O.S.T. As soon as I'm gone, she wants to change the philosophy of our little organization. Like her friend Madame la Directeur, Dr. Magnum is driven by greed. So she'd like to fill your uncle's chair with someone who's like-minded. Not with another honorable and honest Pudding."

Dog suddenly barked. "Drat. Here she comes," Lord Mockingbird said as Dr. Magnum hurried around the bend at the end of the cove. "I must speak quickly." He grabbed Homer by the shoulders. "I shan't be around forever. Who knows when my time will come, so I want you to know something."

"What?" Homer asked.

"You remember how I said that the true self will always reveal itself?" Homer nodded. "You revealed your true spirit on this quest. You are the future of L.O.S.T. I am happy to know that Drake's chair has been filled by someone who will truly keep the spirit of L.O.S.T. alive." Lord Mockingbird looked deep into Homer's eyes.

"I will," Homer said. "I will keep the spirit of L.O.S.T. alive."

Dr. Gertrude Magnum stomped up to the rowboat and stuck her reddened, sweaty face right in Homer's. "What have you done?" she said. "WHAT. HAVE. YOU. DONE?" She grabbed Homer by the collar of his green shirt. "Where are they?"

"Where are what?" Homer asked, trying to sound innocent.

She couldn't, of course, answer that question. Her chins shook with rage. "You know, don't you? You little brat. Where have you put them?"

"I don't know what you're talking about," Homer said, pulling out of her grip.

Lord Mockingbird shoved his teeth into his pocket. "What's the hoopla?" he said with a grumble. "Get me a muffin."

"I can hear the crystals," Gertrude said, pointing a finger at Homer. "I can hear them."

"What crystals?" Homer asked innocently. But he could also hear the music.

Gertrude stepped away from the rowboat. A soft crystal melody filled the air. She stumbled over a rock as her head whipped left, then right. "What's that?" she asked, spit flying from her mouth. "Where's that coming from?" The sound grew louder as a small puffy cloud appeared directly overhead.

"It's a hootenanny," Lord Mockingbird said, tapping his toes.

"It's a cloudcopter," Gertrude snarled. She pointed her finger at the sky. "That's Zelda's cloudcopter. The music is coming from Zelda's cloudcopter." She jumped up and down, her face going as red as a radish. "The girl! The girl took them." She stomped around in a full circle. "She took all of them!"

Homer stifled a laugh. Lorelei must have gone back to the cave and taken the rest of the crystals.

"Who took what?" Lord Mockingbird asked. "The muffins? Did she take the muffins?"

Gertrude stopped stomping. She inhaled a long, angry breath. The music faded as the cloudcopter flew toward the horizon. Then Gertrude turned slowly and glared at Homer. She ran her hand along her diamond necklace and forced her face into a smile. "Yes, Your Lordship, that's right. She took the muffins."

Lord Mockingbird plunked his top hat onto his head. "You're a bumble-headed nuisance, Gertrude. Back to the ship. The whippersnapper and his droopy dog are coming, too."

"And why is that?" Gertrude asked.

"Because we are going to escort them home."

"But Baldwin was going to come back and get me," Homer said.

"The namby-pamby kid's butler?" Lord Mockingbird grunted. "We'll radio him. Tell him it's not necessary. Now shove off!"

Gertrude leaned against the end of the rowboat. With a grunt, she pushed it back into the water. Homer moved to Lord Mockingbird's bench as Gertrude climbed aboard. "I'm the newest member of L.O.S.T.," Homer told her.

"That's got to be the most wonderful thing I've ever heard," she said as she clenched her teeth. She grabbed the oars. "Another Pudding in the membership."

"Not pudding," Lord Mockingbird said, smacking his lips. "Muffins, not pudding."

The summer sun danced on the water as they moved toward the yacht called *Cave Woman II*. A harbor seal swam toward the rowboat, pushing something through the water with its nose. "Hey, it's my backpack." Homer reached over the side and pulled his backpack out of the water. He hugged it to his chest, not caring one bit that it was soaking wet. After all, Mr. Tuffletop, who was a visionary in his field, had designed Homer's adventurer clothing to be sunproof, bladeproof, *and* waterproof.

"Have you ever had your fortune told?" Homer asked. Gertrude said nothing. "I did once, by this guy named Excelsior. He told me that I had a treasure hunter's line on my hand."

"That is so very interesting," Gertrude said, rowing faster.

"It was interesting."

"I suppose you think this is the best day of your life," she said, her eyes blazing. She squeezed the oars until her hands turned completely white.

"One of the best," Homer said, beaming. "Definitely one of the best."

40

Back to Milkydale

I t is not necessary to go into all the messy details about how the membership coin was retrieved. Suffice it to say the world has made great advancements in sterilizing and deodorizing products. And once the coin was polished and hung from a chain, no one would have guessed that it had seen the inside of a basset hound.

On board the *Cave Woman II*, there were many congratulatory hugs from the L.O.S.T. membership. Zelda actually beamed with happiness. Torch even shook

Homer's hand. Professor Thick stuttered his congratulations, and Jeremiah Carson slapped Homer's back so hard that Homer thought his teeth might fly out.

Dog and Homer each ate an overflowing plateful of macaroni and cheese. Even though they were provided with two sleeping berths, they shared one and fell into a deep, welcome sleep. Once the yacht reached the mainland, Lord Mockingbird flew Homer, Dog, and Zelda back across the country in his private jet. "I sure hope I get my cloudcopter back," Zelda said.

During the plane ride, Homer changed into his farm clothes, carefully folding his professional adventurer clothes and hiding them at the bottom of his backpack. If Mr. Pudding saw the treasure-hunting clothes, he'd probably get upset. And if any of the kids from school saw the clothes, well, they'd surely laugh. Too bad he'd lost the Panama hat. Maybe Mr. Tuffletop would make him another. Homer tucked Dog's vest into the backpack, too. More secrets to be kept beneath his bed.

Before they parted at the train station—Zelda to head in the direction of Gloomy Moor, Homer and Dog to head back to Milkydale—Zelda knelt and scratched Dog's rump. "I'm so very sad that we must part," she said. "I do hate good-byes."

"When will I see you again?" Homer asked.

She pushed her silver hair from her eyes. "Most likely

we will reunite when you are ready to begin your next quest."

"You mean for Rumpold Smeller's treasure?" Zelda nodded. "When do you think I'll be ready?"

"I cannot answer that question. As you know, he was the most ruthless pirate who ever sailed the seven seas. His legend lives on because of his dubious deeds. And there are many who want to find his legendary treasure. You will need much preparation." She placed her oversize hand on his shoulder. "Your time will come, Homer."

And so it was that after a short ride on the local line, Homer and Dog arrived at the Milkydale depot on Saturday morning, one day earlier than expected. His entire body ached from the bumps and bruises of the week's adventures, so he was not looking forward to the walk home. After attaching Lorelei's blue leash to Dog's collar, they started down the road. The fairgrounds came into view. Nothing had changed. Kids screamed with glee as they did the loop-de-loop. Vendors hollered, advertising their wares. The tin can music of the Ferris wheel and the *oompa* of a brass band mixed together in melodic chaos. Life in Milkydale had gone on without Homer. His life as an adventurer was a secret, but he thought about how nice it would be to tell the world his story. To see amazement in the faces of his classmates when they learned that he'd become a member of a secret society. To see awe in their eyes when they learned that he'd jumped from an airplane. Was it wrong to want just a little bit of glory?

No. It was not wrong. It is a nice thing to be patted on the back every once in a while.

But Homer would not share his story. Not that day or any day in the near future. The safety of Dog depended on their adventure remaining a secret. And the promise he'd made to his uncle Drake—that he'd continue the search for Rumpold Smeller's treasure—was more important to Homer than a pat on the back. Or a town parade. Or an article in the newspaper.

"Hey, Homer, did you see the article in the newspaper?" someone yelled from across the parking lot. It was Twyla, the mail lady. She leaned out of her mail truck window.

"Hi, Twyla," Homer said.

"Lookey here," she said, shoving the newspaper in Homer's face.

And here is what it said on the front page:

PUDDING GUNNYSACK SLIDE IS A HIT

Last Sunday, this newspaper reported the loss of our beloved gunnysack slide—an almost unbearable tragedy following the burning of our library just three months earlier. Both disasters were entirely the fault of twelve-year-old Homer Pudding and his droopy dog.

But from tragedy comes triumph, for today a new gunnysack slide was unveiled. The builder of the new slide, a mysterious foreigner with an unpronounceable name, said, "By Jove, Homer Pudding is the very fellow you should be thanking. He asked me to build this great bloomin' contraption. He is a fine chap, that lad."

This editor has never laid eyes on a more magnificent piece of engineering than the new gunnysack slide. According to Mayor Sneed, Homer Pudding and his dog are no longer banned from the fair.

There was no doubt in Homer's mind who had built the slide. He knew only one person who said *by Jove*.

"Well, I'd better be going," Twyla said. "Got a few more stops to make, and then I'm going to try out the new slide." Her wandering eye did a loop-de-loop. "Oh, for your information, I just delivered your Map of the Month Club tube. It's waiting for you at home."

"Thanks," Homer said.

"See ya later." Twyla barely missed a garbage can as she drove off.

"Come on," Homer told Dog. Forgetting all about his bumps and bruises, he and Dog raced across the parking lot.

The Pudding Gunnysack Slide was indeed a wonder to behold. The old gunnysack slide had consisted of two steep sets of stairs and four identical slides, each with a little bump halfway down for extra excitement. But this new gunnysack slide, well, it appeared to be right out of a movie. The six slides were in no way identical. One looped around in a figure eight. Another shot the slider straight into the air like a cannon. The third zigged and zagged, the fourth bounced the slider off the sides like a pinball. The fifth went through a tunnel, and the sixth, the pièce de résistance, spun the slider in such a tight corkscrew that vomiting was absolutely guaranteed. And the entire thing was surrounded by a foam moat.

But what made Homer smile was not the magnificence of the new ride, but the person who stood next to it.

"Hello, Ajitabh," Homer said.

His uncle's dear friend grabbed Homer's hand and pulled him into a hug. "Homer," he said. "You have returned. I'm dreadfully sorry I wasn't here for the meeting. Family emergency and all that. But my father has recovered and all is well."

"I'm glad," Homer said. He pulled out the chain and held up the membership coin.

"Well done, lad," Ajitabh said, slapping Homer's back. "Well done indeed." He reached down and patted Dog. "And your hound, too. Well done." Then he stroked the ends of his mustache and gave Homer a long, concerned look. "You look like you've been to the ends of the earth and back."

Homer tucked the membership coin under his shirt. "I feel that way."

"You can tell me all about it later, when we've got some privacy. Those wouldn't happen to be leech-proof socks, would they?"

He'd forgotten to take off the socks, which were visible below the hems of his too-short jeans "Yep," Homer said proudly. "From Mr. Tuffletop."

A group of kids from Homer's school ran past, heading for the slide. "Hey, Homer," they called. A boy shot out of the tunnel and landed in the foam moat. Then he ran to a garbage can and vomited. "That is the best ride ever!" he hollered as he got back in line.

"Ajitabh, how did you do this?" Homer asked, shaking his head in wonder.

"Zelda called me and told me about your predicament," Ajitabh explained.

"Yeah, but how did you build it so quickly?"

"My dear boy, have you forgotten who I am?" Ajitabh put his hands on his hips. "I invented the cloudcopter. Building a gunnysack slide is as easy as making toast."

"Homer!" Mr. Pudding and Mrs. Pudding hurried to their son's side.

"You're home early," Mrs. Pudding said as she hugged Homer.

Max and Lulu, the farm dogs, licked Dog's face and sniffed him all over. Blue ribbons hung from their necks. "It was amazing," Mr. Pudding said. "I wish you could have seen it, Homer. They did right fine. Right fine."

"I wish I could have seen it, too," Homer said.

"And your mother won two blue ribbons for her pies. And your sister . . . well, I don't know what to think about your sister."

"She has a boyfriend. It's natural," Mrs. Pudding said. Mr. Pudding rolled his eyes. Mrs. Pudding kissed Homer's forehead, then kissed both his cheeks. "We missed you. How come you're so dirty? When's the last time you had a bath?"

"Stop pestering the boy. Boys get dirty when they go on camping trips," Mr. Pudding said. Then he winced. "But you don't exactly smell like a bed of flowers, son. Maybe we should get you home and into the tub."

Homer started to introduce his parents to Ajitabh.

"We've already met Mr. Ajitabh," Mr. Pudding said. "He's a genius. A genius. Would you look at that slide?"

"And he named it after our family," Mrs. Pudding said. "The Pudding Gunnysack Slide. Wasn't that nice of him?"

"Yes," Homer said. "Super nice."

"I admit that I'm not usually fond of my brother's friends," Mr. Pudding said. "But I'm much obliged to you, Mr. Ajitabh. Much obliged."

Another kid shot out of the tunnel. "Homer!" Squeak, Homer's little brother, landed in the foam moat, then staggered to his feet. His legs wobbly, he ran up to Homer and hugged him. "You're back."

"Hi, Squeak," Homer said. "Do you like the new slide?"

"It's great. I'm so glad you broke the old slide." Squeak grabbed Dog's leash. "I'm gonna take Dog on the slide. Come on, Dog. Come on, Homer."

"Go on, give it a try." Ajitabh took Homer's backpack and motioned toward the slide.

Homer followed his brother up the steep stairs, pushing Dog's rump the entire way. "Try this one," Squeak said when they got to the top. "It's called The Cannon. I'm taking Dog on The Corkscrew."

Dog didn't seem to mind when Squeak set him on a gunnysack. Homer grabbed his own gunnysack and set it at the entrance to The Cannon. "You ready?" he called to Dog as he positioned himself.

"Urrrr."

"GO!" Squeak yelled.

There are times in life when soaring through the air is an absolute necessity. Like when you need to get to an island to finish your quest, or when you need to save a free-falling dog. Or when you just need to have a bit of fun.

Down, down, down Homer slid, and when he shot out the bottom he looked over to see his dog, his friend, flying alongside him, his ears soaring like wings. Homer reached out and grabbed Dog's paw and they landed on the foam the way they'd always land.

Together.

41

It's Official

About a week later, a letter came in the mail addressed to Homer. He opened it in the privacy of his bedroom because he'd recognized the return address:

THAT NAMBY-PAMBY KID WHO'S AFRAID OF EVERYTHING
The Simpleton Palace
Lofty Spires

And here's the letter:

Hi, Homer,

Guess what! I broke my ankle in two places, so I've been able to hang out in my room the entire time and haven't seen my brothers or sister once. Baldwin brought me the newest edition of The Complete Dictionary of the English Language, *so I've been studying for the next spelling bee, which is in September, so I hope you'll come. But maybe I'll see you at a L.O.S.T. meeting before then. You never know.*

I've enclosed your official certificate of membership. I filed it in triplicate so we will not have any confusion at the next meeting.

Oh, and one other thing. I signed up for skydiving lessons. I know, very unexpected, but Baldwin thinks it will be good for me. And I think so, too. I don't want to be afraid of everything anymore.

See you soon.
Hercules

Homer reached under his bed and lifted the plank. Then he set the official certificate right next to the hidden copy of Rumpold Smeller's treasure map. He set the plank back in place and smiled.

42
Rumpold Smeller
the Pirate

She stood on the ship's deck, the salt water tingling her nostrils. What a lovely scent, the salty air. What a lovely feeling, the motion of the water. She leaned against the ship's rail. The crew was busy hoisting sails and coiling ropes as the harbor faded into the distance. The ocean awaited.

"Captain Smeller?" one of the men said. "We done what you ordered, sir. We removed all the embroidered pillows from your stateroom."

"Excellent," she said, deepening her voice. "I never want to see an embroidered pillow again."

Dear Reader,

Your teacher may decide to assign you a book report about the secret Society of Legends, Objects, Secrets, and Treasures. But here's the problem—because it's a secret society, you won't find any information about it in the library. So, because I like you very much, I've provided you with this handy-dandy list. I hope it's helpful.

CURRENT ROSTER FOR THE SECRET SOCIETY OF LEGENDS, OBJECTS, SECRETS, and TREASURES

Ajitabh: Received his doctorate in inventology from Cambridge University. Invited to join L.O.S.T. because of his unique inventions, which include the cloudcopter. Resides in a secret tower in the sky.

Jeremiah Carson: Renowned fossil hunter and excavation expert. His most famous discovery was the missing link's foot. Resides in Montana.

Sir Titus Edmund: Renowned archaeologist who unearthed the only known Egyptian toaster. Current whereabouts unknown.

Angus MacDoodle: Invited to join because he found a substantial stash of Celtic coins in his backyard. Currently living in an undisclosed location.

Dr. Gertrude Magnum: Doctor of Subterranean Worlds. Offered membership after she discovered the Great Crystal Cave. Lives on her yachts.

The Honorable Lord Mockingbird XVIII: Current president and eldest member. Renowned mapmaker who inherited his membership from his father. Lives in The City.

Hercules Simple: Official records keeper. Offered membership after he became the World's Spelling Bee champion. Lives in the gated community of Lofty Spires.

Professor Thaddius Thick: Professor Emeritus of Egyptology at Cairo University. Famous for finding more mummies than anyone else. Lives in Cairo.

Torch: Inherited her membership from her mother. Has a keen interest in the lost civilization of Atlantis but has yet to find anything. Lives wherever she feels like living.

The Unpolluter: No information available at this time.

Zelda Wallow: Archaeologist. Invited to join because of her expertise on forgeries and artifacts. Lives in Gloomy Moor.

And if you've read this book, you know who the twelfth member is.

Acknowledgments

Huge thanks to my first draft readers, Robert Ranson, Carol Cassella, and Elsa Watson. And to my wise editors, Julie Scheina and Jennifer Hunt, and my agent, Michael Bourret, for continuing this journey with Homer, Dog, and me. I'm very grateful to the entire Little, Brown staff for their support and enthusiasm. Victoria and Zoe, you know what I'm talking about!

I love to hear from my readers, so please write to me at mail@suzanneselfors.com.

CALLING ALL SCALAWAGS
AND SCUTTLEBUGS!

Join Homer and Dog as they embark on a swashbuckling
third adventure to uncover their biggest treasure yet!

Turn the page for a sneak peek of
Smells Like Pirates, the exciting sequel to *Smells Like Treasure*
coming in November 2012.

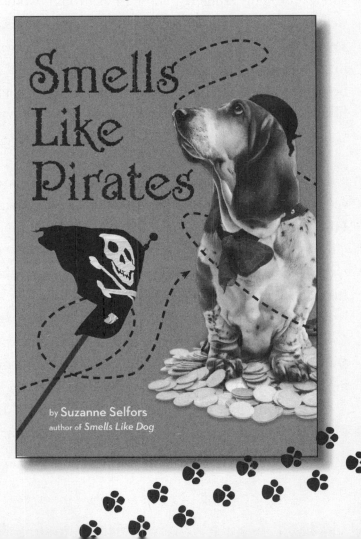

1 : Sweet and Sour Sixteen

It was a nearly perfect morning on the Pudding Goat Farm.

The sun rose with the rooster's crowing, then gently shone through Homer Pudding's bedroom window, tickling Homer's cheeks with its long, warm fingers. A songbird settled on the windowsill, the notes of its sweet melody dancing through the air. The scents of huckleberry pancakes and sizzling bacon wafted up the stairs, filling the bedroom with deliciousness. And a loving voice called—

"Get out of bed, you big dork!"

Okay, so it wasn't a loving voice. It was a moody, bossy voice, and it belonged to Homer's sister, Gwendolyn Maybel Pudding.

If she knew my secrets, Homer thought, *she wouldn't call me a dork*. He yawned and rubbed crust from his eyes, then stared up at his sister's scowling face. "What time is it?"

"Do I look like your personal alarm clock?" she snarled. "Mom told me to tell you to get out of bed. So *get out of bed*." She stomped out the door, her white lab coat billowing behind her.

Gwendolyn's foul personality was, according to Mrs. Pudding, a direct result of her age. Fifteen years, three hundred and fifty-nine days, to be exact, which made her a teenager. "Just because you've got pimples is no reason to be so rude," Homer mumbled as the lab coat disappeared around the corner.

"Urrrr," agreed the dog lying beside him.

Although he looked like an ordinary basset hound, the dog lying next to Homer was not one bit ordinary. An ordinary basset hound has a highly tuned sense of smell. Because the world tends to be a smelly place, an ordinary basset hound spends a great deal of time being led around by its nose. Homer's dog, however, had been born with a nose that didn't work quite right. Dog's nose didn't smell rotting garbage or frisky rabbits or grandma's pot roast. Dog's nose smelled only one thing—treasure. And that was Homer's most treasured secret. Dog rolled onto his extra-long back and stuck his extra-short legs straight up in the air, presenting his white belly for a morning scratch. Homer obliged. Ever since Dog came to the Pudding farm earlier that year, he had spent almost every night sleeping next to Homer. Some of those nights had been filled with danger and excitement as Homer pursued his dream of becoming a famous treasure hunter. The month of August, however, had proven to be a bore—day after day of the same blue-sky weather, day after day of the same old farm chores, and day after day of wondering when adventure would come knocking.

"Urrrr?" Dog complained when Homer stopped scratching.

"We'd better get downstairs," Homer said, "or Gwendolyn might eat our pancakes."

While many kids get to sleep in during the summer months, dreaming of bike riding, swimming, and kite flying, the Pudding kids always got up early. This was the reality of life on a goat farm.

After dressing in his work clothes, a pair of jeans and a plaid shirt, Homer did what he did most mornings—he checked under his bed. Lying on his belly, he pushed aside a pair of dirty socks, then pried free a loose floorboard. He peered into the hole and counted. His secret items were all in attendance: his L.O.S.T. membership certificate, his professional treasure-hunting clothes, and a book called *Rare Reptiles I Caught and Stuffed*, which contained the most famous pirate treasure map in the world. Why was it the most famous pirate treasure map in the world? Because it had been drawn by Rumpold Smeller, a pirate who spent most of his life traveling the world, amassing a treasure said to be greater than anyone could imagine. And Homer secretly owned this map.

With a smile, he returned the floorboard to its place. All was well beneath his bed.

Homer led Dog down the hallway, down the stairs, and into the kitchen. The swirling scents of breakfast pulled

Homer like a leash. The Pudding kitchen was a charming place. Checkered curtains framed a window that overlooked a vegetable garden. Farm-animal magnets covered the refrigerator, and a blue pitcher of field flowers sat on the counter.

Mrs. Pudding bustled around the stove, her brown curls bouncing. Mr. Pudding sat at the end of the kitchen table reading the Sunday *City Paper*, his overall straps hanging at his waist. Gwendolyn sat slumped in her chair, slurping her orange juice. Across from her on a bench sat Squeak, Homer's little brother. He stopped pushing his toy truck around the table and smiled. "Hi, Homer."

"Hi, Squeak."

Dog waddled to his dish, his tail wagging. Because Dog couldn't smell anything but treasure, he wasn't a picky eater. In fact, he'd been known to eat shoes, wood, worms, and toenail clippings. Mrs. Pudding often filled his bowl with leftovers, but sometimes Squeak tried to sneak in weird things—which is why Homer always stopped at the dog bowl first. "Squeak," he scolded as he picked out a snail, "please don't feed gastropods to Dog."

Squeak snickered.

As Dog inhaled his meal, Homer sat in his usual chair at the table's end, opposite Mr. Pudding. He sighed and stared at his empty plate. He sighed and stared out the window. He tapped his fingers on the tablecloth. Another long, hot, boring, totally routine August day.

To an outsider, this scene in the Pudding kitchen would appear normal—an ordinary family sitting down to an ordinary breakfast. But this was no ordinary family. Although Homer looked like a regular kind of kid, at twelve years of age, he was the youngest member of the Society of Legends, Objects, Secrets, and Treasures—a secret organization dedicated to treasure hunting. Though Homer's family knew Homer wanted, more than anything in the world, to be a treasure hunter, they did not know that he actually *was* a treasure hunter, for Homer had sworn an oath of secrecy. It made him kind of sad that he couldn't tell his family about how he and Dog had jumped out of an airplane, or how they'd found a cave of harmonic crystals, or how they'd defeated the evil Madame la Directeur. But Homer knew that an oath of secrecy was nothing to mess around with.

"I've been thinking about a theme," Mrs. Pudding said as she slid pancakes and bacon onto her family's plates.

"A what?" Mr. Pudding said, turning a page of his newspaper.

"A theme for Gwendolyn's sweet-sixteen party."

Sweet sixteen? Homer thought as he poured syrup on his pancakes. *More like sour sixteen.*

"I was thinking a butterfly theme, or a pony theme." Mrs. Pudding smiled lovingly, the gold flecks in her brown eyes sparkling. She sat down next to Gwendolyn. "How about a teddy bear theme?"

"Mom," Gwendolyn groaned, sinking lower in her chair. "I'm not a baby. Those themes are creepy."

"I like teddy bears," Squeak said, syrup dripping down his chin. Dog moseyed across the room and stood right under Squeak's feet. Since nearly half of Squeak's food ended up on the floor, this was a rewarding place to stand.

Mrs. Pudding stirred her coffee. "If you don't like my suggestions, then what theme would you like, Gwendolyn dear?"

"Roadkill," Gwendolyn replied.

Mrs. Pudding gasped. Squeak giggled. Mr. Pudding closed the newspaper and scowled. But Homer didn't flinch. It made perfect sense that his sister suggested a roadkill theme. She wanted, with all her heart, to become a Royal Taxidermist for the Museum of Natural History. She had her own laboratory out in the shed, where she practiced the art of stuffing dead animals.

"And it's got to be fresh roadkill," Gwendolyn said. "No maggots."

"Now, sweetie," Mrs. Pudding said, "you can't expect me to decorate with roadkill."

"Why not? It's my birthday."

"Forget it," Mr. Pudding said, slapping his hand on the table. "No daughter of mine is going to have a roadkill party. You'll choose one of those nice themes your mother suggested."

Gwendolyn darted to her feet and uttered the same statement she'd uttered yesterday, and the day before, and the day before that. "You are totally! Ruining! My life!"

"No one is ruining your life," Mrs. Pudding said. "We want you to have a special sweet-sixteen party. In fact, your father and I bought you a very nice present. And Homer went to town last week to shop for you, didn't you, Homer?"

This time, Homer flinched. He'd gone to town to buy Gwendolyn's birthday present—that much was true. But he'd taken his shovel and metal detector with him and, well, because the detector kept beeping and because Homer kept digging, he forgot all about Gwendolyn. The search for a birthday present wasn't as interesting as the search for treasure, even though that day's treasure had turned out to be nothing but a bunch of rusty tin cans.

"Uh, yeah, I got a present," Homer lied. He'd go shopping that afternoon, as soon as he'd finished his chores.

Gwendolyn peered at Homer through her long brown bangs. "You got me a present?"

"Yep." He stuffed a whole pancake into his mouth, just in case she asked any more questions.

Gwendolyn smiled wickedly. "If you bought my present, then it's hidden somewhere in the house, isn't it? I bet I can find it."

"Gwendolyn Maybel Pudding," Mrs. Pudding said. "You'll have to wait for your party to open your presents. Now sit down and eat your breakfast."

Huckleberries burst in Homer's mouth as he chewed the pancake. His mind raced. What kind of present do you get a moody sister who spends her summer days stuffing dead squirrels and gophers? A gift certificate to Ice Cream World didn't seem quite right.

Just then, barking arose in the yard. Max, Gus, and Lulu, the farm dogs, were upset about something. Dog, who'd been licking syrup from Squeak's fingers, scurried to the kitchen door and joined in the barking. "What's all the ruckus?" Mr. Pudding asked.

A knock sounded on the kitchen door. Mr. Pudding pulled his overall straps over his shoulders and went to answer it. "Well, hello there," he said. "What are you doing here?"

The rest of the Pudding family turned and looked toward the open doorway, but Mr. Pudding was blocking their view. *It wouldn't be the mail lady*, Homer thought, *not on a Sunday. Maybe it's one of the neighbors.*

"Good morning," a voice said. "I say, is Homer up and about? I have rather important news."

Homer's heart skipped a beat. He knew that voice.

2 : A Once-in-a-Lifetime Opportunity

A man stepped into the kitchen. He tucked his long black hair behind his ears and looked around. His gaze landed on Homer.

Homer scrambled out of his chair. "Hi, Ajitabh."

Ajitabh (pronounced AAAH-jih-tahb) did not return Homer's smile. He narrowed his dark eyes and ran his hand over his thin mustache and pointy beard. A doctor of inventology, Ajitabh was a fellow member of L.O.S.T. He'd been a trusted friend of Homer's treasure-hunting uncle, who had died earlier that year, and was now Homer's trusted mentor. The rest of the Pudding family knew Ajitabh from the Milkydale County Fair, where Dog had led a wild chase that resulted in the destruction of the beloved gunnysack slide. Ajitabh, inventor extraordinaire, built a new and improved slide, to everyone's approval.

"Hello, Homer." His tone was serious. He leaned over to pet Dog. "Hello, Dog." Dog *thwapp*ed his tail against Ajitabh's leg.

Mrs. Pudding hurried over to the cupboard and grabbed a plate. "You'll join us for breakfast?" She set it on the table, but Ajitabh shook his head.

"That would be delightful, but time is of the essence," he said.

"What's your important news?" Mr. Pudding asked.

"Quite right." Ajitabh rolled up the sleeves of his white shirt, then reached into the back pocket of his khaki pants and handed an envelope to Homer. "It's an invitation."

Homer half expected the envelope to be secured with a L.O.S.T. seal, but that wasn't the case. The envelope was as plain as could be—no seal, no return address, nothing. He opened it and pulled out a piece of paper.

"What is it?" Mrs. Pudding asked.

Homer read the letter aloud.

To: Homer W. Pudding, Pudding Goat Farm, Grinning Goat Road, Milkydale

From: Lewis Dimknob, Royal Cartographer, Map of the Month Club Headquarters, Boulevard of Destinations, The City

Congratulations, Mr. Pudding.

Your name has been drawn at random from our list of sub-scribers. I am pleased to inform you that you have been awarded a VIP tour of our headquarters. This tour is a once-in-a-life-time opportunity that will not be offered again.

We eagerly await your arrival on Monday, August 20, at noon precisely.

Signed,
Lewis Dimknob, Royal Cartographer

"Wow," Homer said. "This is really cool. I love the Map of the Month Club."

"VIP?" Gwendolyn grumbled. "How come Homer keeps getting these VIP invitations, huh? What's up with that?"

This was, in fact, Homer's second VIP invitation. *VIP* stands for "very important person." The first invitation had come from the Museum of Natural History and had led Homer to the discovery of Madame la Directeur's lair and a near-death escape from a man-eating tortoise. This invitation sounded a bit safer. "Can I go?" Homer asked. "I'd really like to go."

"August twentieth is tomorrow," Mrs. Pudding said worriedly. "That's not much notice."

"Sincerest apologies," Ajitabh said in his lilting accent. "As a board member of the Map Club, I was asked to deliver the invitation last week but was waylaid by circumstances beyond my control." He shot a serious glance at Homer. "We need to leave immediately, old chap."

Homer looked yearningly at his father. Was the boredom of August about to end?

"How long will he be gone?" Mr. Pudding asked.

"A bit of uncertainty there," Ajitabh said. "The Map of the Month Club's library alone covers three floors. I have reserved a room for us at a very nice City hotel. I'll act as Homer's guardian. You needn't worry about a thing."

"It sounds like a wonderful opportunity," Mrs. Pudding said to Ajitabh. "Homer loves maps. He's always loved maps. But he'll need to be back for his sister's sweet-sixteen party. It's a week from today."

"Righteo. That shouldn't be a problem."

"I can go?" Homer beamed, the corners of his smile nearly reaching his ears. But Ajitabh didn't smile. His eyebrows knotted as if troubling thoughts were twisting them. Why wasn't he happy? Homer stepped closer to Ajitabh. And why didn't he smell like cloud cover? Homer glanced out the kitchen window. Instead of a cloudcopter, Ajitabh's usual method of transportation, a black limousine waited in the driveway.

"You can go," Mr. Pudding said. "But Gwendolyn will have to cover your chores."

"No way!" Gwendolyn blurted out, her cheeks turning red. "Homer gets to go on another vacation and I'm stuck here doing his chores? I'm too busy to do Homer's chores."

"I'll do Homer's chores," Squeak offered.

"I'll make it up to you when I get back," Homer told his sister. "I'll do your chores for a whole extra week."

Gwendolyn chewed on her lower lip, her eyes narrowed in thought. "You really want to go?"

"Yes."

"Then tell me where you hid my present."

"Gwendolyn Maybel Pudding," Mrs. Pudding said.

"You will wait until your birthday to open your presents, and that is final."

"Fine!" Gwendolyn pointed at Homer. "But he's doing my chores for an entire month."

"Agreed," Homer said. He held back a sigh of relief. He'd expected to do his sister's chores for an entire year.

"I'll help you pack," Mrs. Pudding said.

If Homer had packed on his own, he would have reached into one of his drawers, grabbed some random clothes, then stuffed them into a backpack as fast as he could. But Mrs. Pudding didn't want her son going anywhere without clean underwear and socks. "Wait," she said as he grabbed the backpack. "You almost forgot your toothbrush." She slid it into one of the pockets. "You'll get cavities if you don't brush."

Homer didn't care if moss grew on his teeth. He just wanted to jump into that limo with Ajitabh and get off the farm.

"I had dreams of becoming a cartographer," Mr. Pudding was telling Ajitabh when Homer hurried back into the kitchen. "Homer gets his love of maps from me."

"Let's go," Homer said, grabbing Dog's blue leash.

After hugging everyone good-bye, except for Gwendolyn, who'd disappeared, Homer flew down the front porch steps. With a grunt and a heave, he pushed Dog into the limousine. Then he climbed in and settled on the soft leather seat. Ajitabh climbed in next to him. "Drive on," Ajitabh said. The driver's outline was blurry through the dark glass panel that separated the front and back seats. The engine started.

"Did you bring your coin?" Ajitabh asked.

Homer reached under his shirt, where a coin hung from a chain. It was his official membership coin with the letters *L.O.S.T.* engraved on one side and a treasure chest engraved on the other side. "Yeah, I've got it."

The goats watched as the limousine headed down the Pudding driveway and onto Grinning Goat Road. Homer looked back at the house. Mrs. Pudding and Squeak waved from the front porch. Mr. Pudding headed toward the barn. But why was Gwendolyn standing in Homer's bedroom, staring out the window? She didn't wave or smile. Was it because he got to go on a little vacation and she didn't? He'd be sure to bring her back a nice birthday present.

"Hey, Ajitabh," Homer said as Dog settled at his feet. "Why do I need my membership coin if we're going to the Map of the Month Club?"

"We aren't going to the Map of the Month Club, old chap. The invitation is fake. I lied to your parents."

"You lied?" An eerie tickle crept up Homer's spine. "Then where are we going?"

Ajitabh frowned. "Homer, I'm afraid I'm the bearer of bad news."

Ready for more excitement?

More magic?

More FUN?

Collect all the adventures by Suzanne Selfors!

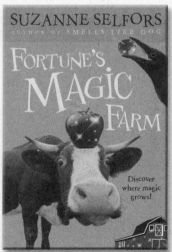